# Eleven

# Eleven

by

Donald Samson

Illustrations by
Heidi Nisbett

Star Trilogy
Publishing

Title: *Eleven*
Author: Donald Samson
Illustrations: Heidi Nisbett
Layout: Ann Erwin


ISBN 978-1-732537-25-5

*I, Benedictus Waisel, record this memoir in the year of our Lord 1392. I solemnly swear, in the name of the Son and the blessed martyred saints of Solodurum, Ursus and Victor, who suffered for our sins, that what I write here is a true and factual account of the events that occurred during my lifetime and in which I played a humble part.*

*I leave this testimony as a legacy for my sons and daughters that they might learn from what lineage they descend. Although they may take no public advantage of that lineage, they can enjoy the personal satisfaction knowledge gives, and I urge them not to undervalue that power. Knowledge is more compelling than the blow of a hammer, or the swiftness of the arrow, for it is knowledge that directs them both.*

*And yet, more powerful still is the guiding hand of God that directs our destinies when the force of our arms and the knowledge in our hearts fail us. Without God's guiding hand, I would have repeatedly, as my story will show, fallen by the wayside never to rise again.*

When I was young and inexperienced in the ways of the quick and the dead, I suffered a severe battle injury. I was filled with foreboding that I might not survive the wound, and if I did, that I might never walk again. I lay in the Guard's House of Healing, still in my battle tunic, stiffened with blood and battle filth. I alternated between delirium and intolerable, scalding pain. I would awaken from a drug-induced slumber in a sweat-drenched panic that the surgeon had come to saw my leg off while I was benumbed from the poppy.

In unguarded moments, the nightmares of that suffering still visit me to this day. At the time, I plagued myself with reproach for what an impulsive idiot I had been, and had I only heeded the sound advice of my parents, I would have been spared my injury and the subsequent unbearable pain and struggle to remain among the living.

Little did I know that this injury was but an unsentimental love-tap from the hard hand of Fate compared to the pounding I later received from that French forest troll at Eleven. But I get ahead of myself. You have asked me to write about my youth, and that battle wound was before I knew Joseph, or his beautiful daughter Zipporah, or even Baron Roland. Connie, of course, I knew, but all young men my age knew Connie.

# The Face on the Tower Wall

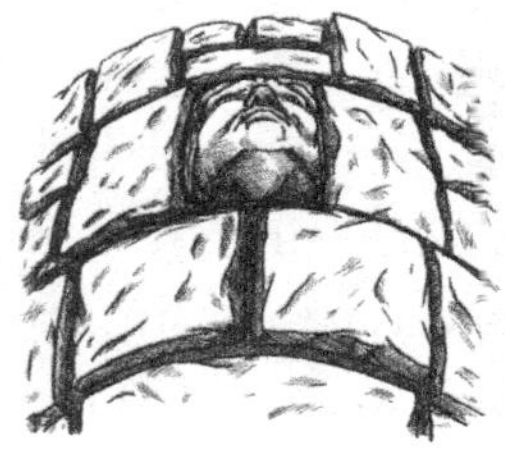

I will begin with this, otherwise none of it will make sense: Long before I was born, a protective high wall of artfully dressed and masoned limestone was built around our noble town of Solodurum, a wall which stands to this day, and will continue to stand as long as there is the will among our people to remain an independent, free city in the rich alluvial plains near to the foot of the Whitestone Mountains along the banks of the Arola River.

Along the north side of our city, rounded watch towers, also of cut limestone, were built into those high walls. These bastions were set 111 paces apart. Every 100 paces would have been adequate, but our noble town of Solodurum has an odd superstition around the number eleven. There are eleven major fountains situated throughout the city from which the different neighborhoods draw their water for cooking, drinking, and washing–there had once been twelve, but I will explain more about that later. There are eleven steps leading up to the great portal of the Saint Ursus cathedral. There are eleven members of the Elder Council from eleven noble households who direct the destiny of our laws and treaties. Two times eleven members form the Younger Council, chosen from the leading tradesmen and artisans to conduct and guide the commercial and internal affairs of our city.

There are eleven guilds that oversee the craftsmen of our town. The city and surrounding countryside is divided into eleven distinct bailiwicks, each district with its own bailiff to oversee law and order and the collection of debts and taxes. We have two larger churches and six small chapels within the city walls, and three monasteries on the periphery outside the city, two for men and one for women, each with its own dedicated chapel, altogether making a count of eleven Houses of Prayer within the larger defined boundaries of Solodurum. We are a devout people.

Solodurum boasts three major gates to enter or exit the city in the Upper Town, one main gate in the Lower Town on the other side of the Arola River, and seven minor gates spread between them, making a total, not surprisingly, of eleven city gates. Just as in other towns, they each have their special name, often derived from the trade that has grown up around them, such as the Tanners Gate, since it is in the quarter where hides are tanned, or the Potters Gate, for a similar reason. Other gates are named for the destination toward which the gate opens, such as the Basel Gate and the Berne Gate. However, there is one minor gate, hardly more than a door in the wall, that has a double name. It is officially known as the Forest Gate, for it opens to the woods that have been left to stand—some insist incautiously—beneath the city walls. But it is also more affectionately known as the Eleventh Gate, or more colloquially, as Eleven. Everyone knows what is meant. It is a popular trysting place for sweethearts who want to steal time to be alone for a walk in the woods. It is a common thing to say, "At nine bells, see you at Eleven," which is a way of saying that when the church bells ring the ninth hour, meet me at the Forest Gate.

When I was young, and some still keep the practice today, we had the dubious custom that when someone wanted a dozen of something, whether it be apples, onions, or turnips, we gave a Soldurmer dozen, which was actually only eleven. Other towns derided us as cheats, but we were fine with asking for a dozen and getting eleven. Like I said, it's a superstition. Eleven is our lucky number. We believe there is hidden strength and magic in that number that keeps our city safe and, as my account will show, that may not be far from the truth.

With that I return to the eleven rounded towers in the city wall. Recall that those on the north side are 111 feet apart. I measured them myself to make sure. It's a matter of family pride. You see, my grandfather was a Master Stonemason. In fact, he was *the* Master

Stonemason of his day. He supervised the construction of the towers along the north wall and likely helped lay many of the immense stones in place with his own hands. He succeeded in bringing the building of the walls to completion, a project that had consumed the efforts of stonemasons for over two generations.

In fact, on the first tower to the west of the Armory Gate—the tower on which I once regularly stood guard—my grandfather mortared into the wall, several span below the top rim of the tower, a stone image of his face. He did this, he told me, so that he would always be gazing north, toward the mountains. Today, people mistake that image for Stephen, patron saint of stonemasons, blessing the fine work of the tower and the surrounding walls. It is an understandable mistake. Others see in it the Green Man, legendary protector of the woods and forest animals. But the face on the wall is clean-shaven and lacks the wild hair and beard of the Green Man. Besides, there was no reason to honor the Green Man on the city walls. The Green Man is the protector of the forest. The protector of Solodurum is my grandfather.

He always said that if there was going to be a threat to our city, it was more likely to come from the north than anywhere else. Considering that the Forest Gate lies on the north side, it seems he knew what he was talking about, as this chronicle will show.

The south side of the city is also walled along the broad Arola River. Across the Chapel Bridge, the Lower Town is but a small foothold on the other side of the river. If it should be taken despite its own sturdy walls, Solodurum would still be protected by the natural barrier the fast flowing Arola provides.

The walls on the east and west sides of the city are not as long, since the city is built a bit like a ship at sea on which the prow and the stern are narrower than the body of the boat. Solodurum is somewhat wider in its middle and gently tapers off toward the ends, much like the bulging waistlines of the prosperous merchants who sit on the Younger Council. For this reason, Grandfather said the north is more vulnerable to attack. The gradually curving walls stretched far too long for his comfort. He set his visage in place with his own hands so that he could for all time gaze sternly out over the land, defying any who might want to scale or break through these walls. If you squint your eyes, you can even see what appear to be two horns on Grandfather's head. I asked him once about that.

"I want them to think the devil himself is guarding these walls," he said with a wink. Then he added, "And you know how to say *horns* in French, don't you? It is *les cornes,*" and he winked again. At the time, I puzzled why it mattered how to say *horns* in French. It was years before I discovered that Grandfather had a secret that he was sharing with me.

I should mention that Grandfather placed his visage not once, but twice, on the city walls. This second visage is not in plain sight for all to see and does not have any horns. It is visible only from the windows of the Privy Council Chamber, and I first saw it only after I had joined the Guard. But I will come back to the reason for that second face later.

My father followed in his father's footsteps, as is the custom of all God-fearing folk, and also became a stonemason. He oversaw the remodeling of several of the patrician palaces as prosperity spread among the noble families. My two older brothers, in accordance with family custom and obedient to the wishes of our father, also became master stonemasons. They directed the project to place immense monolithic troughs at each of the city's public fountains. These limestone troughs are the envy of all neighboring cities. My brothers are sought after and highly regarded in their profession.

Not so I.

I could have followed the tradition of our family. I would have been embraced by the Masonry Guild as an equal to my brothers, descended as I am from an illustrious line of masons. But I was not respectful of custom, I was disobedient to my father's wishes, and I turned my back on family traditions. My parents and my brothers openly accused me of being willful, and I could not dispute this judgment. I wanted something different than eating a mouthful of stone dust every day.

I don't wish to be misunderstood. Stonemasonry is a highly regarded profession in Solodurum. All of our buildings and the defensive walls of the city are made from the limestone quarried from the Whitestone Mountains standing tall and proud to the north. Limestone has many irregularities and is not easy to work with, yet due to its durability and pleasing appearance, it is nearly as sought after as marble. Since it is so readily available, it became a popular stone with which to build, and over time it earned the name *Soldurmer marble*. For this reason, the masons are considered more than workers in stone, they are viewed as artisans.

My decision not to follow in the family profession was personal. I did not want to spend my life chipping and laying stone.

My mother believed that I was trespassing upon God's own law. A son followed in his father's profession, no questions asked. This ensured that society would continue to flourish and not collapse as a result of the headstrong, willful, self-serving, rash impulses of youth. She did not keep this opinion to herself, but spoke it loudly and repeatedly. Nor did she keep secret that I was an embarrassment to our family, and she was ashamed, on my account, to show herself in public. As much as I disagreed with her, I had to honor that she sincerely viewed it as her duty to keep me from erring in the eyes of God and our fellow citizens.

However, there was little chance my parents could convince me to abandon my youthful dreams. And as for God, well, my friend Martin was the closest I came to hearing divine opinion regarding my decision to break with family tradition. Fortunately, Martin voiced genuine respect for our ability to exercise what he called *Free Will*. Had he not applied it himself, he'd have become a soldier like his father had been before him, rather than living a hermit's life as our local mystic in the holy gorge of St. Verena.

# *Something More*

It was all my grandfather's fault, really.

Grandfather was unique for a stonemason. He could read and write. You know how uncommon this is, even now in our times. Imagine how much less common it was at the time when my grandfather was a child. When he was a boy, only the clergy and some nobility acquired these skills. And the members of the Scriveners Guild, of course.

Grandfather had grown up an orphan in the care of the Benedictine monks at the monastery that lies within sight of the eastern gates to the city. He said that they raised him as they lived, on prayer and the labor of their hands, or, to use the Latin phrase, *ora et labora*. They taught him to pray and, when he was not praying, to work. Since he was a bright boy, they also taught him how to read his prayers as well as remember them. Grandfather said he took to the working, enjoyed the challenge of learning how to read, but never warmed up to the amount of praying they did throughout the day. So when he reached majority, instead of taking orders and finding his place as a brother in the monastery, he left and took up stonemasonry. He had already learned the craft while helping to build the monastery's long eastern border wall around the pastures that held their dairy cattle. Learning how to read stuck with him and he never forgot. It ended up serving him well. As a result of being able to decipher words, complemented by his ability to give directions as easily as he could receive them, he was raised to the status of Master Stonemason.

Grandfather tried to teach my father how to read. But Father's joy was working with his hands, and he found it arduous to make sense of the "dancing scribbles," as he called them. Grandfather did not give up. He attempted to teach each of his grandsons. My two older brothers took after our father in their enthusiastic lack of interest. But with me, Grandfather found fertile ground: I could not get enough of learning. Most likely, I was drawn to reading because it meant I could spend more time sitting in Grandfather's lap or, later, beside him at the table, for I was wildly fond of him. In his later years, he called me his "bed coals," for we shared a bed in our cramped home, and my youthful heat warmed his aged bones through the damp winter nights. My brothers teased me for my fondness of reading, but Grandfather always defended me and scolded them to let me be and learn. Secretly, he told me that I warmed his soul more than I did his body. My child's heart was devoted to him.

Grandfather was convinced that I was born to do something more than lay stones one on top of another. He never said what that *more* might be, nor did it occur to me at that young age to ask.

I don't remember when the dancing scribbles began to make sense to me. I don't remember a time when they did not. I would sit on Grandfather's lap and he would read to me out of a prized psalm book he had from his childhood days in the monastery. It was precious to him and I was never allowed to touch it. But his finger moved from word to word, and the more he read, the more the scribbles made sense. It was not long before his finger followed the words, but I was the one reading. It was not a big jump to go from there to writing. And since the prayers were not in our native dialect, I also gained, as an added benefit, a basic understanding of Latin.

As I grew older I got my first tastes of stonemasonry doing odd chores for my father and later for my brothers, for we all worked before we were properly apprenticed. I soon realized that I did not want to follow in the family tradition. I was careful to always praise stonemasonry as a noble profession. It provided a living for Grandfather, for my father, and my brothers. The fruits of their labors protect the city and provide dwellings for our townspeople. But I found it ponderous, boring work after the worlds that reading opened up to my imagination. I got it in my head that since I could read and write I had two choices. For one, I could enter the monastery and take orders. I rejected that path for the simple reason that I could not imagine living a life of celibacy. Already by the time I was fifteen, I fantasized having a sweetheart and thought there could be nothing more fulfilling than raising children of my own. Fortunately, I knew there was a second path for those who can read. I would become a scrivener, a maker of correspondences and legal documents, such as contracts and wills, as well as a transcriber of certified copies. Because I had learned my lessons so well from Grandfather, I thought it would be a simple thing to set myself up as a scrivener. All I needed to do was enroll in the Scriveners Guild. I felt certain this was the *something else* Grandfather had always whispered in my ear.

# The Assurance of Failure

"Do you want to bring the wrath of the Lord upon our heads?" Mother screeched. She did not stop there. She declared that I was bringing disgrace upon the whole family from which we would never recover, and predicted, "Your sister will find no man willing to wed her and your brother no bride willing to bear him children. Our family tree will wither and die." Mother always had a way of dramatically making her point. My siblings and I found it entertaining when we were not the immediate focus of her fury. Not wanting to risk her accusing me of being impertinent as well as rebellious, I did not point out that the family tree was not likely to die out because my eldest brother Anton had already given her three grandchildren, two of them boys.

It had taken a lot of courage to tell my parents of my plans. Grandfather had long since been laid to his eternal rest, so I did not have his support to fall back on. But I had to speak up. Father was getting ready to apprentice me, and the thought of dressing stone from sunrise to sundown was a sore burden on my heart.

When I revealed my plans, my father's face went blank. I had seen that happen only once before when my older brother Anton confessed to us that his sweetheart was with child—his child. But that was relatively easy to resolve. Their marriage was joyfully celebrated after the banns had been read in church three times. Besides, brides with a bulge were not uncommon.

What I was proposing did not have an easy fix. Father took a number of breaths while he summoned coherent thoughts. He looked as if a donkey had sidled up and given him a swift kick. Then he muttered, "I should have seen this coming. I blame myself. After all, I let your grandfather put foreign thoughts into your head."

"They weren't foreign to Grandfather," I protested, wanting to defend him.

"Foreign to our family's chosen work," Father said quickly, stopping me from going further.

"But before Grandfather, no one in our family was a stonemason," I persisted.

"We have no way of knowing this since Grandfather was an orphan," he pointed out. Then he said firmly, his face in a frown, "It is an honorable profession."

"And I will never say otherwise," I said quickly. The last thing I wanted was to ruffle his pride. "The stonemasons of Solodurum are true artisans. I am only saying that Grandfather chose his profession, and he prospered at it. I want the same freedom to enter a profession of my own choice."

"And bring shame upon our family and stumble along a downward path that will lead to poverty and starvation," Mother interjected sharply. I rolled my eyes before I could stop myself. I only hoped she hadn't noticed.

Father held up a warning hand. "Marta, he is not bringing any shame upon the family. Nor will he starve."

"He will die a pauper," Mother insisted. "And be buried in a ditch. You must stop him."

"Mother, please," I protested. "It's not always that dramatic."

"The streets are filled with the poor and hungry," she quickly pointed out.

"And none of them are failed scriveners," I nearly shouted.

"There is no way for you to know that," her voice rising higher than my own.

Before I could respond, Father's warning hand shot up a second time. "No bickering. I will have peace in my home." He looked at me severely to keep me from saying more. He took a deep breath. "You know that my wish is for you to follow the family profession. What you are proposing will require great courage. You have no assurance of success. Are you prepared for that?"

"The assurance is of failure," Mother inserted.

Father looked up at her, "Perhaps, you're right," he said with a nod. My heart sank like a stone in water. Then he continued, "But I say, let us wait and find out." The sinking stone suddenly became a fat duck and bobbed to the surface. "Marta, you have had your say and Benedict knows what you think. I suspect the neighbors also know by now as well. I ask for restraint, and that we keep our voices down. There is no reason for the whole street to hear our quarrel."

"Then you accept that I try—that I *find* my own path?" I was bubbling with excitement.

He looked at me in that particular way he has and laughed. "Do I have a choice?"

"You could forbid me," I said honestly. It was never any use avoiding the obvious with Father. He was direct in his dealings with his children and approached life along the lines that any problem can be reduced to a simple solution. It was how walls got built: simple solutions. Complication was a luxury for the wealthy. The poor could not afford it.

"Forbid you? That I could," he mused. "But then, you are different from your brothers. Even your build. You take after your mother's family, lean and wiry. Go on with you. Follow your foolish dreams! I can always apprentice you in the spring when you see the error of your ways." He said this with a sideways smile, so I knew he was, without saying it outright, giving me his blessing.

Not so Mother. Her eyes grew wide at Father's words and she worked herself up like a pot ready to boil over. "You're not going to forbid him?" she started.

Before she could steam up, Father stood and walked to the door, pulling Mother by the arm with him, speaking in a quiet and calm voice. "Come walk with me, Marta. Let's take in the evening air. It's grown stuffy inside with so many harsh words of fear and failure." He led her to the door and they went out together. Even with the door closed, I could hear Mother's shrill voice and Father's soothing baritone until they walked out of earshot.

That left me at the table with Sebastian and my sister. I looked up at them silently, waiting to hear what they had to say. Seb was pushing some crumbs around the table. His fingers were thick and stubby, perfect tools for his chosen craft.

"It doesn't matter to me," he said, but he didn't look at me. "You always were a fool. Like in the stories, third son, dumb one." He flashed me a brotherly grin. "Besides, I already have a sweetheart." He then smiled broadly and pushed himself up from his chair. "And she's waiting to meet me at Eleven." He walked to the door, snatched his cap off its peg, and let himself out.

I turned to Veronika. My sister and I had a very special bond. In many ways, I was closer to her than anyone else. We were born eleven months apart, such a Solodurum number, so it was easiest to share everything with her.

"That went better than you expected," she said quietly. "Father took it quite well."

"But Mother ..." I began.

"Did you expect anything different from her?" she asked, making big eyes at me.

I laughed. "No. I expected no less."

"Father will calm her down," she said nonchalantly. "He always does."

I fidgeted a moment trying to find the right words. "Mother did say something I hadn't thought about."

"About my not finding a husband?"

"I really hadn't thought about that, Veroni," I explained. "What if she's right? What if I do bring shame upon our family and no man will consider you a worthy bride? I could never forgive myself."

Veronika smiled broadly and reached out to place a hand on my arm. "First of all, I am too young to marry. Nor do I wish to think about sweethearts. And by the time I am old enough and interested, you will be a famous scrivener and my suitors will be lining up at the door. That's what I think." And she gave me a wink. "Now that's finished, would you like an extra helping of stew? I saved you some."

# The Guild House

The day I turned sixteen, I scrubbed myself from head to foot, dressed in my best hose and tunic—hand-me-downs from Seb that fit his large frame but were too big for me—and presented myself at the Guild Hall for Scriveners. It carries a coat of arms over its entrance with the symbols of all scribes: a quill, a scroll, and an inkpot. I proudly carried my own goose quill, scrap of parchment, and a small inkpot tucked in a pocket of my tunic.

I walked boldly inside and reported to the registrar who sat on a high stool at a raised wooden desk that was ornately carved. He wore a plain doublet and a felted cap perched on his head. His hair was graying and his beard looked like it could use a trim. His fingers were stained with ink, which was the certain sign of a man of letters. I could not wait until my own hand proudly bore those same tell-tale stains.

Our conversation went something like this:

"What do you want?" he asked brusquely, briefly glancing down at me from his high perch and the text he was transcribing. "A marriage document? You can have that done in the market."

"No, not at all," I replied. "I am not ready to marry. I came to enter the guild as a scrivener." I stretched to my full height, trying to fill out my clothing.

Now I had his attention. He lay down his quill and stared at me. "Who are you?" he demanded.

"Waisel," I replied. "Benedictus Waisel. Son of Lorentius."

"I've never heard of you," he said, sounding puzzled. "Why have I never heard of you? With whom did you study? Who administered your exams? Why do I have no recollection of your name?" He started pushing scrolls around on his desk, opened a drawer, pulling out more, apparently looking to find the missing document with my name upon it.

"I studied with my grandfather," I replied. I was puzzled about his last question. I didn't know there was an exam.

"With your grandfather?" the scribe repeated, pinning me with his gaze. "And exactly who is your grandfather?"

"Was," I clarified. "He is no longer living."

"Was, then," the scribe snapped at me. "Who was he, already?"

"Valentinus, the Master Stonemason," I proudly informed him.

Instead of being impressed, the scribe burst into laughter. Then he barked at me, "Out! For the sake of the entertainment you've given me, I won't call the Watch on you. But if you don't leave promptly, I will see you sitting below the Tower Gate for your insolence. Shame on you for mocking your betters. A stonemason! Out! Go write sonnets to your stones. Go! Now! Out of my sight!" With a rolled-up parchment clutched in the fist of his ink-stained hand, he vigorously swept his arm up and away from himself as if swatting at a pestering wasp.

Chased by the vehemence of his words and gestures, I beat a hasty retreat. I did pause with the intention of pulling out my quill and ink pot as proof of my skills and my sincerity, but at the last moment thought better of showing them to him. He did not seem in the least interested. His threat of the dungeon below the Tower Gate had unnerved me. Was it just an idle threat? I couldn't take that risk. Everyone knows that whoever has the misfortune to disappear below the Tower Gate does not see the light of day again. It is as certain as entering one's own grave. Little did I know, before three years were out, I would get to know it intimately.

In the innocence of my youth, I could not fathom what I had done to incite his anger. Nor did I know where to turn for advice. I dared not speak to my family of this incident. To tell my mother I had been threatened with the Tower Gate would give her apoplexy. My brothers would just mock me. Father would knowingly shake his head and arrange my apprenticeship. Veroni would be sympathetic, and then try to comfort me with a bowl of stew. She thought all problems could be solved by an extra helping of food. In truth, it worked for my brothers and often for me as well.

At this moment, I needed answers. Apparently, learning from my grandfather was not enough. It seemed that I had to take an exam and have papers to prove it.

I pondered who I could ask to unravel this riddle. Then I had an idea. Twice a week, on market days, at either end of the marketplace, a scribe set up a small table. On the table stood a quill, inkpot, and a selection of small parchments. The scribes served the merchants, farmers, craftsmen, and laborers by writing up legal documents, whether for the sale of a cow or a parcel of land. They even wrote up the papers for a term of indenture. Regularly, couples sought the scribes out for marriage contracts. People paid them in coin, but more often than not in goods bartered. I had the inspiration that these scribes held the key to what I needed to know.

At the next market day, I again put on my best hand-me-downs and went to get answers. The first scribe I approached was sour and unfriendly. A middle-aged man in a doublet that had seen better days, he barked at the people who came to him, letting them know in no uncertain terms that they were unlettered, ignorant, inferior, and at his complete mercy. It was obvious that he loathed serving the needs of the common people. I watched him for a moment and knew that I'd get nothing but abuse from him. However, I was in luck with the scribe at the other end of the market. He was a young fellow wearing his first beard and a cheerful disposition. I watched at a distance as during the morning hours he had a steady stream of townsfolk who wanted him to write up documents.

Toward noon, as the market crowd was thinning out, he finished with his last two customers, a shy young couple seeking a marriage contract. When they happily scurried off arm-in-arm, the scribe sat alone, ordering the remaining parchments on his small table top. A bag with his bartered goods sat at his feet below the table. I could see him eyeing the large clock tower, likely wondering if he had fulfilled his allotted time and could slip away. I sidled over and started a casual conversation. When he saw I was not bringing him a document to write, he relaxed and accepted me as an entertaining way to wait out the end of his post. I wove into our conversation that I had a cousin in Berne who had a friend who was studying to become a scrivener, but always acted mysterious about what the steps were to gain entry into the guild.

"Is there any reason why he couldn't tell me what the requirements are?"

The scribe laughed. "I think your cousin's friend is just trying to make himself seem important. Either that, or he has failed to fulfill one of the steps and is embarrassed to speak about it. He likely failed his exams and has to apprentice longer. That happens all the time, you know."

"Truly?" I asked.

"More often than not. Although there are no great secrets, fulfilling every requirement is not always easy. The steps are straightforward. First, your cousin's friend must find a Master Scribe who will take him on as an apprentice and train him. It is just like any other profession: You must learn the trade from a master. Then, the candidate must have enough money to see him through the time of his apprenticeship. That is not always easy. You can always tell a scrivener apprentice by his lean and hungry look. When the apprenticed scribe is thoroughly versed in creating all manner of documents and contracts, the guild administers an exam to prove his knowledge. The exam is not easy, and most fail at least once. I did."

So there it was. I needed to find a Master Scrivener! As casually as I could, I asked, "Who did you study with?"

"Oh, that I can readily tell you. I studied with Master Cornelius right here in Solodurum. He lives in the upper end of Chapel Way near the Basel Gate."

I was overjoyed that I had discovered the path to success so easily. In my giddiness I wished the scribe long life and happiness, and that his ink never run dry. Then I hurried on my way.

I wasted no further time. I went directly to Chapel Way and by asking around found the door to Master Cornelius' dwelling.

# Master Cornelius

I knew that I had found the right door. To the left hung the guild shield for scriveners. It was dirty, covered with cobwebs and the remains of flies and gnats stuck in the silky threads. It had obviously hung there a long time. The front door was also dirty and scuffed. Clearly scriveners did not become wealthy, but they could afford a home. I knocked at the door and waited. When nothing happened, I knocked again. I finally heard heavy footsteps on the stairs within. An elderly woman opened, most likely the Mistress Cornelius. Her face had a pinched look, as if I had roused her from her nap, and she gave every impression that she was not happy to have been disturbed.

She looked me up and down before saying, "Master Cornelius is taking his noonday rest, as you should be doing as well. He will write no documents until after the clock strikes half past two. Return at that time." And then, without giving me a chance to say anything, she shut the door. I could hear her heavy footsteps going back up the staircase inside.

I decided to wander about town until I could return to speak with him. I was too excited to do anything else. Although the air had the chill of the coming winter, inside I felt bee-buzzing, birdsong springtime. I went down to the river and, just to have something to do, helped a boat unload its cargo. I even earned a copper penny for my efforts. I counted every quarter hour bell with anticipation.

As the clock tower rang half past two, I was back at Master Cornelius' door. The mistress opened to my knocking and her look was full of disapproval. Wordlessly, she let me in and, with a gesture, indicated that I should proceed up the stairs.

"Door on your right," she murmured behind me.

I must have floated up the steps because I did not hear a single one creak beneath my feet. At the top, I knocked at the door on my right, and a tired voice from within bade me enter.

I paused with my hand on the door handle. A thrill passed through me that my future was taking form before me and that by opening this door, I was about to enter it. I took a deep breath and stepped into Master Cornelius' workroom. Although curtained, it was well lit from windows looking out on the street below. I could see the windows of the house directly across the narrow way. Master Cornelius sat behind a stout wooden table covered with scrolls and neat piles of documents.

"What can I do for you?" he spoke in a slow deliberate voice. He was graying and pale. He looked as if he had not yet fully awakened from his noonday nap. He was clothed in multiple layers, common for the elderly trying to stay warm in our damp stone houses. His topcoat had a yellowish stain on the lapel, most likely from his noonday soup.

"I've come to inquire after an apprenticeship," I said. I saw no advantage in not being direct.

Master Cornelius perked up and looked at me with interest. "You're old to start an apprenticeship, so I assume that you have already learned your letters. Where have you taken your schooling?" he asked.

"I studied under my grandfather," I replied.

"Ah, and what is his name?"

"Waisel, Valentinus Waisel ... *was* his name. He is no longer living."

"I'm sorry for your loss," Master Cornelius murmured tonelessly. He had a puzzled look on his face. "Waisel? Was he known by another name? I know the names of all the members of the local guild for the past thirty years, as well as most in the surrounding regions, but Waisel, I have never heard of him. Did he move here from another town and never register?"

"He was not a member of the Scriveners Guild," I added quickly.

"Not a member?" Master Cornelius looked at me with interest. "If not a scrivener, what was he then?"

"My grandfather was a stonemason."

Master Cornelius drew his brow together trying to understand this riddle. "So, your father, then, is a scrivener?"

"No," I replied meekly. "He is also a stonemason." I suddenly grew uncertain. Was he also about to banish me with the same fury I had been met with at the guild?

Master Cornelius' puzzled expression turned to bemusement. "This is rather irregular." He scratched his bearded chin. "So, if I understand you correctly, you wish to change the profession of your family and become a scrivener. Is this correct?"

"Yes," I said, relieved. Finally, someone who understood exactly what I wanted to do.

"Irregular, but not impossible," he said more to himself than to me. Then he looked up and engaged me with his gaze. "And do you have the necessary fees?"

I hadn't expected this. Recounting this now, I marvel how green I was then. "Fees?" I stammered.

"Your apprenticeship fees. A Master Scrivener requires a fee for training an apprentice, as is his right. Although there are guidelines, I feel that my fees are reasonable enough and slightly below the going rate."

"H-How much?" I stammered. I felt a weight on my chest like one of the stones my father worked on. It was pressing all the air out of my lungs.

"Eleven silver groschen a year. In any other city I could demand twelve, so there's a discount right from the start," he grumbled with a smile. "An additional two pennies a week if you take your meals here. Three if you sleep here. Since you claim that you can already read, the apprenticeship would last about two years—if you are a quick learner. It ends when you take your exam or run out of money."

The stone pressing on my chest now had a donkey balanced on top of it. A very stout donkey.

"Any questions?" he asked.

"Can I work it off?" I asked in a strangled voice. I had no source of groschen. My brothers were happy to earn four pennies a day.

"Work you will the whole time you are with me," Master Cornelius said with a shrug. "As for working off what you'd owe me, we could talk about helping the mistress of the house with cleaning, shopping, and cooking to defray the costs of your food. If you work hard, even your lodging. Those are the terms."

I stood there, unable to speak.

Master Cornelius continued. "Money is always an issue, so I wanted to bring it up at the beginning. You see, if you cannot afford my fee, you have to consider how you will pay for your exam."

"The exam has a fee?" I stammered.

"Ten schilling. They want to discourage frivolous attempts at entrance into the Guild. You take the test only when you are confident you will pass." He barely paused before pressing on. "Once you do pass the exam, then there is the fee for entrance into the Guild."

"The Guild has a fee?" I gulped.

"All guilds demand a fee. Certainly your father and your grandfather paid the guild fee for stonemasons."

"I suppose," I faltered. I had honestly never thought about it.

"Of course they did," he continued. "Because unless you pay the guild fee, you cannot apply for work anywhere. It is really that simple, you know."

"Of course," I agreed weakly.

When I just stood there speechless, he prodded, "Anything else?"

"I don't have that kind of money," I said, shaking my head.

"There are, of course, moneylenders."

"Moneylenders?" Jews. The general belief was that if you could not pay back in coin, they demanded you pay in Christian blood with which they were rumored to bake their bread. He shook me out of my dark reverie.

"Your other choice is to return to the profession of your family," Master Cornelius said, not unkindly. "You said you're a stone cutter?"

"Stonemason," I corrected.

"All the same," he shrugged.

"The stone cutter cuts the stone in the quarry and then roughly shapes and dresses the raw stone, making it into the approximate shape for the intended purpose," I explained, my voice a faint monotone. Every profession has its pride. "The stonemason plans and designs the wall, gives the stone its final form, finds the perfect stone for the need of the wall, and sets it with mortar in its permanent position. It takes great skill to cut Soldurmer limestone and know how to build a wall that will stand against weather, time, and assault ..." My words drifted off. I hardly heard what I was saying. My mind was racing to find some way to talk him into taking me on as an apprentice without paying fees that were beyond my reach.

"Wonderful. I never knew there was a difference. I recommend you go practice what you know best. Is there anything else I can do for you?"

Wordlessly, I shook my head. The next thing I knew, the Mistress Cornelius was letting me out the front door. The stairs had creaked loudly as my feet plodded heavily the whole way down. My hopes shattered, numb, I wandered aimlessly through the streets, not paying attention to where I was going.

I wandered along the riverfront, my head hanging, when I nearly collided with Crazy Connie. Just in time I saw him out of the corner of my eye and jumped aside. His feet were bare and filthy, and over his shoulders he wore a worn surcoat that had once been finely brocaded. His eyes were wide with rage, his beard and hair wild and unwashed, Crazy Connie screamed at me, "Go away! Get out!" Normally, I would have spoken gently to him, taken him by the arm and calmed him down. We all looked after Connie, particularly when he was wrought up. But this day, shaken by my interview with Master Cornelius, the bright picture of my future dissolving before my eyes, Connie's words struck me as if coming from the mouth of the Almighty God. *Get out!* I staggered back and hurried away.

Behind me stood the wooden bridge that crossed the Arola. Without thinking, I fled from Connie and sprinted across to the other side, to the Lower City that flanks the southern banks of the river. I followed my feet, wandering through the crooked lanes until I found myself standing before the Berne Gate. I didn't stop there and kept going, out through the open portal to the meadows beyond.

There is a soldiers' camp in those fields, not far from the city walls where the City Guard marches and practices and spars. They take their meals in low pavilions and sleep in wooden barracks at night. I came to the edge of the field and stood vacantly watching them at their exercises. Their marching in perfect unified step caught my eye and stopped me from wandering further. I stood there dumbly, stunned by the suddenness of my failed future. I needed time to gather my thoughts. A protected part of my mind assured me that I could stand there until my head cleared.

It wasn't meant to be. Suddenly, out of nowhere, a soldier, magnificently dressed in shining armor and polished leather, was walking directly toward me. With a raised hand, he hailed me loudly. He was a large man and stood at least a head taller than I.

"You there!" he bellowed. I turned to him. He was a glorious sight in his Guard uniform. He walked right up to me and placed both of his huge hands on my shoulders. "Just the sort we need," he exclaimed, grinning down at me. "You've come to the right place. We've been waiting for you." *Waiting for me?* These were welcome words to my confused heart. I yearned to hear that I was welcome somewhere.

"Come with me and we'll get you set up. You'll be right at home with us." Without waiting for my reply, he wrapped his massive arm around my shoulders and steered me toward the nearest pavilion. I was too bewildered to resist. But then, why should I? They needed me. I was welcome. There was no talk of a fee, no exam, no guild requirements. Thus, in this effortless manner was I recruited into the City Guard.

My friend, the hermit Martin, has always assured me that whenever a door closes, it is because the wind of God is blowing from an open window beckoning us to find it. On this day, the door to my plans of becoming a scrivener slammed shut, and my new life in the ranks of the City Guard opened wide and welcoming before me.

# Rodrigo

"Waisel, Benedictus," I said to the scribe writing names into the list of recruits. Then I described where I lived. I was told my family would be informed not to expect to see me for three moons. I was restricted to camp for that long. Although until now I had never been away from home for longer than three days—once I had traveled with my father to Berne—a part of me was relieved that I would not have to face my mother's "told-you-so" or Seb's ridicule. Even Veronica's pity would be too much to tolerate right now.

As I watched the scrivener writing my name, I mumbled, "I can do that, too." The guardsman standing with me mistook my meaning, thinking I was looking beyond where the scribe sat to the guard standing at the doorway to the pavilion with a halberd in his hand. "You will, soon enough," he assured me.

I was taken to a tailor who measured me, jotted some numbers down on a slip of paper, and then handed it to me. "Don't lose this. Take it to the armory and they will suit you up."

Somewhere along the way I was introduced to a guardsman, older than me—but then they all were. His name was Andreas, and I trusted in his honest face. I was told he was to look after me until I learned what I needed to know. Andreas said he had an errand to run and would catch up with me in the mess. I watched his receding back until I was nudged to continue my tour of the camp.

I was then taken to the barracks to find an empty cot. It was so dark within that lanterns were burning. There was no one inside, but the strong, stale smell of men lingered in the air. The cots were set so close together that there was only enough room to stand up between them. I was shown an empty one, down a middle aisle and toward the back. They all looked alike. The guard told me to count how many cots it was away from the end, to make sure I would find it again. I wondered vacantly if there were piss pots for nightly needs. Surely so, or men would be falling over one another all night trying to find the door. I wanted to ask my guide, but the words didn't come out. I was still numbed from the suddenness of everything.

Last of all, I was taken to the mess. A large, airy pavilion, heavy with the smell of food, it was filled with low tables and long benches. Off in one corner was a knot of men with their backs to us. Men regularly emerged from that mass with a bowl in one hand and a hunk of bread in the other. Obviously, that was where food was served up.

The meal was already in full swing. The pavilion was loud with conversation, occasional bursts of laughter breaking forth from different pockets of men. The guardsman who had been escorting me around pointed toward the knot of men. "Pick up your meal from over there. Sit where you like," he said. "But use some common sense." Then he left me.

I stood a moment to orient myself. My mind was still reeling, the full consequences of what I had just done struggling to come to consciousness: I had joined the Guard. There was no going back. I took a deep breath. Food first, I thought. That would help to clear my head. I went to stand in the mess line when I thought I heard someone call my name. Assuming it was Andreas, I turned my head to look over my shoulder and made the mistake of continuing to walk. I rammed right into a wall.

At least, that is what it felt like. I hit an immovable barrier and crumpled to the ground. Surprised and stunned, I looked up at the largest man I had ever seen. Being around stonemasons all my life, I was accustomed to large men. This one dwarfed them all, and he was peering down at me.

"Who's the fresh meat?" he bellowed to no one in particular. There came no answer but a hush in the conversations around us. The behemoth bent over and with one hand on the back of my tunic, heaved me to my feet.

"What's your name, little tadpole?" he asked. He hadn't let go of my shirt and gave me a little shake.

"Waisel," I replied, uncertain. "Benedictus Waisel."

"Waisel?" The behemoth rolled the word around his mouth, as if tasting it. "I know that name from somewhere."

"What is your name?" I asked suddenly. I wasn't sure where my bravado came from. I figured I had to show him, even if I was not his equal in size, that I was not afraid.

The behemoth smiled broadly. "He wants to know my name!" he called out loudly to all standing around. Then he bellowed, "What's my name?"

That is all the prompting the crowd of guardsmen needed. They began chanting, "Rodrigo! Rodrigo! Rodrigo!" It went on until he held up his free hand, and it died away immediately. It was obvious that he commanded respect. He turned his attention back to me. "Do you know my name now?" he asked, baring his teeth.

I nodded, but said nothing.

"Never forget it. What does your father do, Waisel?"

"He's a stonemason," I said, all bravado vanished from my voice. I saw his eyebrows briefly shoot up, as if he recognized something. But if he had, he didn't reveal it to me.

"Little stonemason," he said to me, "your father should have taught you better than to walk into walls." There was a sprinkle of laughter around us. I realized far too late that I had become part of the evening's entertainment.

I wanted to end this as quickly as possible. "I will watch where I'm walking," I said quickly.

"That's good, little stonemason," he said. "Because if this wall falls on you," he said, pounding his chest, and with his other hand lifting me by my tunic bodily straight off the ground, "You don't get up again very quickly." He let me fall. I landed on my feet, but would have collapsed had Rodrigo not grabbed me by the shirt again.

"You need to strengthen yourself, tadpole. Get something to eat," he said. "Make room for the little stonemason," he bellowed, and propelled me forward. I was caught by many hands and, obedient to Rodrigo, they pushed me forward to the front of the mess line. I felt humiliated by this rough handling, but what could I do? I quickly collected my supper, a bowl of stew and a fist-sized hunk of dark bread.

All eyes were on me and they were having a good laugh at my expense. I'm tougher than this, I told myself. I wasn't going to get chased away by some hazing.

There was a massive plane tree with its heavy limbs and splotchy-patterned bark growing in the middle of the mess pavilion. The canopy over our heads had been fitted around the broad girth of the tree. There were more seats available there than anywhere else. If I had taken a moment to consider the best thing to do, I would have just plunged into the thickest gathering of men and disappeared among them. Instead, I sought some solitude to settle my wounded pride. One of the benches backed up to the immense tree trunk. I was drawn to it because there were cushions along the bench. I didn't stop to think why there were cushions there and nowhere else. I did notice the smirks of the men I passed by, but I thought it was because of Rodrigo's taunting.

I sat down, took several deep breaths to calm myself, and tasted the stew. It was neither good nor bad, just slightly over-salted. It would do to fill the emptiness in my belly and distract me from the ridicule I had endured. I was just beginning to wonder why no one else was coming over to sit at the tree when I heard Rodrigo's booming voice.

"Now this little stonemason is beginning to annoy me." I looked up. He had a bowl of stew in each of his massive hands and was making straight for me, flanked by several other guardsmen, also carrying food, all of whom looked like seasoned veterans. I froze, watching them slowly approach. Suddenly, Andreas was standing in front of me, blocking my view of Rodrigo.

"Get out of there, now," he said steadily. "Do it. Just get up and leave."

That's when it dawned on me that the benches were empty because they were reserved for Rodrigo and his friends. "Use common sense," the guard who delivered me there had said. I had used none. I grabbed my bowl and bread and vacated.

"Andreas," Rodrigo boomed, "is he your charge?"

"He is, Battalion Master," Andreas said, turning to face him. Wonderful! I had managed to annoy a Battalion Master on my first day.

"Then do what you've been given to do," Rodrigo bellowed. I wondered if he had any other way of speaking than shouting. "And take charge of him!"

"I will, Battalion Master," Andreas said, deferentially. By this time, he had me by the arm and was propelling me away from the benches around the tree.

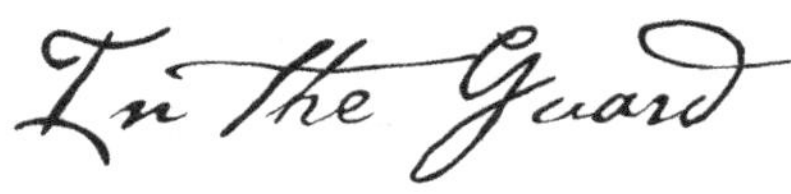

"You sure know how to make friends," Andreas said, after he had settled me safely at another table. We were sitting with other guardsmen who leaned forward listening.

"I had no idea," I started.

"Well, now you do. Stay out of his way the next week. In fact, stay out of his way the next three weeks. Otherwise you'll become his newest favorite target, and you don't want that."

"Best entertainment all week," one of the guardsmen commented with a smile.

"Only because it wasn't you, Fredi," Andreas said drolly.

"You're right about that," Fredi nodded solemnly.

"Just keep your wits about you," Andreas continued, addressing me. "There are many who would enjoy seeing Rodrigo make you his personal whipping boy. You don't want to go there."

"No, no, no," I said.

"Just stay close and don't wander off. Understand?"

"Understood," I said. I was glad to have found a friend.

Andreas took me the next day across town to the armory to get suited up. We returned to camp with my gear and he cleared a space to store my armor next to his own station in the dressing rooms, so we could cinch each other up. At supper the next evening, Andreas pointed out different guardsmen as they passed by our table.

"That's Christian. His father is a poor landowner. He has four older brothers, so all he was going to inherit were the shoes on his feet. The joke was that he came here barefoot, anyway. That there is Christoph. His father's a tailor. He didn't want to spend his life bent doubled over, sewing other people's clothing. That's Paulo. His father died when he was young and his mother took over his job cleaning the latrines in the Lower Town. That's one job he did not want to inherit." After several more, I asked, "And what about you, Andreas? What brought you to the Guard?"

"My father's a tanner. Have you ever passed through the Tanners Gate?"

"Not often," I admitted. "An unhealthy air lingers there."

"Unhealthy is kind. It stinks! Everyone avoids it. Ever wonder why?"

I realized I had never thought about it. I had simply gone a different way.

"It's because tanning's a stinking, ugly business. I wanted the adventure—and the *healthy* air—of the Guard."

"Is everyone here running away from his father's profession?"

"Far from it," Andreas explained. "Many are third or fourth sons like Christian, with little chance of following the family line. They have had to strike out on their own. The Guard offers that independence. Many spend their lives here."

A guardsman joined us at our table. "Andreas," he said in greeting. Then to me he said, "And the little stonemason. Say, Andreas, is he even old enough to be a guardsman?"

I bristled, but Andreas put his hand on my arm to stop me from saying anything. He looked the guardsman in the eye and said, "Bug off, Felix. When you arrived, you were afraid of the dark."

Felix shrugged. "Still am," he admitted with a smile.

Then Andreas turned to me. "When they tease you, don't react," he said. "You've been branded, and nothing will change it until Rodrigo himself changes it. Some will use it neutrally, because that is how you will be known from now on. Others will use it mockingly, because that is how they show their superiority. Just take it with your head held high. If they see it gets under your skin, they will use it as a weapon against you."

"Why did Rodrigo do that?" I asked, exasperated.

"You're not the first, as you'll soon figure out. If he knows you don't like it, he will go out of his way to make your life miserable. You're in the Guard. Time to grow a thicker skin."

With Andreas' guidance, I came to know the camp routine and what was expected of me. I learned quickly that our life was regular and predictable. We rose to a trumpet call at the crack of dawn, when there was just enough light to keep from tripping over one another. We were given time to use the latrine and wash before we had to report to the drilling field. While we were fresh, our first drills were in the use of the pike in battle, the primary weapon of the Guard. It was not so heavy as it was long and unwieldly. Longer than two men lying head to foot, it took considerable skill to keep it balanced and pointed in the direction I wanted. We learned that in battle, due to its weight and length, the pike rested on the shoulder of the man in front of us. We practiced many hours taking turns kneeling and holding the weight of the pike on the shoulder, and then learning how to aim it by thrusting it at a hay target many feet in front of us. It was a tricky business to get it to balance on the fulcrum of a comrade's shoulder and pierce the target.

After three hours of these exercises, we were sent for a drink and a first bite of the day, often just a hunk of bread, and some days, a cold barley cake, barely enough to fill the hungry hole in our stomachs. The break never lasted long, just time enough to refresh before reporting back to the drilling field. We lined up in ranks eleven men wide and eleven rows deep. To begin with, we carried nothing. We had to learn how to walk as a unit, keeping our ranks straight. A drill master called out the orders to walk straight, turn right, about face, turn left, wheel right, wheel left, and walk straight again. We practiced until we could follow the commands without a single man stepping out of order.

New recruits like myself were tucked closer to the center of the ranks so our missteps had less impact on the whole. There were many times in those first weeks when I turned the wrong way and the men around me shoved me back into position, roughly, but not unkindly. I had to learn. We were told over and over again that in battle our lives depended on being able to fight unified, as a single man. We stood or fell as a unit. Otherwise, as individuals, we would all fall.

Our daily practice turned into weeks, until we learned to march in order, turn in order, retreat in order, stand still in order, run in order, and wait in order doing nothing while listening for the next order. The veterans stoically waited for new recruits like myself to catch on. Every week there were always a few new faces, and soon I felt myself swell with pride at my growing confidence as I watched the brand new recruits stumble.

We also drilled with the long pike balanced on our right shoulder. All the skills we had put into place fell apart as pikes clacked against one another, got tangled and went flying. We alternated marching without pikes and then with, as we grew more skilled. It did not take long for me to realize that the key to success was repetition, and our drill masters made sure we had plenty of that.

We practiced until we could anticipate the moves of those around us both with and without pikes, and everything we did was as one man. There was something invigorating and oddly empowering to feel myself an integral part of a fighting unit so much larger than just myself. At such moments, I was surprised by how little I missed my family. I reasoned that I was growing up and taking my own place in the fabric of our town's community. It was not the place I had wanted, but the camaraderie of the Guard took some of the bitterness out of that disappointment.

Rodrigo came out regularly to observe our drilling. Most of the time he just watched, but there were occasions when he yelled out his disapproval at how a row of men were managing, or worse yet, an individual. One day, he actually grabbed one of the men near the edge of our ranks and tossed him tumbling into the fields away from our unit.

"Out! Out!" he yelled at the poor recruit. "I don't want to see you again! Get out of my sight!"

"Keep marching!" Our drill master bellowed. I wanted to catch a glimpse of the one he had singled out, but I could not risk falling out of rhythm.

Rodrigo turned back to us and ordered, "Man down! Close ranks!" It was a move we had only just begun to practice, how to fill in the gap when a man for any reason fell out of his rank. Sadly, we made a mess of it and both the Drill Master and Rodrigo yelled themselves hoarse. As a result, we were later than usual breaking for our noonday meal.

Once I had my bowl of stew, I sought out Andreas. I wanted to know if he understood what had happened.

"His name is Hannes. The rumor is that he was caught stealing food. He had been warned, yet did it again. And not small amounts, either. The gossip is he was making a little business for himself turning around and selling food to hungry first-years like yourself. Those who enabled him will likely be dealt with harshly. Rodrigo was generous toward Hannes. He could have had him lashed, or even hanged. There is a virtue in making a punishment harsh enough to prevent anyone else from trying to get away with it."

"Why do you think he spared him?"

"A cousin, most likely," a guardsman at our table snorted. There was a sniggering agreement from others. I looked to Andreas for an explanation.

"We have among us a number of illegitimate sons from patrician families. Whether we like it or not, these bastard sons are favored over regular recruits like the rest of us. And it's no secret that Rodrigo is one of them."

"What's his story?" I asked, eager to know more about my tormentor.

"All that seems to be agreed on is that Rodrigo wanted to be a knight, but his family did not want to acknowledge him by fronting the money for horse and armor. Here in the Guard, he's risen as high as he could expect as our Battalion Master. He's hard on all of us, but he's hardest on those bastard sons and vents at them his anger at his noble family. They get no special privileges from Rodrigo. They have to earn their keep like the rest of us. As it is, he did no favor by not hanging Hannes. He has thrown him out of the Guard. Hannes will return home disgraced. He was a persona non grata before. Now he will be disavowed. He may wish he had been hanged."

ৎ ৎ ৎ

The regular routine after our simple noonday meal was time for a rest. Most everyone slept. Around three bells a trumpet called us back to the drilling fields. In addition to more practice in ranks, we were introduced to our other weapon, the short sword, and how to effectively use it for hacking, less for stabbing. Over time, we also learned to wield the deadly halberd with its razor-sharp axe blade.

Supper came late as it was designed to be our last activity before dark. Our days were as long as there was light, and physically demanding. By evening, I dragged myself to mess and forced myself to stay awake and eat. Food was not plentiful or often enough to miss a meal. We always complained of being hungry. I understood why the disgraced Hannes tried to make a profit selling food to new recruits. He had probably made a brisk business.

After supper, we had some time to gossip, and on the shorter winter days there were many games of knucklebones. Although we all welcomed a diversion, I stayed away from playing. Guardsmen were eager gamblers, and the stakes were always our wages, but I had other plans for my earnings than risk losing them at knucklebones. As it was, I had had to give my first month's wages to pay for my armor, and I inwardly bristled at the loss of the money. By ten bells, all gossip and games ended as we were expected to retire to our sleeping cots.

The barrack I slept in had several dim lanterns burning all night. This way, men who needed the piss pot did not end up falling over their sleeping comrades. The rank smell of unwashed male bodies persisted, but once I lay down, I didn't notice it any longer. All night, the barrack was a gentle roar of men snoring. There was something oddly comforting in it and strangely sleep inducing. I awoke every morning refreshed in spite of sore muscles from the exertions of the previous day.

The change in weather with the seasons altered our routine little. When it was cold, we were worked harder to keep us warm. Rain and snow did not keep us indoors. We knew we had to be prepared to fight in all weathers. In this way, my life in the Guard followed a daily, predictable rhythm.

We were given Sundays to rest. This was the one day that many of the Guard went to spend time with their families. Those who had no one they wanted to visit remained behind with the new recruits like myself who were restricted to camp for our first three months. There was no early morning bite on Sundays. Instead, a priest from town came to give prayer and confession to those of us remaining in camp. After the service was a large noonday meal, followed by light chores and hours given over to washing clothes, resting and gossiping. Inevitably, several of us would be volunteered by an officer gathering a work group for some sort of chores or repairs. If chosen, we grumbled, but complied. We relished the chance to laze around in a sunny, protected spot and either visit or get some extra sleep.

The days unfolded with drilling, drilling, and more drilling until we could move without thinking and with precision. We drilled with a pike until it ceased being clumsy and awkward and became a natural appendage. In the afternoons, we practiced with sword, pickaxe, and halberd. Then, when I thought that we had mastered everything we needed to become a fighting unit, we were ordered to put on our armor.

Following Andreas' guidance, I learned that the armor of a guardsman consisted of several layers. First came quilted trousers and the thick arming doublet. This padding was important to keep the metallic upper layers from chafing the skin raw. Over the doublet we wore a shirt of chain mail. This weighed a good twenty pounds and hung heavily on the shoulders. It was a weight we endured, as the mail could take slashing blows and save the guardsman from a fatal injury. Over the mail, we fitted the collar, a piece that protected our neck, shoulders, and upper arms. This was cleverly fashioned with a hook over the shoulder so it could sit tightly around the neck. Then the harness, which was our upper body armor, was lifted over the head. It had buckles at the shoulders and waist to accommodate the stature and girth of the guardsman. Hanging from the waist of the harness was the apron that protected the vulnerable belly and groin. Plating hung down half-way to the knees of both legs. Crowning it all was a helmet.

This armor was designed for maximum protection while allowing for maximum movement. Our torsos were covered front and back. Our lower legs, hands, and forearms were exposed, and we were schooled that this was where a guardsman received most of his injuries. Actually, we were instructed to strike an enemy at these exposed places, and only by inference realized that was exactly where we were also most vulnerable. The backs of our legs were also exposed, but then, the enemy would have access to them only if we retreated, and by that time, we'd be running.

Knights had even more armor plating, but that took a great deal of money to afford. We were grateful for what we had. With this added layer of metal, we started our drills from the beginning. Those of us doing this for the first time returned to that initial clumsy state, out of step and out of touch with one another. Our first attempts had all the new recruits and even some veterans tripping over each other, and our Drill Masters worked themselves into a froth. At this point, thankfully, Rodrigo stepped in. He ordered us all back to our dressing stations to remove our outer armor. Clothed just in chain mail, we were able to establish a semblance of the perfect marching harmony we had achieved before. We marched this way for two weeks before we were ordered to put on our outer armor layer again. It was still a challenge, but at least it was not chaotic. Then we had to get accustomed to doing all of this with a pike on the shoulder.

I was grateful that Andreas had so good-heartedly taken me under his wing. More than once he kept me from a misstep that would have left me open to ridicule from our comrades, or worse, reminded Rodrigo that I existed. Our Drill Masters were strict, and not following their orders drew loud criticism as well as blows. But we endured it, knowing that learning these forms would keep us alive in battle. Our survival demanded that we move and think as one.

Our life felt like an endless routine of one drill ending and a new one beginning. Worked to near exhaustion every day, I took to heart the soldier's creed that Andreas taught me. I followed it whenever orders did not contradict it:

*Why run when you can march?*
*Why march when you can walk?*
*Why walk when you can stand?*
*Why stand when you can sit?*
*Why sit when you can lie?*
*Why lie awake when you can sleep?*

It made perfect sense.

# "Benedict is back!"

The three months' confinement to camp passed quickly. It helped that I was kept busy from the time I rose in the early morning until I collapsed on my mat every evening. Those of us on confinement had not been allowed out even for Christmas, although we were given the day off with extra rations. Otherwise, we drilled daily with the explanation that war knows no holidays. I was surprised that I did not mind. Skipping lifelong customs made me feel quite grown up.

I had not been paying attention to the passing of time and was surprised the day I was told I was allowed to visit home for the first time. Getting ready to leave, I was suddenly nervous how I'd be received at home, and walked slowly through the town. It felt odd to see the familiar streets after so long. It was as if I had been away on a long journey, but in truth I had been just outside the city walls, still within hearing of the church bells.

I was passing the riverfront when I saw Crazy Connie. His head down, he was staring at his feet as he walked. Unlike the last time I saw him, he was wearing shoes against the winter cold, but they were old and broken. As I approached him, I could hear him haltingly count his steps. "Seven, eight, nine," then turn suddenly, retrace several steps and begin again. "Eight, nine," pause, retrace, "nine, ten, eleven." Then he began with "one, two, three, four, five," turn and start again. He was not agitated, but clearly obsessed with counting his steps. "Connie!" I called out to get his attention. He looked up, smiled, and waved. He hurried over to me in his loping gait.

"Ben-nie," he called out to me. He looked me up and down. "Bennie's in the Guard," he cooed with awe in his voice. I could not deny it. I was wearing the tunic of the City Guard, with a blazon of red and white on the shoulder. Hearing him say it out loud, though, gave me a sense of pride.

"That's right, Connie," I said clapping him on the back. I wanted to tell him that he had played a role in my joining the Guard, but I knew that would be hard to explain, so I let it go. "What were you doing, just now?" I asked.

Connie got a serious look. "Counting, Bennie. To eleven. Always eleven. Most important number, Bennie. You know?"

I laughed. "Sure, Connie. It's our number, isn't it? But what of it?"

"Today's eleven," he announced, as if it were self-evident. I thought for a moment what he could mean. Then it dawned on me.

"Of course, it's the eleventh day of the month, isn't it?"

"Count eleven, on eleven," Connie chanted. "Count eleven on eleven, on eleven, count eleven."

It was a childhood superstition we all played out when I was a child. On the eleventh of every month, wherever we went, we counted eleven paces, over and over again. Our obsession with it drove the adults mad. Obviously, Connie still played it.

Connie was staring at me, admiring my tunic. He reached out and his hands traced the red and white blazon.

"How about you, Connie? Would you like to join the Guard?"

"No!" Connie said with sudden vehemence, withdrawing his hands as if my tunic had burnt them. "Connie can't touch swords. No! Never!"

I was not prepared for such a strong reaction. I hadn't meant to excite him.

"Sure, Connie. No swords." I decided to change the subject. "Are you doing all right? Are you getting enough to eat?" Others my age took advantage of his limitations and made mockery of him, teased him, or played mean jokes on him. I hate to admit that when I was younger I thought it was wildly funny and did the same. Being the butt of Rodrigo's ridicule had taught me more compassion.

"Connie's fine," he said. He wore tattered hose and a doublet that had once been brocaded, but this had mostly fallen off and now the cloth was frayed, torn, and dirty. He was usually dressed in cast-off finery. I often wondered where he found such fancy clothing, worn out as they were.

"You want to sit with me?" he asked. In spite of living on the streets, I got the sense that Connie was lonely most of the time.

"Can't right now, Connie. I'm going home to see my family. I've been away a long time."

"Bye, Bennie," he said. Abruptly, he turned his back on me and walked away. That was just Connie.

The first thing I heard as I was walking down my lane was my sister Veronika. "Benedict!" she cried out. "Benedict is back!"

I saw her racing toward me and she flew into my arms. Then she ran circles around me, chanting, "Benedict! Benedict!" It warmed my heart to see her again and be infected with her exuberance. She linked arms with me and brought me to our front door. Both my parents were there and gave me a welcoming embrace. When she turned away, I saw my mother wiping tears from her eyes. Seb was there as well and put me in a quick headlock, ruffling my hair. It was so good to be in the family circle again.

Veronika had baked her best Sunday treat, a heavy cake with raisins and nuts, sweetened with honey. We sat down at the table to enjoy it together. "We've been counting the days until you'd come home," Veronika said with a wink. Mother's tears had dried by now and Father was giving me an appraising look.

"Guardsman, eh?" he said. "The livery looks good on you, though you know what I would prefer."

"At least he has let go of that terrible idea to become a scribbler of letters."

"It's called a scrivener, Mother," I said, holding down my desire to scold her. My time in the Guard had at least taught me some restraint. "And I have not exactly let go of it."

I placed two silver groschen on the table. "We're paid a silver groschen each month," I said. "I used my first month's pay for my armor. This is my second and third month's pay. I am giving two-thirds of my earnings to the household that fed me and cared for me until this day. I will continue doing this, giving two of every three pay periods."

"And what will you do with your third month's pay?" my father asked, eyeing the coins, but leaving them lie where I had placed them. He had a smile on his face as if he already knew the answer.

I took a deep breath. I knew I was expected to give all my money to the support of the household. This was common practice with every young man until he set up his own. Seb handed over all but a few pennies of his earnings. "I'm saving it," I said. I watched my father's face carefully, but could read nothing, which I took as a good sign. Not so, my mother. Her mouth shot open, but before she could say anything, my father held up his hand. "Marta, let the boy speak."

"I still want to become a scrivener," I continued. "But I learned that I have to take an apprenticeship, and apprenticeships cost money."

"Well, what did you think?" my mother interrupted shrilly.

"Marta," Father warned. "Let him finish."

I mumbled the next. "And then I'll need to pay a fee to take the Guild test." I didn't mention that the Guild had an entrance fee as well. I did not want to give my mother any more fuel for predicting my failure. I took a breath and steeled myself to continue. "When I've saved enough money, every third month's pay, I will apprentice myself. I've already spoken with a Master Scrivener." I was not being completely honest with this, because I was giving the impression that I had made arrangements with him, which I had not.

Father heard me out and nodded his head in approval. "That sounds fair to me." He reached out, took the silver groschen and pocketed them. "Now that's settled. Veronika, pass me that last piece of your irresistible Sunday cake."

As easily as that, I was back in the good graces of my family.

In the afternoon, when everyone else was settling down for their midday rest, I excused myself.

"Martin?" Mother asked.

I nodded. "It feels like forever since I last saw him."

"Take this with you," she said, handing me a small bag. Inside were some carrots, potatoes, fennel, and half a loaf of bread. "It's from our winter store. It will just go bad anyway with warmer weather coming," she said quickly. "We won't go hungry, and neither should he." Mother always puzzled me. She never had a kind word to say about Martin's choice to become a mendicant, yet here she was sending him food. There was even one piece from Veronika's cake that she had put aside. "I don't know how he keeps from starving," she said with a disapproving shake of her head, "in spite of the mild winter we're having."

"He says he lives on prayer," I offered.

"Then tell him to garnish his prayers with my vegetables."

I thanked her and headed north out of the city.

# Martin

I left my guard tunic on. I knew Martin would want to see me in it. I hiked half an hour through the woods until I came to the entrance to the gorge. Jagged cliffs and a wooded hillside rose on either side of a fast flowing stream that splashed down a series of cascades. The cliffs hemmed in the stream, framing it, yet not so close as to rob the space of light. Trees grew along the bank as well as on the hillside. The last snow still lay in the shaded places beneath trees, but the path was free. I followed it upstream. I breathed in the moist, brisk air and felt a quiet peacefulness settle on my heart. This gorge was famous for bringing stillness to one's thoughts and feelings. Perhaps that was why it was considered sacred. I was certain that was why my devout boyhood friend had chosen to live here.

As I turned the corner around an outcropping of boulders, I saw Martin with his back to me, standing motionless in a grove of trees. A single ray of sunlight broke through the thick branches, and he stood bathed in its warming glow, illuminating his long hair and thin frame. He wore a shift that had seen much wear. It reached down below his knees and was tied at the waist with a short piece of rope. Around his shoulders was draped a tattered blanket. On his feet was an old pair of sandals.

Happy to have found him so easily, I called out his name. He did not respond. Was he that deep in prayer? I came closer and called out again, "Martin! It's me, Benedict." Still, no reply. By the time I reached him, I expected him to at least hear my footsteps and turn around, but he did not react to my approach. I stepped in front of him. He looked up at me, his face glowing, not just from the sunlight. He raised his hand and in the air made the sign of the cross.

"Benedictus," he said warmly, "I am blessed to see you again." We fell into one another's arms in a brotherly embrace.

We walked further upstream side-by-side along the path. "Martin," I asked. "Didn't you hear me call out to you?"

"Indeed I did, my dear friend."

"Then why didn't you return my greeting?"

"It is my newest discipline," he explained. "I am practicing strict inwardness. If I manage to silence the voices from without, I can focus on silencing the voices from within."

When Martin saw the puzzlement on my face at this remark, he laughed, and added, "It is a great pleasure to be able to converse with one's friends in this world, but I have also come to realize it is also a great distraction."

"A distraction?" I asked. "From what?"

"From meditating upon the true pictures of the world."

Martin had spoken to me before in such terms, but I never quite got to the point of understanding what he meant.

"I have long wondered," Martin continued, "how life is different for one who cannot hear what is said to him and cannot share his thoughts with others. To experience this, I am practicing being both deaf and dumb toward my fellow human beings. In this way, I am able to limit my worldly distractions."

"Isn't living as a hermit in the woods enough separation from the world?" I asked.

"I will do whatever I can to sharpen my spiritual eyes and ears," he replied with a gleam in his eyes. "I wish my prayer to become more authentically mine own. Your appearance was a great test for me, although it was not one I had planned, but was planned for me by a greater power."

I had grown accustomed to Martin referring to his life being guided by the hand of the Divine.

"A test?" I asked. "What do you mean?"

"Whether I could resist the temptation of the outer world of the senses. You know, I have often told you, what we see before us is but a pale reflection of the one true world. Nature speaks most purely of that world. The speech of man, on the other hand, is often a great distraction. I have shared this with you before, have I not?"

I suppressed a smile. "Yes, Martin, you have spoken of these two worlds with me before." As in every time we met. "So how did you fare in your test?"

"I heard your voice call to me, and I felt great joy in my heart. Then, with an immense effort, I turned a deaf ear to that joy and focused alone on the voice of my Lord."

When Martin would not say more, I had to ask, "And? What did you hear?"

"I clearly need more practice," Martin smiled with an endearing embarrassment. "It is for this reason that I will live deaf and dumb to the word of Man, listening only to the voice of the Lord as it speaks to me through Nature. I will have succeeded when people who visit will come to believe that I have lost the power to hear and speak."

"Oh, Martin, you are always so extreme," I scolded.

"Our incarnated life requires extreme measures," he replied with a smile.

"I am learning there is truth in that," I agreed. "So, if that is the case, that you will soon live deaf and dumb, then I must speak with you quickly, before you lose the power to hear me or speak with me. I have been gone a long while and wish to catch up with you."

"I know," Martin said. "I would have worried about your absence, but I was told by the wind not to be concerned."

I laughed. I never knew if Martin was making these things up. "And what else did the wind tell you?"

"That it had blown a door closed for you."

I grew serious when he said that. "In truth, it had. I was very desperate." We walked a few moments in silence, but I could not contain my words and they poured forth as quickly as the water flowed in the stream running beside us. "I tried to join the Scriveners

Guild. They turned me away. I sought out a master to learn from. I had no idea it would cost so much. I can't afford an apprenticeship."

"It was a strong wind, to shut that door so harshly," he mused.

"I had to choose another path."

"Indeed, it was necessary," he replied with a nod.

Hadn't he noticed? I couldn't contain myself any longer. "Martin, you've said nothing about my uniform!" I gestured to the tunic identifying me as a member of the Guard.

"It is clear to me that the wind that blew the door closed to all your hopes came from a window that wanted you to find it."

I was astonished at his words. "Are you saying that it is God's Will that I joined the Guard?"

"I'm glad you have come to realize this without my having to say it."

I had stopped in my tracks, trying to make sense of what he wanted me to believe. Was it my destiny to enter the Guard? Martin turned to me. He reached out and tugged at my tunic, straightening it.

"It fits you much better than Seb's hand-me-downs," he said, sizing me up.

"Is that all?"

"It fits you better than plans you cannot follow, or rattling at doors that are closed to you. Is your family content?"

I nodded my head. "It is something they can understand, although Father would still prefer to apprentice me."

"I am happy for you and for your parents. I am certain this will lead you to your next window." He caught my attention with this remark.

"So, you think there is still a chance that I will study to become a scrivener?"

"The Good Lord will open the next window when the time is right."

"I'm saving a third of my pay. Father has not objected."

"A wise man," he nodded. "As wise as your mother is generous." Martin gestured with a disarming smile at the bag slung over my shoulder. "Now, tell me, did you bring the mendicant a gift?"

I handed him the bag Mother had given me. "It is sent with her love."

Martin opened it and took a quick look inside. "Blessings on her winter stores. While you were gone, she sent your brother Seb to deliver her gifts to me. He was not terribly gracious about it, though. He does not approve of your mother's generosity to the hermit of the gorge. I will feast well from this. Thank her for me, please."

At Martin's request, we walked in meditative silence along the stream. The water, running low in winter, at intervals iced over, fell along multiple cascades filling the air with a cheerful sound, and the surrounding fir trees filled the air with their pungent aroma. It was a place of serenity. I could better understand how this gorge was Martin's chosen refuge.

We had by this time reached the far end of the ravine where Martin had a protected place out of wind and rain to lay his head at night and a corner against the rock wall where he could cook his meager meals.

Martin's chapel was nothing more than the ruins of an ancient building that had been hardly more than foundation stones marking the perimeter of walls that had once stood there. He had been painstakingly and slowly rebuilding it. He had constructed a coarse stone altar tucked against the canyon wall with nothing but a roughly formed wooden cross sitting upon it. In this place of wild nature, it was a powerful gesture. I had to admire the work he had already put into creating a holy place. He saw in my face that I was impressed and smiled broadly.

"I believe you once told me that you are sustained mostly by prayer."

"I am," Martin said with a nod.

I made an exaggerated point of looking him up and down. "I have seen beggars in town who look better fed," I said. "If you are sustained by prayer, my friend, you are clearly not praying enough."

At my words, Martin burst into laughter.

"Too true, dear Benedictus. Come, help me nourish myself, lest I starve to death. Enter my chapel with me and let us pray together. Just one rosary, mmh?"

Martin was so clever turning my teasing around. He was always trying to get me to pray more. How could I refuse? I joined him in singing the Lord's Prayer followed by a decade of Hail Mary. He then took my joke a step further. As we finished the tenth Hail Mary, he cried out piteously how hungry he still was. In the end, we sang the decade three times.

"Martin," I said. We had gone to sit in the sun against the limestone walls of the ravine. I had tempted him with Veroni's piece of Sunday cake. I had wanted him to have it all, but he said he would eat none unless I shared it with him. I broke off a corner and gave him the rest. "I have a question."

"Speak," he said. "With Veronika's cake sweetening my tongue, there is the danger that I break out in prayer again."

That made me laugh. "This is a serious question," I began.

"As all should be viewed in God's manifested world."

"Martin, why do you not take orders? No one could question your commitment to God. I know when you first moved here, people mocked you and said you'd run scared back home with the first thunderstorm, but you've weathered nearly a whole winter here. You've begun repairing the old chapel and tend it with your prayers daily. People take your devotion seriously now. But why live here in solitude when you could have the company of others without the distractions of the venal world. You would not have to struggle as you do now to keep yourself fed, or to keep the iron grip of the cold from your bones. You are thinner than ever before, and I will say honestly that I am worried about you."

"Dear friend Benedict, I am warmed by your brotherly concern. Be at peace to know that I have seriously considered the path of joining the Brothers. I have spent many an hour in my solitude arguing back and forth the virtues of their path versus my solitary way. It is a worthy step to join a holy order of Brothers, but I have concluded that it is not for me."

"But why?"

"It comes down to this. Once among the Brothers, I must submit to the yoke of their discipline, without variance, without objection. Just as you must submit to the yoke of the Guard and follow the rules they set forth. The Brothers have their order, and to live among them and follow their ways, one must bow to that order."

"But isn't that what you want? You are always telling me about your latest discipline. With the Brothers, there need be no more trial and error."

Martin gave me one of his special smiles. "It is by trying and erring that we find our way to God."

"You truly believe this?"

"I believe that as the crown of creation, we were given a gift that was withheld from all other creatures. That gift is the freedom to make choices. We call it *Free Will.* We see it for the first time when Eve accepts the forbidden apple from the serpent. She could have refused. We see it with Adam, when he accepts the apple from Eve. He could have refused. Cain, instead of slaying his brother in a fit of jealousy, could have chosen to act with humility and curiosity instead of violence. Free Will was a gift given to us, yet it is also a great responsibility. Every time we use this gift and make a choice, there are consequences. So we owe it to ourselves to use it with great caution and awareness."

I pondered this a moment. I have always been troubled by the stories Martin had referred to. "But by exercising Free Will, Eve disobeyed the direct commandment of God, and that led to the Fall. To the expulsion from Paradise. The First Sin. Are we not taught that this disobedience led to all the struggle and pain we now experience? What sort of gift is that?"

"The gift is that we are allowed to learn through our mistakes."

I must have frowned, because Martin laughed and said, "It does sound like an odd gift to be allowed to make mistakes. But isn't that the only way to raise a child? At one point we have to stop holding his hand and let him stand or fall on his own. And we are all God's children." He let me ponder this a few moments before continuing.

"Life among the Brethren would, without question, be more comfortable and regular, feed me and keep me warm in winter, but it would rob me of that unique gift of Free Will. It would be like having my hand held, although I am a grown man. The Holy Brethren do not believe in our right to trial and error. Out of an extreme caution that we would err too greatly, they have removed choice. The activities of the Brothers are ordained from the moment they rise in the morning until they lay their heads down at night. They live a very ordered life. Obviously, this appeals to many. I prefer to live in the simplicity of nature, where the lessons and consequences are immediate and unequivocal. And living here, I am free to follow a discipline until it no longer serves me along my path. Then I am free to let it go and find a new one."

I took a deep breath and thought about his words. "It makes sense, when you say it that way, although it will not warm you in winter."

Martin laughed openly. "God will provide. Don't forget that I have nearly survived this one."

I glanced up through the trees. The sun had sunk low, and I was required back in my barracks by nightfall. "Martin," I explained, "we will speak more of winter another time. Right now, I am compelled to go due to the restrictions of the order I now belong to. I must return by nightfall. I am confined to camp during the week, but Sundays are my own. I will return every Sunday, when I can."

"Wonderful," he exclaimed. "You can help me stay my hunger for prayer."

I had to laugh. "Look for me in a week." When I rose to leave, Martin held me back and told me to bow my head. He placed his hands upon my shoulders and spoke a quiet prayer that I go in peace and with the blessings of the eternal God, under the protection of the ever-watchful angels. Walking back along the stream, warmed by our conversation and stirred by his parting gesture, I realized that, while I had enlisted as a soldier, my boyhood friend had become a holy man.

# *Walking the Periphery*

I returned to camp in time to slip into the mess hall to snatch a bowl of stew and a fistful of bread before they closed down for the night. The pavilion was mostly empty by now, just a handful of men like me who had made it back to camp just in time to grab a bite. That is where Andreas found me. I watched him come bustling into the pavilion as if he were looking for something he'd lost. As soon as he caught sight of me, he made a beeline to where I sat.

"Where have you been?" he demanded.

"Home," I replied. "What's the problem?"

"The Watch Master wants to see you. Don't make him wait any longer." Before I could ask him what this was about, he was gone.

I looked up at a guardsman sitting at the table. "Don't mess with the Watch Master," he said. "You'd better go."

I wolfed down the rest of my stew, wiped my bowl clean with my remaining bread, stuffed it into my mouth, and headed out of the mess hall. I knew where the Watch Master's station was, although I had never paid it any attention. The Watch Master set guard duty in town, but since I had been, until now, confined to camp, I had had nothing to do with him.

The ceiling of the small tent that was his station was high enough for me to stand up in. A lit lantern stood on a small table. Behind the table sat two men, one a scribe with his quill and a sheaf of loose papers, and the other the Watch Master. I presented myself. "Waisel," I said. "I was told you were looking for me."

"About time," the Watch Master grumbled. He looked sleepy. "Been waiting all day to see you."

"Watch Master," I explained. "It's Sunday, my first day off. I went to see my family."

He waived me off as if what I had said was irrelevant. He turned to the scribe. "What's Waisel's duty?"

I watched the scribe shuffle some papers, all of them lists, by their appearance. I thought to myself, I could do that job, but knew better and bit my tongue.

The scribe studied one of the papers and said, "Periphery. Basel Gate."

"Check him off," the Watch Master grumbled. To me, he said, "Tomorrow, immediately following the noonday meal, report to the Basel Gate. They will explain your duty. Simple enough. You walk the periphery. Afternoon, next morning, day off to train, then repeat afternoon, next morning, then off again. Understood?" He glanced up and must have seen the bewildered look on my face. "They'll explain," he continued. "You will dress in full armor, with chainmail, and carry a halberd. Understood?"

"Yes, Watch Master," I replied, not in the least clear. "But—"

"You can go now," he interrupted me. "They'll tell you what you need to know at the gate. Go immediately after the noonday meal. Full armor. Halberd."

"But Watch Master," I began again.

He wouldn't let me speak. "It's soon lanterns out. Good night." He turned to the scribe. "Anyone else?"

"He's the last, Watch Master."

"Then secure the lists before you go." With this, the Watch Master stood up and left the tent.

I looked to the scribe. "What was that all about?"

"You've been assigned. Simple enough. You heard what he said. Full armor, Basel Gate, tomorrow after the meal. You better get to your barracks now before they count heads."

He was right about that, and I hurried away. They place a heavy fine on us if we are missing when heads are counted at lights out, and I needed every groschen I earned. As I jogged across the open ground to my barracks, it hit me what had just happened. I was considered ready to draw a shift in the Guard. A broad smile crossed my face. No more endless, mindless drills all day long. I would stand guard in the city. *This is good,* I thought to myself. How little did I know.

The next morning, at first bite, I told Andreas that I had been assigned to guard duty in the city.

"Lucky you," he said dryly, and moved on.

I hadn't expected his lack of interest, and I caught up with him.

"Hey, Andreas, aren't you happy for me? Isn't that why I've been drilling all these weeks?"

Andreas turned to face me. "We've been drilling how to move as a single unit in battle. You will now learn how to be a single guard at a post. Sorry for not celebrating your new assignment. You'll understand later. I'm content to pull shifts here in camp."

"What do you mean?"

"Have you been ordered to report in full armor?"

"As a matter of fact, I have. Is there a problem with that?"

"Talk with me again this evening."

I couldn't figure out what bothered him, but I was not going to let it dampen my good spirits. Our morning drills passed quickly and I rushed through the noon meal. I did not want to arrive late. Although I was clumsy putting on my armor without help, I consoled myself that it would get easier with time. I slipped on my helmet, grabbed a halberd from the rack along the wall, and headed into the city to report at the Basel Gate.

My heart swelled with self-importance when people glanced at me as I passed through the narrow streets of the city, my halberd perched jauntily on my shoulder. I arrived at the Basel Gate and presented myself to the Captain of the Guard.

"You the new watch?" he asked, looking me up and down. "Name?"

"Waisel. I'm happy to meet you, Captain," I added, wanting to be on friendly terms.

This caused him to take a serious look at me. "I'm sure you are," he said, one eyebrow raised. "Anders!" he called out. Another guardsman stepped forward. "Show our friendly guardsman here his route." With this he turned away from me.

I turned to the man he had summoned. "Hello, Anders," I said, still determined to be friendly.

Anders gave me a quick glance. "Follow," he said curtly, turning and walking away at a fast clip. I fell in a couple strides behind him. I soon realized that he was speaking, but I could not catch what he was saying. Was he talking to himself? I quickened my pace to walk beside him.

"... in order to arrive at the same time. Understood?"

"Sorry," I said. "Could you repeat that? I didn't know you were talking to me."

Anders stopped in his tracks and turned on me. He had a surly look on his face. "When I'm speaking you listen and remember, understand? I'm not saying it twice, understand?"

Uncertain what I had done to annoy him, I nodded vigorously, causing my helmet to rattle against my neck piece. I felt like a fool.

"You start beneath that postern up there," he said in a loud voice, gesturing vaguely behind me. "You march steadily along the outer periphery of the wall. You time yourself to meet the guard walking toward you at the midpoint. Every third meeting you can stop for a drink and a piss, otherwise you keep going—all the way to the Tower Gate. You turn around and march back. You do this until relieved. Understand? You abandon your post for any reason, first offense, twenty lashes. You do it again, second offense, you'll be hung from the wall by your feet until the Guard decides you are no longer a threat to the city, and your family can bury your rotting corpse. Understand?"

I was taken aback by his forceful words. "Yes," I stammered. "I understand."

"Great. Now follow along and I'll show you your route. show you only once." Turning away from me, he cursed under his breath, "Wish they'd stop sending these green recruits. Such stupidity."

I walked beside him and said nothing. There was no jauntiness left in my step. He'd taken the wind out of my sails. We walked along the base of the wall on the north side of the city. We came to one portion of the wall that made a little turn. He paused at this place.

"This is where you take your break. Only every third time you come here, understand? You time it so you arrive at the same moment as the guard coming from the opposite side. Put your water flask here." He pointed to a shallow indentation in the wall at shoulder height. "Over there," he gestured to a stand of trees, "is where you piss." Then he started walking again, and I hurried to keep up. He walked me all the way to the Tower Gate.

"Here is where you turn around. Understood?" He looked me up and down, utter disapproval on his face. "Where's your horn?" he demanded.

"Horn?"

"Yes, horn. Are you deaf? Yes, I said horn."

"No one told me about a horn," I stammered, not wanting to kindle his anger again.

"You pick one up at the gate. You leave it when your duty ends."

"What's it for?"

He cursed again under his breath. "I swear, they send up children. To blow the alarm, of course! In case you have to blow the alarm!" he shouted. As if nothing could be more obvious.

"I'll make sure to pick up a horn," I said quickly.

Anders shook his head in disgust and started the long walk back to the Basel Gate. I hurried to keep up.

When we reached the midpoint, there was a guardsman standing there. He must have come down from the gate where we were headed.

"Here's your other half," Anders barked. "Hope he has more brains than you. Figure it out." He did not stay any longer, but kept walking.

When he was out of earshot, the other guardsman said in a quiet voice, "Don't mind him. He's always sour about something."

I recognized him from camp. Andreas had pointed him out in the mess before. His name was August. We discussed briefly which direction to go. I noticed that August already had a horn hanging at his side, so I had to return to the Basel Gate to pick up mine.

"I'll give you an extra count of thirty before turning around," he said. "That should give you enough time. Find someone to show you where the horns are kept. Don't ask Anders, otherwise he will chew you out all over again." I nodded my agreement. He added, "You've never done this duty before, have you?"

"I admit, first time. I just finished my three-month confinement to camp."

"Let me show you how to walk, so we can keep pace with one another and arrive here at the same time." August showed me how to walk at a leisurely, though regular pace, each stride taking three counts. "Don't get too fast, otherwise, with all this armor, you'll wear yourself out. It's a tedious shift. Try not to daydream too much. Anders checks in on us every once in a while. You want to see him coming before he sees you."

By the time my shift was finished, I understood why Andreas had shown no enthusiasm for my new assignment. I dragged my feet all the way back to camp. I had barely enough strength left to stow my gear. At the wash station, I stripped and poured a bucket of water over my head. This would keep me awake long enough to eat something. I was famished and at the mess hall gulped down my bowl of stew. I went to my sleeping mat before the final lights-out call, and I was sound asleep the moment I lay flat. The next morning, I felt like I had fallen out of a window. Everything hurt. Andreas found me at the mess, where a substantial breakfast was set out for those going into the city to their posts. He didn't have to say anything. The pained expression on my face said it all.

Andreas patted me on the shoulder. "Welcome to the Guard," he said with a wry smile.

So began a rhythm of two days walking the perimeter of the wall, the first day walking the afternoon shift, and the next day the morning shift. Then I had one day off. It was not a rest day as I rejoined the ranks drilling to march as a company of soldiers. At least it was a break from the tedium of walking the periphery. I looked forward to the short breaks with August, but only every third time we met in the middle. Fellow guardsmen consoled me that every new recruit pulled this kind of duty. The intention was to build up stamina by wearing full armor. If we ever went into battle, we would go suited up. They assured me that if I kept eating the solid meals the canteen offered, with time I would bulk up.

It was a lonely shift and gave me plenty of time to consider what Martin called the consequences of my free choice. Since the only other option I could think of was becoming a stonemason like my brothers, I was content with my lot, and if I complained it was not out loud.

As the days spread into weeks, I grew comfortable with this shift. My armor seemed to wear lighter and I took pride in keeping the perimeter of our town safe, keeping my eyes open for suspicious activity, none of which I ever saw.

The farthest point in my tour along the walls brought me under the imposing Tower Gate. There are slots in the walls of its rounded tower. More than once, I heard cries of distress coming from inside. The first time I heard them, I wanted to go to their aid. But then I realized that I was hearing the troubled cries of men imprisoned, beyond any help I could offer. It sent shivers down my spine.

It did not matter the weather—sun, heat, rain, sleet, cold. We walked the perimeter, always in a slow three-count step. I prided myself that the protection of the city depended on us. Just the same, for the first time since joining the Guard, time passed slowly.

Sundays were still my own. I wondered whether there was a shift on Sunday as well. When I asked, Andreas explained that the city walls get no day off. However, extra pay was offered to those willing to pull duty on the Lord's Day. When he saw my eyes light up, he laughed and said, "Get in line. There are a lot of guardsmen who covet the extra pay. For now, be satisfied with your regular duty."

So I spent my days off with my family, with the added treat of time with my dear friend, Martin. Days and weeks passed following a regular routine, and I was pleased to realize that I was indeed bulking up, as my comrades had told me I would. Not only Veroni commented on the added girth to my chest and arms, but even Seb, normally short on words, commented that I was starting to get the build of a real stonemason.

Life in the Guard had one added perk. With great satisfaction, I watched as my little treasure of savings grew, and I could imagine the day coming when I would be able to once again seek out Master Cornelius, but this time with my apprenticeship fees in hand.

In this manner, spring passed into summer, and when the heat had peaked and began slowly to fade toward autumn, Veronika turned to me with a twinkle in her eye.

"In case you had forgotten, it's berry picking season," she said. "When are you free to go?" For years Veronika and I had gone in search of berries, which Mother turned into jam for the winter months.

"I'm off duty next Sunday again," I said. "Will that do?"

"It will do very well," Veronika replied. "That will give the berries another week to sweeten. We'll leave right after our noonday meal."

# Berry Picking

The following Sunday, I rose early so I could join my family in church and return home with them for an early noonday meal. After a short rest, Veroni announced that we were going berry picking. I could tell that Mother was in a good mood, for she hummed as she prepared us two baskets, and put in one of them half a loaf of bread, a wedge of cheese and a bottle of weak ale to see us through until evening. We didn't say anything, but Veronika gave me a look that said we would stuff ourselves with berries and never touch the food. We took our baskets from the table.

As we were walking out the door, Mother warned us sternly, "And bring enough berries home so I can make several pots of compote. We need them to sweeten our days in the darkness of winter. Serves no one to make yourselves sick and have nothing to show for it." She had read our minds! Veronika and I looked at each and broke into giggles as we ducked out the door and hurried down the lane.

"How does she do that?" Veronika marveled.

"She knows us way too well."

"I think it's part of being a mother."

"Reading minds?"

"Something like that."

"Do you think you'll be able to read minds when you have children?"

Veronika blushed. "Don't know if I ever will," she said under her breath.

"What's to stop you?"

Veronika pressed her lips together and gave me a dark look, blushing even more.

"What did I say?"

"Just stop," she insisted. "It is not seemly to speak so with a maiden."

I was puzzled what she meant. Veronika was my sister. We always spoke about everything. I opened my mouth to speak, but she held up a warning finger. "Don't," she said commandingly. I let it drop. What else could I do? My little sister, it seemed, was growing up.

It was a brilliantly warm day. There were billowy white clouds over the mountains, but they threatened no rain. We passed through the city until we came to the river and crossed Chapel Bridge to the Lower City. We followed the riverfront until we came to the Beggars Gate with its tall, crooked pointed roof, like a gnome's cap. We walked through it out of the city. True to its name, outside the gate were gathered a dozen or more of Solodurum's unfortunate. Ragged, filthy, haggard and hungry, they huddled in small groups. The moment we appeared, a dozen grubby empty hands were raised in supplication, looking for a handout. I waved them off and they let us pass unmolested. They knew better than to be too insistent. It could cost them entrance into the city. They had learned to suffer in silence.

"I feel so sorry whenever I see them," Veronika murmured.

"And so be grateful that Father keeps a roof over our heads and food on our table."

"If only we could lighten their suffering," she said, glancing over her shoulder back at them.

"They have the Church to turn to when their need is that great."

"Not so," Veronika said. "Many are gypsies. The Church will not offer a helping hand until they accept the true faith."

I shrugged my shoulders. "Then they could go pick berries, as we are doing," I pointed out.

"Why do you think they do not?" Veronika wondered.

"I think they do," I replied. "See how they collect at this gate. They don't gather here because it is named so. The gate is named after them. They linger here because this is where the open fields and the orchards begin. Even though they may be non-believers, the Church gives them the biblical allowance to glean the corners of the fields and eat what fruit drops to the ground. They have learned how to forage."

We were following a wooded path along the Arola, walking upstream.

"Have they no better choices?"

"I once spoke with Martin about them," I said. "Since he has chosen to live the life of a mendicant, I thought he might know something about their situation, and I was not disappointed. He knew quite a bit."

"What did he say?"

"He said that, aside from the gypsies who wander from town to town, some are homeless by choice, others by birth, meaning they are orphans. The gypsies come and go, but our local homeless wander from place to place around the town, begging, foraging, and looking for any opportunity. Martin explained that they are nearly as outcast from society as the Jews, except the Jews live among us, lead an ordered and productive life, but keep to themselves. When the homeless have a coin to spend, they visit the Jews' tavern house, since one outcast group is drawn to spend time with another. In this way, Martin said, they have developed a language all their own, with words borrowed from the gypsies and the Jews, a sort of secret beggar's language."

"I had no idea," Veronika marveled.

"Nor I, of course. Our saint Martin is a treasure trove of information."

We were coming through the woods, passing a dense hedge, when I happened to see something through a gap in the thicket.

"Hold on a second," I called out to Veronika. "This is strange." On the other side of the thicket were several rows of trees in an open glade, as orderly as any orchard. I was puzzled, because this orchard appeared to be hemmed in on all sides by either forest or thicket. "What farmer would plant an orchard and make it inaccessible on all sides?" I mused. "Let's see if there's a way in." We followed the edge of the dense growth until it turned a corner, and we continued walking along it until we found a very small gap, just large enough to let us pass inside.

"Strangest thing," I said, as we gazed at the three rows of trees, about one dozen total in number. I was ready to let the mystery pass when Veronica called out.

"Now that's odd."

"Exactly. I can't figure out what an orchard is doing out here, as if it's hidden away."

"Not that," she said, shaking her head and looking up into the branches of one of the trees. "That," she said, pointing.

"What do you see?"

"Berries. There are berries growing in the tree. Trees don't bear berries."

I looked where she was pointing, and indeed, there were berries hanging from the branches of the tree.

"The rowan does, but this is not a rowan." I circled the tree. "Now how's that possible?" I asked out loud. "Maybe there is a vine growing up into the branches." We both looked, but could find no vines growing up the side of the tree. We looked into the neighboring trees and saw that they, too, bore fat berries in their branches. "That's the oddest thing," I concluded. "I thought I knew all trees and what fruits they bear." I laughed out loud. "Well, here's a new mystery on God's earth that I can bring to Martin's attention. I suspect he won't disappoint me and will tell me all about these trees and how they got here, and why I've never seen them growing anywhere else."

"Do you think they're edible?" Veronika asked.

I reached up and plucked one. It was dark purple in color. "Only one way to find out," I said, popping it into my mouth.

"Wait!" Veronika tried to stop me. "They could be poisonous."

I laughed. "No one plants an orchard with poisonous fruit. And if they are, then it is a deliciously sweet poison. This berry is very tasty. We will keep our eyes open, and if we see berries such as these for sale at the market, we will know from what tree they come, and be able to ask for its name. For now, let us keep our eyes open for the berries we've come to pick."

We slipped back through the gap in the thick hedge and continued our walk upriver. We didn't have far to go.

"Well, there's what we came for," Veronica said, pointing. I looked up and saw ahead the first hedge of blackberries growing close to the river bank.

"Now we can begin our own foraging. Race you," and I broke into a trot. Veronika caught up and with a laugh of glee gave me a shove as she passed me, throwing me off balance and I tumbled into the grass. I jumped back to my feet, shouting, "You cheat!"

"I can't help it if you trip over your own feet," she called over her shoulder as she reached the hedge. "I win. Hurry up. They're ripe."

She was right. The hedge was filled with blackberries ready for picking. In an instant, Veronika's fingers were stained blue.

"Remember, for every one you eat, three into the basket," I said.

"Yeah, yeah," she said. "Three in the mouth, one in the basket," and she shot me a saucy smile.

We picked for some time in silence, stuffing our mouths with the juicy berries while making sure not to neglect filling the basket. It was a glorious, perfect late summer day of warmth and sunshine. Out of the corner of my eye, I noticed, back in the direction of the grove of mystery trees, three men watching us. They were not dressed in the ragged fashion of the beggars, so I concluded that they were bound land laborers, our local peasantry. Someone was caring for these trees, even if they were hidden away. The men stood rather awkwardly, staring at us. Or rather, I was convinced, they were staring at Veronika. There was a reason we had come together. It was not safe for Veronika to go out alone. She had nothing to worry about as long as I was with her, but just the same, I was not going to let them out of my sight.

"I'm going around to gather on the river side of the hedge," Veronika called out to me.

"Do you see what I'm seeing?" I said, inclining my head in the direction of the gawking peasants.

"I see them," she said casually.

"You still carrying the blade I gave you?" I asked.

"Yes, I carry it in my waistband. And a lot of good it will do against three of them."

"It will give them pause, and that may be all the time you need to get away."

"My poor brother, always seeing the worst in people."

"My poor sister, not seeing people for what they are."

And with that Veronika slipped out of my sight around the hedge on the river side. I continued my picking, keeping tabs on the three men. For a while, they sat in the grass, watching me watching them. I was annoyed when two of them got up and wandered off to my right and out of my line of sight. I had berries enough to keep me busy, but I was growing uneasy about the two rascals I could not see. I was just about to go around the hedge to continue picking nearer Veronika when I heard her call sharply.

"Benedict!" Her voice had urgency in it. Then, "Benedict, come. Quickly!" I forced my way through the high grass, cursing that I had not thought to bring my short sword with me. But when I rounded the hedge and came to the banks of the river, I saw Veronika standing there alone, staring into the water.

"What?" I asked "What frightened you?"

"That," she said, staring into the river.

I followed her gaze, and what I saw made my hair stand on end. Bodies. Bodies floating in the water, lazily carried downstream on the current.

"Who are they?" Veronika asked. I saw immediately that some were dressed in the colors of Solodurum's Guard, but two wore uniforms I did not know. Clearly there had been a battle upstream. Why did I not know anything about this? And if I didn't, that meant no one else knew. Had we been invaded?

I reached out and grabbed Veronika by the wrist. "We have to go. Now!"

"Who are they?" she shrieked at me.

"Some are our own. We have to alert the Guard. We have to go." I had to bring this news back as soon as possible, yet I could not leave Veronica in the fields alone. I started yanking her away from there. "Come on!"

"Leave me," she insisted. "Take the news back to town. Go."

"Not without you," I yanked harder to pull her along. "Time to show me how fast you can run." I linked elbows with her and we rushed back to the wooded path that would take us to the city walls, our baskets dancing wildly on our arms.

"Our berries," Veronika wailed. "We're losing them all."

"Can't be helped," I grunted. "We have to get back."

We made it within sight of the crooked steeple of the Beggars Gate before Veronika sank to the ground, spent. "I can't ... any farther," she panted. "I must rest."

"Veronika," I insisted. "You can't stay here." I looked around at the knots of beggars gathered here. I had to get Veronika safely behind the city walls. I also had a duty to alert the Guard to an attack on the city.

"Can't," Veronika sighed. She was breathing heavily, her head sinking down.

I was trying to tug her to her feet when an elderly woman left a group of women and girls sitting in the shade of a tree and approached us. She knelt down and put her arm around Veronika's shoulders.

"Poor thing," she said, her voice full of sympathy. "She is overheated. She needs to rest." She looked up at me. "If you must hasten, leave her with me. She will be safe. I will see her safely back inside the gate once she has regained her strength."

Her voice had an unfamiliar accent that I could not place. Was she a gypsy? I stared into her face, trying to read something that would tell me if I could trust her. I noticed that she was not dressed in the same rags as the other beggars. Nor did she wear the bright colors gypsy women favor. Her shawl was finely woven and without tears. At least she did not seem to be one of the homeless. But what was she doing here? What was her accent? I was far too distraught to ask questions or make a rational decision. Veronika did it for me. She glanced up at the woman and decided she was trustworthy. "Go," she pleaded. "I will be fine."

How was I to choose? Was my duty to my city greater than to my family? Then I realized the truth. If we were in imminent danger of invasion, city came first, otherwise we were living every man for himself, and few would survive. I had heard too many horror stories from the men in the barracks of towns surprised and overrun by an invading army, the old and the youngest put to the sword, the women raped, and every child and man left standing sold to the east as slaves.

"Fine," I said. "Promise me you will make your way inside the city gate as soon as you find your legs again. Promise me."

"I promise," she said weakly. "I just need a few moments. Go now."

Pushing aside my fears how this could all go terribly wrong, and leaving my basket with my sister, I turned and rushed headlong to the city gate.

At a sprawling run, I barged into the Guard Room underneath the crooked tower of the Beggars Gate. I was relieved to find five guardsmen lounging about, three of whom I knew. They stared at me with wide eyes.

"You, Johann!" I shouted, pointing at one of the men. "To the Wait Room. Report to the Watch Duty that there has been a skirmish upriver. Don't know how far away. Dead on both sides. Floaters are coming downstream. You! And you!" I pointed to the two I didn't know. "Grab poles to pull the dead that are near the shore out of the water." For a moment they just stared at me until I bellowed, "Now!" Then they scurried off. I looked at the other two. "Christof, is there a flatboat tied up below the gate?"

"Always," he nodded.

"You and Jakob, grab some grappling hooks and we'll pole out to midstream and pull the bodies to shore before they float through the center of town and cause widespread panic."

We scurried down the slope to the water's edge and jumped into the flatboat tied up below the tower. Christof unhitched us as Jakob and I grabbed poles and we pushed ourselves out into the river's current. We arrived in time to grab the first few bodies that were floating down. We hooked two and Jakob poled us close enough to shore that the men with the long poles could land them. Then we turned around to get more. I still was not making sense of the colors or design of the blazon on the enemy uniforms. They were nothing I had seen before. There were far more of our own colors, which likely meant that a guard post had been taken by surprise and overrun.

We were just bringing the next two corpses to shore when we heard the trumpets. It was the call for all off duty guardsmen to report immediately to barracks.

"I've got to answer to that," I panted. Once Jakob had poled the boat close enough to shore, I jumped off. "I expect they will lock the city up next. Look, I was with my sister Veronika on the other side of the gate. I had to leave her behind. Make sure ..." My voice faded at the realization that I had abandoned her.

"We'll keep an eye out for her," Christof assured me. "Be off now."

By the time I reached the barracks, men were milling about everywhere. I grabbed one soldier by the sleeve. "What news?" I asked.

"There's a general call to arms," he answered brusquely. As he hurried on, he barked, "Suit up."

# Muster

As I entered the dressing room, there was a press of men jostling for space and helping one another lace up. I snaked my way to my station and found Andreas already waiting for me. "Took you long enough," he said severely.

"I was fishing bodies out of the Arola." I watched his eyebrows shoot up. I knew that would get his attention. "I was out east of the Beggars Gate and saw them floating toward the city."

"Who are they?"

"I didn't recognize their uniforms," I said. "What are the rumors?"

"Some say French. Others say Scots or Danes. Does it matter? It could be Saracens, for all I care. Whoever they are, we stop them."

As we spoke, Andreas was putting the collar of his harness over his shoulders.

"Wait," I said. "You've forgotten your chain mail." He was putting the collar right over the doublet we wore to keep the metal from chafing on the skin.

"We're to leave it behind," he said flatly.

"What for?"

"The rumor is that we have some marching to do and they don't want men keeling over before we engage the enemy." It made sense. A hauberk of chain mail weighed over twenty pounds. I helped him settle his collar with its shoulder armor around his neck, then I lifted his harness with its long apron over his head so he could slip into it. I tightened the buckles at his shoulders and waist to hold it in place.

"So you sounded the alarm?" he asked over his shoulder. "That was gutsy for a first year guardsman."

I grinned at the compliment. "I obviously was not the only one. It's not my place to give a call to arms. Word of the battle must have reached town some other way as well. What are our orders?"

"The Guard is to arm with pike and short sword and be ready to march to battle."

"Rations?"

"We are to take two days' rations, no more. Rumor is that the Council has decided that we go meet whatever is coming rather than to wait for it to lay siege to our walls. With only two days' rations they can't be far away. But in the end, it doesn't matter. If we are longer gone, we live off the land."

"Who stays?"

"The guardsmen who are already at their posts on the gates and walls. Every other available man is being sent into the fray."

"Have they called out the citizenry?"

"Not yet. Obviously, they believe we can hold them off."

Once I finished tightening Andreas' buckles, it was my turn. I pulled on the thick padded arming doublet and breeches we wear under our armor.

"It's going to be hot in this," I muttered.

"You'll be grateful for it when it comes to blows. Stop complaining."

"Wasn't complaining," I defended myself. "Just saying."

"In case no one else had noticed that it's a hot summer day and the sun will bake us? Here, let me help you put on your chain mail. The metal will cool you down." He was already reaching for my hauberk. I held up my hand to stop him, realizing I had earned that bit of rough handling for my foolish words. "Lesson learned," I said. "I will be silent." There is a code among soldiers: Don't talk about the obvious. Don't complain about what you can't change. Just endure it.

Andreas helped me settle the collar into place and latch it. Then he lifted the harness over my head. As he tightened the buckles, I asked, "Have you done this before?" He was several years older than I and always wore the air of experience about him.

"Buckle you up? Several times last week, as I recall. And the week before. And the week before that. Should I go on?"

"I didn't mean that," I said, but hesitated to say more.

"You mean, gone out to cross pikes with an enemy force?"

"Just that," I answered tersely.

Andreas laughed in a carefree way. "I'm as much a virgin as you, my young friend. We go out to lose our innocence together. Have courage. We don't go alone. There will be blood, but we will make theirs flow harder." He turned me around and tugged on my armor to make sure it was secure. "Eleven times harder," he added. That got a broad smile out of me. "Short sword," he said, gesturing at my piece still hanging on its hook. Once I had buckled it around my waist, he said, "Time to join the muster. Let's grab our rations, long pole, and line up. Don't forget your head." By which he meant my helmet.

Rations were already prepared and waiting on a long table. Normally, we would be responsible for feeding ourselves on a march, but since this was at such short notice, the Guard was supplied at the cost to the city. We each grabbed a small food bag. I peeked inside and saw a two-fist hunk of rough bread, a large wedge of hard cheese, and two small apples. We each had our own leather flask filled with weak beer. With the food bag tied on one side next to the short sword, the flask on the other to balance it, our pike over the right shoulder and our helmet tucked under the elbow on the opposite side, we went to join the growing ranks in the open field.

It was a magnificent sight. Colorful banners fluttered and snapped in the breeze. They showed the city's red and white coat of arms, our colors, and each battalion had its own banner with specific colors and designs. Seeing our own battalion flag, the Snarling Badgers, we knew where to go and stand muster.

Knights in full armor were already prancing their horses about the perimeter. At the front marched the archers with crossbows. They had the shortest range and would have to be close to be effective. As soon as we closed ranks with the enemy, they would melt away. Behind them, forty-four rows deep, marched soldiers with pike along the core and with halberds on the edges. We were there to battle pike to pike and then hand to hand. The ranks behind the pike-bearers were held by archers with regular bows. They had a greater range and could shoot more quickly, although their arrows struck with less force. Their bows were the easiest weapons to make and the majority of the bowmen carried them. Behind them, however, stood the archers with their longbows, each bow extending a head or more higher than the bowman. Their arrows were the most destructive, and they boasted the farthest range, but the effort to pull the string was so great that they had to rest a moment between arrows and could not shoot rapidly.

I knew all of this because we had met up with a crossbowman in the tavern one evening and by his second mug of ale, he went into such detail about the quality, skill, advantages, and disadvantages of each of the rankings of bowmen that we began to regret we had ever asked. But after that evening we knew everything we could ever wish to know about the archers. None of the bowmen wore any armor whatsoever. They did not meet the enemy hand to hand as we would. Of course, the enemy would have an equal number of their own bows to thin out our ranks. We counted on our armor to protect us from the worst of that onslaught.

We knew we were at the mercy of the crossbows and longbows. Their bolts and arrows were shot with such force they could pierce our armor. Our consolation was that their primary targets were the knights, who were more heavily protected than we were. The regular bowmen targeted us, and we were assured that chain mail, helmet, and breastplate would stop most of their arrows. *Most* was not particularly encouraging, and for this skirmish, we were without chain mail.

I must have been wearing my worry on my face. Either that, or he simply had decided to once again single me out for derision. Rodrigo, our Battalion Leader, was ambling through our gathering ranks, checking armor and giving words of encouragement. I heard him chiding a soldier at the end of a line formation for having brought a pike instead of a halberd. He passed another and gave him hell because in the rush of dressing he had forgotten to fasten his short sword to his belt.

The moment Rodrigo saw me, he pushed through the ranks to reach where I stood. Towering two heads-length over me, he sized me up with a pained look on his thickly bearded face. I had hoped that he had forgotten all about me. He hadn't.

"Knees buckling yet, little stonemason?" he jeered for all to hear. Many turned and knowing what was coming next, they shuffled closer. After all, this was entertainment, a welcome distraction from what lay ahead, and it was I, not any of them, who was the butt for his derision.

"You're looking like this is a lot for you, little stonemason. After all, you're not used to having to carry more than a trowel. And a pike is a bit heavier and longer than a trowel, wouldn't you men agree?" He looked around and winked at the circle of soldiers guffawing and snorting. "Maybe you'd like someone to carry your armor for you? It's a hot day. You're already awash in sweat." He bent over to peer at my legs. "Or maybe you just pissed yourself is all." The harsh laughter around me was worse than his words.

I refused to look at him, or give him the pleasure of knowing that his needling got under my skin. It didn't help. He pressed on, as a prelude to the forced march we were about to take. "This is the real thing, little stonemason," he sneered. "You can still back out and run to mommy. I'm sure she'll hide you in her bed until this is over."

When I refused to respond or even look at him, he said, "All right, you can come with us, youngster. We're in need of a mascot." More laughter. "Our little Badger baby!" Rodrigo declared loudly. Even greater laughing. Then he sneered, "When we get into the fray, though, don't worry if you crap your pants. It will save us all. The smell alone will keep them at bay." Now the rough snorting laughter was all around me. I could tell from the heat in my cheeks that I had turned red. I wanted to smack him in his arrogant face, but that would only make it worse. You can't hit a rock and expect your hand to come away in one piece.

Rodrigo turned away from me and bellowed at the surrounding soldiers. “Snarling Badgers, form ranks! We march to defend Solodurum! Be worthy of the honor!” A loud huzzah arose from the soldiers around us.

# On the March

Before the drums began to beat, we were ordered to take our pikes to several waiting carts. We had miles to march, and there was no sense in using up our strength carrying the long, heavy weapons. The rumor along the line was that scouts were riding far enough ahead to give us warning when we were approaching the enemy. The trick was to give us enough time to fetch the pikes and make ranks in an orderly fashion. For this we hoped our archers would give us the edge we needed to re-form ranks in time to engage.

The sun was beastly hot, and, beating down on our metal armor, I felt like I was trapped inside a baking oven. It wasn't long before I was sweating profusely. I was not alone in my misery. No one complained out loud, but that did not prevent men from muttering into their beards. We marched seven across at a quick pace, which made sense. We wanted to stop whoever was coming against us as far away from the city as possible. Before long, the muttering stopped, but tempers began to flare. If I wandered a bit to my left or right in the ranks, I was sharply shoved as men defended the little marching space our crowded ranks gave us on the narrow road.

We had left before midday, marched right through noon and into the long second half of the day, roughly following upriver the meandering flow of the Arola. I had fallen into a silent rhythm of putting one foot in front of the other and thinking of nothing. The drummers kept up a brisk cadence for us to march to. I had just pulled out my drinking flask only to notice that it was empty when the trumpets blew the tones to signal that we break ranks and rest. The order to keep the road clear passed quickly. We poured out into the surrounding meadows on both sides of it. I staggered a dozen steps and collapsed in a heap. I pried my helmet off my sweaty head and lay on my back. But the sun was too bright in my face, so I turned onto my side, breathing heavily. There was a slight breeze cooling my sweat-soaked hair.

There were quiet moans around me, but mostly men were sitting up and breaking out their food bags. We needed to put something into our bellies to keep us marching. Word passed along that we were near an elbow of the river. I could see the line of trees that marked the river bank not more than two hundred paces away. I wasn't the only one who had drained his drinking flask. A ragged line of men were dragging themselves in that direction. I heaved myself to my feet and joined them.

One of the battalion leaders was leaning against a tree at the water's edge, shouting at us to fill our flasks deeply but to drink shallow. Puzzled, I wondered out loud why we couldn't refresh ourselves fully. An older veteran beside me grunted one word, "Cramps."

"What?"

"When you're sweated out, if drink too much, you get cramps," he explained tersely. "Splash water on your exposed skin and let it cool you."

I'd never heard that before and was so thirsty I was tempted to ignore it. Maybe he was just intentionally misleading the less experienced. Older recruits did this all the time, trying to embarrass us. Just the same, his advice to splash water on my face and arms to cool down was sound, and I saw others doing it as well. I returned to the field beside the road and sat down again cradling my water flask, taking only sips at a time. I felt a shadow pass over me and glanced up at Rodrigo leering down at me. I braced myself for his verbal assault. "Well done, boyling. Only small sips." That was it, and then he moved on.

Our break was short. We had enough time to fill our flasks, wolf down a few bites of food, and empty our bladders. The muster trumpets sang out and the drums beat the tempo for our marching feet. I found Andreas, and we joined the re-forming ranks. The air around us was filled with the sound of the drums, echoed by our feet slapping on the road in time with the beat. The sun beat mercilessly down on our heads.

I glanced over my shoulder and saw that not everyone had returned to ranks. A scattering of men lay in the grass, their arms wrapped around their stomachs, their faces lined with pain. Some had even peeled off their armor. "They drank deep," Andreas grunted. "The fools. They'll catch hell from the battalion leaders." Guards already stepped out of the ranks to make sure that when their cramps had passed they did not run away back to town.

We marched on, and I was too tired to do anything more than walk, carried by the beating of the drums and the momentum of the men around me. At one point Andreas nudged me and gestured behind us. I looked to see several men breaking ranks, stumbling into the adjacent field, their faces contorted in pain, clutching their stomachs. Rodrigo was already upon them. We could hear his booming voice as we marched on. "Were you not listening, you idiots? Small sips! You're useless to us! Cowards!" I wondered what would happen to them, but was too weary to ask Andreas. I felt a wave of relief that I had followed orders. The little water I had drunk refreshed me and I still had a nearly full flask.

As we marched, it occurred to me how eerily empty the cultivated fields were. Not a soul was seen mowing or gathering hay, a common task this time of year. Small herds of sheep and cows grazing in the meadows—a normal scene beyond our city walls—had vanished. The peasantry, sensing the coming threat, had withdrawn to a safe place.

The sun was making its slow descent to the west when suddenly, I felt tenseness in the air that had not been there before. I lifted my head and looked around. I wasn't the only one to notice it. Many heads were craning in every direction looking for what had caused this palpable change. At that instant the marching drums were drowned out by the trumpets blowing the order to form battle lines. We had found the foe.

The wagons carrying our pikes and halberds had kept pace between battalions. As one man, we sprinted to them and grabbed the first pike that came into our hands. Only the soldiers on the edges of the ranks carried halberds to cut down anyone trying to flank us. Although we made haste, we made haste slowly. It would not do to be careless and skewer or slash a companion in arms. We needed every able body among us. In spite of the care we took, I did get knocked and jostled. At one point, the haft of a pike cracked hard against the back of my helmet, knocking my head forward. The haft of a different pike gave the back of my hand a sharp smack, momentarily numbing it. I didn't see who did it, nor did it matter. We all hurried back to our positions in the line.

Andreas and I stood in the second line. Before us stood the front line of soldiers, and before them, for the moment, marched archers with crossbows. They would melt away once we were close enough to the enemy to release their bolts. It was not due to our skill at arms that we stood so far forward. It was a function of stature. Those in the first row were shortest in height. We were half a head taller than they were. Those in the third line, the one directly behind us, were half a head taller than us. Beyond that, they were all roughly the same height. For those of us in the first rows, we were able to extend our pikes over the shoulders of those in the row before us, and those behind us stretched their pikes over our shoulders, thus creating three bristling rows of spear points. It was comforting to feel that pike on your shoulder. It meant that someone had your back. These three rows of extended pikes meant that anyone who slipped past the first row of pikes faced a second row. If anyone managed to get past them, the third row of pikes would skewer them, and so on back in the formation.

Of course, we expected to be met by the same bristling rows of pikes coming toward us. The question was which line would break first. In deciding this, the archers played a decisive role by trying to create a breach. Once the line broke, our short swords and even our daggers would be our immediate weapons.

Settled in our ranks, everything happened very quickly. Our drums had not yet started up again, but we heard the drums of the approaching army and their chanting to the cadence of the beat. I could feel the ground tremble under my feet. Then their lead line rounded a bend in the road and we saw them for the first time. A murmur of recognition shot through our ranks.

"It's the French! French troops!"

# A Break in the Line

Until now we hadn't known for certain who we were going up against. Several of our men recognized the colors of their uniforms, as did I from the floating dead in the river. I felt a jolt of fear. Veterans often discussed the nature of soldiers we were likely to meet in battle. The French were rumored to be wildly ferocious and impervious to pain. A French soldier with multiple wounds kept on fighting as if he had none. Now I would see if these were just barrack stories—or real.

It was intimidating to see a large force coming toward us, bristling with spears, the sun glancing off the metal of their armor. The French filled the road, as we must have as well. The moment they saw us, they poured out on both sides of the road into the adjacent fields. We mirrored their movement to hold a unified line to meet theirs.

Our archers were not idle. The first row of crossbowmen sent off a volley, then the second row shot theirs, before they all melted away. A crossbowman has to stand in place and use his foot as an anchor to pull back the taut string to load another bolt. If they remained where they were, they would be caught in the vise between the two clashing front lines. We saw men in the enemy ranks fall, struck by bolts, then quickly replaced as men behind stepped forward. They had been trained as efficiently as we had. I puzzled why they did not have archers in front of their first row of pikes. Had they come without any?

The moment our archers let their lethal volley loose, we sent up a loud cheer to give ourselves courage. My own cheer caught in my throat when movement in the field to our left caught my attention. A troop of their archers was crossing the open meadow. They were going to flank us and pepper us with arrows as we were engaging the enemy in front of us, a tactic we had never been warned about. At their appearance, the opposing troops let out an enthusiastic "Huzzah!" It was obvious they saw the battle as already won. These archers would be able to stay in place and reload repeatedly. Would our knights ride up and chase them away? I could hear no approaching horsemen. I felt fear shoot through our ranks as a communal tremble. If even a handful bolted, the rest would follow, and our ranks would crumble. What use was there in standing our ground only to be cut down from our flank? The men beside me glanced left and right, weighing their options to escape.

Over it all we heard Rodrigo's booming voice, "Courage, lads! Hold strong! Your wives, mothers, and sisters count on you. Hold your ground! Give no quarter! The enemy is before us! Stand as one! Eyes forward!"

Whether we fought or ran seemed to hang in the balance. I could feel the warning pound in my head with every heartbeat: Get out of range! Already, their bolts had found their mark. Metal arrow points tickered, glancing off helmet and breast armor. There was also the gasp and cry of men who had been bodily struck, their armor penetrated by the metal-tipped shafts. Panic seized my heart, as I watched men near me crumple. I felt an arrow glance off my helmet, and another struck me at waist level, but when I frantically placed my hand there, I could feel no shaft. My armor must have deflected it. Our own archers were not idle, but returned fire to the enemy archers. Still, based on the loud shouting, it appeared they had been caught unprepared by the enemy's unexpected tactic and were struggling to regroup.

At that moment, I saw movement in the high bushes behind the enemy crossbowmen. A mob of villeins suddenly emerged from the thicket behind the flanking archers. Although they bore neither pike nor sword, they did not come empty-handed. Each man carried a sharpened sickle, a long knife, or a pitch fork. Some bore nothing more than an iron crowbar. They fell from behind on the unsuspecting French archers, hacking at them viciously. They knew better than we town-dwellers the price of an invasion: their cattle slaughtered or chased off, crops ruined, stored grain stolen or burned, orchards chopped down, storage houses burnt. On top of that was the catastrophic loss of wives, sisters, and mothers, raped and murdered, and every male, man or child, put to the sword.

In spite of their loud and constant laments about how ill-used they were by the noble landowners, here the villeins showed their loyalty to their feudal masters. The archers not mowed down by the peasants' sharp sickles, fled in disarray. Now it was our turn to send up a cheer. Rodrigo's voice, echoed by the other battalion commanders, bellowed heartily, "Into the fray! Forward! Strike with courage! Drive into them!"

With a loud cry, we charged against the opposing bristling wall of spears. There was an immediate deafening clatter of wood against wood as we strove to get past one another's guard, our hours of practice turning into automatic movement. There arose the dull metallic thud of spear against helmet and breastplate. The air was filled equally with the war cry and the gasp of agony as spear points penetrated past and through metal to pierce flesh. All the while, men shouted and cursed defiance, and I among them no less. We had practiced endlessly how to parry and stab, parry and stab, and now here it was in earnest. Terror carried me as much as my training and the strength in my arms. More than once I knocked a spear point away that, had I not been fast enough, would have stabbed me in the arm or shoulder, in my face or my neck. Blood splattered across my cheek and nose and I knew not if it was my own or another's. The faces of the bearded men opposing us were a blur. I saw in them anger, rage, terror, pain, fierce intention, and despair. Was this what they saw in us?

Our standing order was to hold our line, while at the same time weaken theirs to the point we could break through somewhere. Our opponents had the same goal. Behind us stood warriors we called *rushers* at the ready with war hammers, battle axes and mauls. Once we could force an opening, they would rush in and create havoc in the opposing line, attacking pikemen from the flank and from behind, causing their line to waver and break. We knew they had warriors on their side waiting to bring the battle chaos to us, and we strove with all our might to keep that from happening.

Standing in the second row, we were not as exposed at the first clash of spears, nor did we have to parry as many thrusts as the front line suffered. The disadvantage of the second line was that it all too soon became the first line as comrades before us fell to the ground dead or grievously wounded.

Without warning and almost at the same moment, the two guardsmen directly before me fell. Without thinking, while their pikes were still entangled in our fallen comrades, I stepped forward to drive my spear point into the face of the man directly before me. I was sickened seeing his blood spurt forth. I felt my knees ready to buckle and my stomach turn. No amount of practice in the camp had prepared me for this. I sensed more than saw that Andreas beside me had taken down the man opposite him. In the passage of a moment we had avenged our fallen comrades, blood for blood, but instead of satisfaction, I felt a growing rage. I bellowed my defiance at the soldiers before me, joining my voice to the chaotic chorus of those around me.

The steady press from all the lines of pikemen behind us was insane. Retreat was not an option. Giving ground was not an option. My feet were not firmly planted when the man behind me shoved into my back. I took a lurching step forward, then another to keep my balance, my pike wildly knocking opposing pikes aside, and at the same time I tried to strike home against an unguarded opponent. Stabbing diagonally was often more successful than a straight thrust, as it was difficult to parry. Just such a one struck my breastplate, but the point glanced off, catching me in the arm. Still uncertain on my feet, this blow threw me off balance. With a roar of helplessness, finding only the rolling limbs of fallen comrades beneath my feet, my momentum took me down. On my way, I leaped onto the hafts of two pikes that were seeking to stab me. My leaping fall was all that saved me, as I collapsed on top of the long pikeshafts instead of under their points.

Although I had for the moment escaped impalement, I realized with a wave of nausea that falling was my death sentence. If our troops continued to advance, I would be trampled by my own comrades, as I had trampled the fallen before me. If the enemy advanced, I faced double jeopardy. I would be trampled by their feet, and if any of them saw me still alive and struggling, I would be dispatched by a knife stroke to my neck.

We had a code of honor among us, much discussed in the barracks. Once fallen, unless grievously wounded, it was our duty to attempt to rise again, and continue fighting, no matter the risk. Anyone lying still until the battle passed over him was a coward. Hearing tales in the barracks, I hated both options.

Falling in battle, I had no thoughts, only frantic reactions. I had lost hold of the shaft of my pike, and out of a desperate sense of survival tried to struggle back onto my feet. In the back of my mind, over the tumult of battle, I could hear the chanting of many voices, "Rodrigo! Rodrigo!" I knew what that meant. A rent in the enemy's line had been made, and they were summoning the giant Rodrigo to enter the fray with his immense spiked maul. I vaguely wondered where the break was, and whether the press around me would lessen or increase, when a foot landed heavily on my neck and pinned me to the ground. I ate a mouthful of dirt and grass. But a foot was better than a knife blade. It meant I was still alive.

I felt all the chaos of battle raging above me, the yelling, the screams, and the clatter of pike hafts. Someone fell on top of me, and then rolled off. Of a sudden, there was a new sound, the violent impact of metal against metal, grunts of pain, cries of outrage, a sudden cheer of success. Theirs or ours? More feet roughly used my back as a stepping stone, knocking the breath out of my lungs, pushing my face into the dirt again. I was half aware of feeling grateful for the armor that kept my back from breaking and my ribs from snapping.

Suddenly, massive hands from behind grabbed hold of the back of my harness and lifted me out of the bloodied tangled mass of arms, legs, and pikes. Rodrigo's rough voice echoed in my ear and I felt his hot breath on my cheek.

"This is payment for the debt our city owes your grandfather, little stonemason, for the walls he built. Be worthy of it. Go lick your wounds."

Like a discarded plaything, he tossed me over one line of soldiers. I landed in the unwelcoming arms of several comrades, knocking them down. How I escaped being impaled on the bristling rows of pikes, I'll never understand. Those around us heaved us to our feet. I had lost my helmet and my pike. I was dazed and wounded. The guardsmen hastily faced me away from the line of battle and gave me a shove. They wanted me out of their way. I staggered in the direction of safety, others making way for me to pass, shouldering by me as they pressed forward into the fray. I stumbled against a wall of guardsmen, pressing myself sideways against them to squeeze between their ranks, each of them giving me a shove toward the back.

Suddenly I stepped into open space, past the shouting, the commotion and confusion. I saw a few others like myself, bloodied, without helmet and pike, wandering about in a daze. I instinctively reached for my short sword. It still hung from my belt. I was battle-stunned, torn and sore, but nowhere did I feel broken. My upper leg felt odd, like I had a severely strained muscle. I decided to favor it until I worked out the problem. I had a slash across the back of my left hand, and although it bled, I could see it was nothing serious. I spit the dirt out of my mouth, and with it came the broken half of a tooth. My right cheek was numb, and my searching hand returned from it covered in blood. I still had all of my fingers. My right arm was bleeding, but I could not find the source of the wound, and I could still move my arm, though with some discomfort. I vaguely remembered the spear point that had glanced off my armor striking me there.

I stared dumbly at the others around me. Many were visibly injured, and their faces had far-away looks. They either sat or lay on the ground. Those lying on the ground were mostly silent, and it was impossible to tell the quick from the dead. Their wounds were obvious, slashed in arms, face, neck, and legs, all of our exposed parts.

I felt a sudden elation that I was not wounded so badly that I needed to lie down. On the ground a few steps away lay a discarded pike. With a surge of energy, I snatched it up, turned and rushed back into the press of battle. Rodrigo had saved me from certain death in the line. How he knew it was me was a riddle I didn't stop to puzzle over. I would be worthy of my grandfather. In spite of the growing stiffness and tenderness in my leg, I felt a frenzy to continue fighting.

In the short time that I had been turned away from the battle, our troops had managed to shift the tide of the fighting. Rodrigo and the other rushers had penetrated through the line and it broke under the press of their swinging war hammers and mauls. The rest of our troops had swarmed in after them, splitting the French forces and creating a general melee. The enemy line had faltered and fled. They offered no more resistance and were on the run. It sounds so simple when I write of it now, but the air was filled with desperate clamor and cries, and everywhere I looked was frantic effort, sacrifice, and blood. Lots of blood, smeared across armor, faces, arms. I never landed another blow.

Very quickly, the battlefield was staged for supporting the wounded and managing the prisoners. A station was set up to give aid. Many of us joined in the task of combing the battlefield for those who were too injured to walk. We carried them between us to where their wounds could be attended by the surgeons who had traveled with us. We also set aside an area for our fallen comrades who we respectfully lay beside one another. The enemy wounded were dealt with differently. Those who could walk were corralled into a field and guarded. Those who, due to their wounds, were not mobile, were put to the sword. It was gruesome work, but I saw there were those who did it with relish. The mania of battle was still upon them, and they were at least merciful in quickly dispatching the wounded enemy. I did not volunteer for that detail, but there were others willing enough to take their fury out on these strangers who dared to invade our land. We dumped the enemy dead in the field in a tangled mass which I was told would be set to the torch. Weapons and armor that could be reused were set aside in a growing pile.

The different battalions set up banners in designated areas where we could regroup with our own battle companions. When my arms were too weary to carry another body, I limped over to the Snarling Badgers. The men there sat either alone or in small groups. They looked spent, with stunned, faraway gazes. I was nauseated by the amount of blood and the scattering of dead bodies lying in unnatural positions. At the same time, I felt a surging elation that I was alive, that I had survived my first battle. I never wanted to be in one again, and at the same time, a part of me hungered for the next encounter. I spotted Andreas and went to him. He was blood splattered and seemed to be staring at nothing in particular.

"Andreas, are you still in one piece?" I asked. I needed him to help me figure out the confusing feelings pulling me in two directions.

He looked up at me and smiled weakly. "Thanks to you, Ben," he said with a nod.

I was confused. "What do you mean?"

"Well, you opened the breach in their line, you know. I saw it all. That took a lot of courage."

His words made no sense. Was he confusing me with someone else?

"Andreas," I said. "I fell."

"Yes, but you fell and took down with you four spears."

I was confused. "It was one, maybe two," I objected.

"It was four, Ben. I don't know how you did it, but I was right there next to you and saw it. Maybe they were just all trying to stab you at the same time, but you collected in your arms four pikes and neutralized them. Then I did my part. Once they were without their weapons, I took down two men facing me. The guardsman to your left must have taken his man down as well. In that one moment there was a large enough rent in their line to call in the rushers. That was a courageous deed. And risky. You had no idea if it would work."

I shook my head. "Andreas, I lost my footing. I fell."

Again Andreas shrugged his shoulders. "I guess you know how to fall." Then he added, "Why else do you think Rodrigo plucked you out of that mess? Because of the love he bears you? Fat chance."

I wanted to tell him what Rodrigo had said to me. I was certain Rodrigo knew I had fallen and was not trying to be heroic. But Andreas wouldn't let me talk. He waved me off and asked, "You got anything to eat? I'm famished." He sounded exhausted. I reached for the food bag tied to my waist, but it was gone, lost in the melee of battle.

"You're bleeding, you know," he said with a tired gesture.

I lifted my hand to look at the gash on its back side. It still dripped blood. Then I touched my arm. It was sore but otherwise felt fine. "It's pretty much stopped by now," I said.

"I don't mean there," he said. "I mean, there." And he pointed at my left leg.

I looked down, but saw nothing concerning. Then I pushed aside the armored apron at my waist. What I saw gave me a shock. The cloth of my trousers above the knee was soaked in blood. "How's that possible?" I mumbled. "It's just a—a pulled muscle."

"When you grabbed the pikes," Andreas said. "And fell on them. The thrust of one must have slipped past the plating and caught you in the leg."

There was a tear in the material of my trousers and I slipped my hand inside. It came out covered in blood. My head swam. In shock, I sank to the ground next to Andreas. I didn't know what to do next. Fortunately for me, Andreas did. Exhausted as he was, he sprang to his feet and ran off. At the moment, I wondered why he was abandoning me. He wasn't. He went to fetch a surgeon.

It turned out that wound was the best thing that ever happened to me. Although if you had told me that at the time, I would have said you were crazy.

# The Draught of Forgetfulness

Andreas insisted that he was standing beside me in the line and would vouch for my courageous deed that, disregarding my own safety, I had leapt onto four enemy spears and opened up the rent in their line. Rodrigo made a point of suppressing that story. He went so far as to threaten to send Andreas to a frontier post if he did not keep his fanciful tales to himself. "He fell," he bellowed at Andreas. "He admits he fell. It was a fortunate fall, full of consequences, but without intention." Rodrigo refused to see me sung as a hero.

At the same time, although he would not give me any credit for turning the tide of the battle, Rodrigo did me the kindness of keeping me in the Guard. The wound in my thigh had been nasty. Treating it nearly drove me out of my mind. Once a surgeon had been fetched, he decided that the bleeding could be stopped. I still shudder to think of those men considered too grievously wounded to treat; they either had the limb amputated, or worse, they were left on the field of battle to bleed to death.

The surgeon cauterized my wound to stop the bleeding in my thigh. It is standard battlefield procedure to cauterize wounds, and it saves lives, although it often leaves the patient deeply scarred and, as in my case, maimed. They carried me to the surgical station where they were treating soldiers with the iron rod. A fire was kept going with a bellows to keep the irons red hot. The procedure is simple enough. The surgeon lays a red hot cautery iron against the wound until the bleeding stops. My wound barely hurt. The agony of the hot iron, on the other hand, was beyond any pain I had ever before endured. Andreas tells me that it took five men to hold me down, one of them sitting on my chest. I cursed, I screamed, I pled with them, and I cried in anguish until I fell into welcome unconsciousness. The stench of my own scorched flesh has never quite left my nostrils, which explains why I gave up eating roasted meat. I lost all appetite for it, which I have since learned is fairly common among men who have endured the cautery iron. I prefer my meat boiled, even if the taste is blander. But the fact is, hot iron stopped the flow of blood and saved my life. It also cleansed the wound, so it did not fester, which would have forced them to cut off my leg as a last resort.

I don't remember much of the return to Solodurum. When I came to from the agony of the iron, a surgeon handed me a cup with a dark brew and told me to drink up. When I made a face at its bitterness, he scolded me to stop playing the child and drink it at one gulp, which I obediently did. It was a sleeping draught, and after this, my memory is vague. I know that together with other wounded, I was loaded into the bed of a cart. On the ride home I was jostled by the rough road beneath our wheels and occasionally shoved by another of the wounded men lying on either side of me. The cart was full and we lay shoulder to shoulder, hip to hip. I crossed my arms over my chest since there was no space beside me. I do remember the sky, spotted with immense, billowy white clouds framed by a blue the color of the mountain gentian, my favorite flower. Its beauty was my only consolation. Of the men around me, there was shoving to claim a less uncomfortable place for painful wounds, some were silent, others moaned incoherently. We all reeked the sour stench of sweat and the gore of battle. For the most part, I faded in and out of consciousness, mostly out.

When I woke up, I was lying on a hard pallet in a dimly lit, smoky room. Around me were the soft moans and sighs of other wounded guardsmen punctuated with the occasional sudden shriek of—what was it? Pain? Terror? Although I have little recollection, I likely added my own grief and hurt to this involuntary chorus. I numbly noticed the immobile figures lying nearby on pallets identical to my own. I was unbearably cramped, restless and achingly sore in every muscle. The room was stuffy and far too warm. Or perhaps it was just my leg that was burning me up; it was on fire. The pain was so unbearable that I wanted to jump up from my pallet and run away, away from my pain, as if I could run anywhere. I attempted to sit up, but ropes had been stretched across my chest and hips to keep me from moving. I felt like a trapped animal and called out for someone, anyone, as I frantically pulled and tugged at the restraining ropes. An attendant appeared, to my muddled mind out of nowhere, and spoke to me in quiet tones. He unfastened the ropes, and with my arm wrapped around his shoulder, helped me to hobble over to a bucket in the corner where I could relieve myself. That effort alone exhausted me, and all thoughts of running away were replaced by the need to just lie down again on my pallet. When I asked him if he had anything for the agonizing burning in my leg, he brought me another cup of bitter brew. This time I downed it quickly, knowing it would soon return me to sleep. Listening to the moans and shrieks of my wounded comrades, I fell into a dark and dreamless pit.

I have no count of the days I lay in that room, waking only long enough to relieve myself in the bucket in the corner. Each time I woke, I begged for another draught of the brew that would take me away from my misery. In the dim light of the smoky room I gazed numbly at the rows of other pallets like mine, each with an injured man lying prone upon it. Some were restless and emitted groans of suffering, others did not move and were silent. Alive? Dead? I cared little. I only wanted my draught of forgetfulness.

# *Joseph*

I awoke to find a stranger kneeling beside me. By this time, I knew by sight all of the attendants. This man was different, and clearly not an attendant. He had opened the bandaging around my leg and was applying something to my wound.

"Are you a surgeon?" I asked groggily.

"Hmm, hmm," he murmured, still focused on my injured leg.

"Are you a surgeon?" I asked again. Then more pointedly, "What are you doing?" A sudden terror shot through me that they had decided to cut my leg off.

When he turned his gaze on me, even in that dim light, I could tell he had a very kindly face. He smiled, nodded his head and said, "I am a physician."

There was something strange in his speech, which brought me more awake. I took a closer look at him. He wore a felted rounded cap of an uncommon fashion. His full beard, although well cared for, was not closely trimmed as was the fashion in Solodurum. Then it struck me, his strange dress and uncommon accent.

"You're a Jew."

He nodded his head, saying, "My name is Joseph." Then he asked, "Do you mind?"

I quickly shook my head. "Not at all. Only surprised. Why does a Jew come to treat Christians? Has the Guard engaged your services?"

"I have not come to treat Christians," he replied. "Only one Christian. You."

When he saw the puzzlement on my face he added, "Your sister has sent me."

"My sister?" I asked, astonished. I was suddenly more awake than I had yet been since arriving in this place. "Veronika?" And then the whole memory of leaving her behind at the Beggars Gate returned to me. "Veronika!" I exclaimed, trying to sit up. "You know her? Is she well?"

He had already loosened the restraining ropes, and he used my momentum to help get me to my feet.

"First things first," he said, slipping my arm around his shoulder. "I suspect you are in need of the piss bucket. Then I have some soup for you, and while you eat we can talk."

Soon afterward, I was sitting on my pallet, my back propped against the wall, with Joseph sitting comfortably cross-legged on the floor beside me. He had brought with him a basket, out of which he took a crockery container bound in cloths. He unwrapped it and handed it to me. It was soup, and still warm. I drank it down greedily, not even using a spoon. I had eaten only bread and cheese since arriving in this dim room, and very little even of that. "It's delicious," I murmured between gulps.

"My wife Miriam made it. It is a bone broth soup, very healing for the sick and injured. It also contains other herbs that will clear up your digestion after all the bread and cheese they've been giving you."

"My thanks," I said sincerely. "While I drink, please, tell me what you can about my sister."

From Joseph I learned that the woman in whose care I had left Veronika was his wife, Miriam. She had not been alone that afternoon at the gate, but had gone there with their daughter, Zipporah. Miriam and Zipporah had escorted Veronika safely into the Lower Town and back across the river. With the trumpets sounding and all able-bodied men rushing to take up arms, it was a frightening time. They could tell that Veronika was worried over my sudden departure. Since the Jewish quarter where they lived was on her way, they took Veronika with them to give her something to eat before sending her home. In this way, Veronika and Zipporah struck up a friendship.

"Is your daughter Zipporah the same age as my sister?"

"Two years older," Joseph explained. "We learned that Veronika has only brothers at home, as does Zipporah, so it was in their nature to be drawn to one another. They have become very fast friends. Veronika has often come to our home."

"And you said she asked you to come see me."

"When the Guard sent word to your family that they were keeping you here while you mended, Veronika asked if I would look in on you."

"You said you are a physician."

"I have practiced medicine in many places. I learned much from the Muslims among whom we once lived. Their practices are far superior to your Christian surgeons."

I bristled at this. "They saved my life with the cautery iron."

"If I had been there, I would have attempted to sew you up first. That way, I could have saved your life *and* your leg."

"Sew up?" I asked with astonishment. "As in a piece of cloth?"

"Yes, not much different than that. It could have saved you the muscle damage that the iron caused."

I wasn't ready to believe any of this. "What's done is done," I shrugged.

"That is true," he agreed with a nod. "You know, you are very lucky."

I looked at him dumbly. I did not feel in the least bit lucky.

"Well, you were wounded, and in that you were not lucky. But your good fortune is that the blade did not cut you here." He lightly traced with his finger a line on the inside of my leg from the groin down to my knee. "There is a vessel that runs here, that if cut, well, you would have bled out in a matter of minutes. That is why I say you were lucky."

I saw his point. We have a saying, *Fortune in misfortune.*

"With your permission," he continued in his comforting way, "I would like to take over your healing from now on."

I shrugged my shoulders. "As long as you give me something for the pain." That was all I cared about. The throbbing in my leg was already making it hard to pay attention.

"I will, but I want to change what they have been giving you. It has too much hemlock for my comfort. You are sleeping too much."

"The sleep keeps the pain away," I protested.

"I know this will be hard to hear, but it's time that you face the pain. It will recede some, but you will have to get used to it. You cannot spend the rest of your life sleeping your days away. I will replace the hemlock with more mandrake root. And I will also lessen the amount of poppy. There is no profit in getting you dependent on the poppy. It will make you a slave to it."

My head was swimming from his words. I was weary from so much talking.

"And it is time to get you back onto your feet. Otherwise your muscles will atrophy—"

"Atrophy?" It was a word I'd never heard before.

"Shrivel up. Then you won't be good for anyone, not even yourself. I want to get you in the fresh air. A warm autumn is in full swing outside. It is time you went out and let the sun shine on you again, before the cold weather sets in. Sunlight helps to heal wounds."

"But, but—" I started to protest. He wouldn't let me talk. He grabbed the sweat- and blood-stained shift that I still wore since being delivered to the sick house. It was the only clothing I had. He pulled it off over my head and threw it into a corner. I was too stunned to be embarrassed by my nakedness. He pulled a fresh shift out of his bag and helped me get my head and arms through it. Then he hoisted me to my feet and slipped under my arm.

"Out we go," he ordered. "I will be your crutch until I can bring you a proper one. We have to get you strong again." In spite of my weak protestations, Joseph returned me to the light of day.

Joseph visited me daily. In fact, I discovered that he had come every day as I slept, and treated my wound with salves he had made himself from herbs he had collected. I looked forward to his cheerful, steady presence in this place surrounded by the misery of other grievously wounded, and I was growing strong again from his care and gifts of food. He always brought a warm bone broth soup, tart apples, some soft goat cheese and occasionally salted fish. In addition, once a week he brought me a fresh shift so I could keep myself clean. His salves were cooling and comforting to my wound. He brought me a crutch so I could be independent and not always need an attendant to use the bucket in the corner.

As promised, Joseph also changed the bitter brew I drank. I no longer descended into mind-erasing sleep both day and night. Dealing with more wakeful hours of pain was hard, but with added mobility, I was able to start learning how to tolerate them. I spent less and less time lying on my pallet, and more time hobbling into the yard outside the sick house to sit in the fresh air and sunshine.

One day, after slipping into a clean tunic, I had to breach a topic which had been troubling me. "Joseph, I cannot pay you for your services. This has been bothering me deeply."

Joseph smiled broadly. "I am glad that you are healing to the point that you are worried about paying me. Let me put your mind at rest. You owe me nothing. I have been doing this for the sake of your sister. She has brought much comfort and companionship to my daughter, Zipporah. Now, on your feet. You have visitors."

I was excited at the thought that someone from my family had come to see me. Until this point I would have been embarrassed to see anyone, but with Joseph's care, I had grown stronger and felt ready to be with others. Supporting myself on the crutch Joseph had brought me, I hobbled out into the bright sunlight.

"Benedict!" I heard my sister's delighted squeal before I saw her. Then Veronika was there in front of me. She danced around me in her joy, finally giving me a warm embrace that nearly toppled me to the ground. I was so happy to see her, all I could do was grin. Then I noticed, standing demurely to the side, a young woman. She wore a blue head scarf tied loosely around her long black hair. One look at her olive skin, black eyes, and long lashes sent a thrill through my heart. At that moment, I was certain she was the most beautiful woman I had ever seen.

Veronika was speaking quickly, most of which I was missing. Something about our parents and brothers and why they were not there as well. But I heard her clearly when she said, “Benedict, this is my friend Zipporah. She is Joseph’s daughter.”

I had not taken my eyes from her since first noticing that she stood there, and this embarrassed me, though I could not say why. I smiled in greeting and said something, although I don’t know what, and felt immediately that I was making a fool of myself. I stammered something, making it even worse. Joseph saved me when he said, “Let us help Benedict get his strength back by walking with him a couple of turns around the courtyard. Then he should rest on the bench while we talk.”

Veronika walked to my left, on my crutch side. Joseph was on my right, and beside him walked Zipporah. I walked as in a dream, trying to follow Veronika’s stream of chatter, and at the same time attempting to glance at Zipporah without her noticing. When we had made three slow turns, Joseph said, “It is soon time for us to go. I wish to give you and your sister a few minutes alone. Veronika, Zipporah and I will wait in the street to escort you home. Benedict is likely exhausted from your visit and will need to rest. Come soon.” And with these words, the two of them walked out of the courtyard. My eyes followed them until they were gone.

I pulled myself back to the moment. “Thank you, Veronika, for sending me Joseph. Without him, I may never have stood again, let alone walk.”

“They are sending you home in two days to finish your healing. The surgeon said you are no longer in danger of infection. Mother is already cooking and baking.”

“Will you come to help me home?”

“Anton is borrowing a donkey cart so you will come home in style.”

I sighed, “I am ready to leave this place.”

"What do you think of my friend, Zipporah?"

"She's beautiful," I blurted out before I could stop myself.

Veronika stared at me. "Benedict, I've never heard you say that about any woman before."

I must have blushed. "I guess I've never seen one as beautiful before." Veronika continued to stare at me until I mumbled, "It's time I went to rest."

Two days later, my big brother Anton arrived with his donkey cart and took me home.

# The Door Blown Shut

Every day, once in the morning and once in the afternoon, I took my crutch and walked as far from our front door as I felt I had strength. I would stop to rest briefly, then return. Some days I would rest and then continue walking a little farther. With every outing, I grew a little stronger. I had a goal in mind, and it motivated me every day to push myself to go farther.

Veronika joined me when she could. Walking with a companion helped me to forget the pain. About once a week, Zipporah came with her. I always talked them into walking with me before they went off alone to chat with one another. It was hard for me to take my eyes off Zipporah, but I forced myself not to stare because every time I did, it made her blush and she would pull her scarf tighter around her hair.

"You really have to stop that," Veronika said once after Zipporah had gone home.

"What?" I asked innocently.

"You know exactly what I'm talking about," Veronika said. "If you don't stop, she will not come to visit anymore."

"She said that?"

"Just stop. The way you look at her even makes me uncomfortable."

"She said that?"

"Just stop," was her final warning.

I couldn't help myself. Zipporah fascinated me. I never had a chance to speak with her alone, and when we were together, she spoke mostly with my sister. As it was, I was too tongue-tied to say much at all.

As the weeks passed, I divided my time between daydreaming about Zipporah and strengthening my leg. Every week the pain receded into the background a little bit more and I was delighted with my returning stamina. Finally, the day came when I was determined to make the trek to see Martin. Around my shoulder I slung a bag Mother had prepared for me. When I came to my first rest, I did not turn back. Nor at my second. I kept going. It took five rests, taxing me to my limits, but I was determined. I finally reached the lower entrance to the Verena Ravine. To my surprise, I saw Martin sitting on a fallen log just where the stream emerges.

"Martin!" I called out in joy. He hurried over to me and took my crutch. He wrapped my arm around his neck and took me to his sitting place.

"Were you waiting for me?" I asked. "Did you know I was coming?"

"The wind told me to sit at this place today," he said, a mischievous gleam in his eye.

When he saw the big eyes I was making, he added with a smile, "The wind has had me sitting here every day this week."

I was relieved. "Not altogether a saint yet?"

"I still have far to go," he laughed. "However, it looks as if you have fully become a soldier."

"Complete with war wound," I added with a sad nod.

"So I see the door that's been blown shut," he said, gesturing to my leg. "Have you found the window that has been opened?"

"The Guard has not released me from service. My physician is hopeful that I will learn to walk again without a crutch or even a cane. Then I will go to serve in the City Guard, manning the walls and the gates."

"That sounds like a very large window," Martin laughed.

"I am grateful that I will still be able to serve and earn my living," I replied.

"And save groschen for your apprenticeship?"

"And save for my apprenticeship," I confirmed.

"So that is still your wish?" Martin asked, holding me with his gaze. I knew that look. I had struggled a lot with this question, and Martin's eyes drew it out of me.

"I lie awake at night. Martin, I can't stop asking myself the same questions. Did I make a mistake? Should I have been an obedient son like my brothers and followed in my father's profession?"

"Should you have?" Martin wasn't going to answer my questions for me.

"If I had," I pressed forward, "I'd still be in one piece. I wouldn't need a crutch or be a burden on my family. Is this God's punishment for being headstrong? This question has been plaguing me."

Martin pondered a moment before saying, "Let me ask this. What if you had become a mason's apprentice and, while working stone, something had gone wrong and a large block had fallen and crushed your leg? Would you be torturing yourself, as you are now, that you should have followed your soul's desire to become a scrivener?"

I thought a moment about what that would have been like. "Probably, yes."

Martin continued, "So let me propose this to take into your sleepless nights instead. What if it was God's design that you limp, for a reason you may never be given to understand, that for the sake of your destiny, it was necessary for you to have injured your leg and to live with a limp. Which would you prefer? Gloriously injured on the field of battle? Or injured in an unfortunately careless accident laying stone?"

I had to laugh. "Well, when you put it like that, I find my current situation preferable."

"At least this way, you can briefly enjoy being hailed a war hero."

"You make it sound so simple," I laughed again.

"Do you prefer complicated? Take simple so you can sleep better at night. Now, tell me about your adventures."

I recounted everything, starting with my berry-picking outing with Veronika. I felt a burden lifted from my shoulders just being able to talk about it. When I told him about Joseph and his daughter, Zipporah, he stopped me.

"I have never heard you speak of a woman this way before, my friend."

"In truth, I have never seen such a beautiful woman before," I said truthfully.

"I hear more in your voice than an appreciation for beauty," he said, giving me one of his penetrating looks.

I was uncomfortable under that gaze. "And what if there is?"

"Then I would have to encourage my friend Benedict to remember that some things are not within our reach."

I thought about this and asked, "Do you mean more out of reach than becoming a scrivener?"

"That is far closer to your reach than what you are now desiring," he warned me.

I bristled that Martin would tell me there was something I should not wish for. "What about *free choice*?" I argued.

"I have never promoted free choice, as that often follows the random vagaries of desire. Instead, I have urged you to lead a life of restraint and discipline, and in that context I spoke of Free Will, and I urge you now to use it in order to keep your boundaries clear. The daughter of a Jew is not within your reach."

"But you are the one who preaches that love knows no boundaries," I said with more heat than I intended.

"I was never speaking of carnal love, Benedict," Martin said severely.

Chastised, I hung my head. First Veronika and now Martin. Why was it wrong to feel desire for Zipporah? I felt confusion and a stubborn anger.

Martin must have seen my dark looks and slapped me sharply on the back. "Cheer up, my friend. Raise your head and enjoy the light of God that shines freely down upon us. Rejoice that your leg is healing and that you have a long life of making mistakes before you."

Martin's words made me laugh. It shook me out of a black funk at being refused his blessing to pursue my feelings for Zipporah. At that moment, though, I made the choice to shrug off his warning. Our friendship was too valuable to be angry with him. Besides, Martin is a hermit, I reasoned. What could he possibly know about love for a woman? I decided that I did not need to take his warning to heart.

Suddenly, it dawned on me. "Martin, you're talking! The last time I saw you, you were under a vow of silence. And deafness, too. Have you given that up?"

"Not in the least. I am very content with my silence."

"But you are speaking with me. And listening to me. Quite a bit!"

"Yes, I am making an exception so we can visit. I shall return to my silence once we are finished. That is the advantage of not living under another's discipline," he said, referring to our previous conversation about joining one of the holy orders.

"What insights has your great experiment given you?"

"Many benefits. The voice of God in nature speaks much more clearly when I am not constantly filling my head with human speech. It has also enabled me to observe some unusual visitors to the holy ravine."

"What sort of visitors?" I asked.

"They have come repeatedly, and they do not come to receive the blessings of this sacred place. More I cannot say now."

"That is mysterious. Can you not tell me more?"

"I will, when I have more to tell. For now, I would like you to tell me what you have in that bag you are carrying. Unless I am mistaken, you bring greetings from your dear mother."

I opened the bag and out tumbled a selection of vegetables from my mother's root cellar.

"Ah," Martin cooed with pleasure. "My cornucopia. You will thank her for me?"

"Not finished," I said, reaching into the bag. At the bottom was a balled up piece of material. I pulled it out. "I brought you something against the cold." It was a pair of hose. "They're my old ones, and Veronika has patched them up. I now receive my clothing from the Guard."

"I am moved with gratefulness," he said with sincerity.

"I know you believe all of your needs are supplied by prayer. But I don't think prayer is going to keep you warm when the wind blows cold."

"Prayer, directly not," he said. "But it was my prayer that brought you to this glorious show of generosity. My thanks to you. And thanks to your generous mother and your sweet sister."

# Zipporah

Having rejected my friend Martin's stern advice, I could not stop thinking about Zipporah: her smile, the black hair that flowed down her back from underneath her head scarf, her dark eyes, her curvy figure. I knew that Veronika was right, and that if I continued to moon over her, I would not have a chance to win her heart. I needed advice, so I turned to my brothers.

"Well, well," said Anton with only a hint of ridicule. "Little brother is growing up. Who is she, Bennie?"

"There isn't anyone yet," I lied. "I just want to be prepared. Tell me what to do."

"Tell her you want to make strong babies with her," Anton said with a big grin. His wife, Giselle, was expecting their third.

"Nonsense," Seb objected. "You tell a girl that and she'll never talk to you again."

"She will if she's ready," Anton replied, elbowing me with a wink.

"Maybe that'll work if she's a cow," Seb shot back.

"Hey!" Anton objected. Giselle had plumped up between numbers two and three.

"You have to court her, Ben," Seb continued quickly.

"With a firm embrace and a kiss to her mouth," Anton interjected. "Just so she knows you have something to offer, if you know what I mean." And he winked again.

"You court her with sweet words," Seb corrected, shooting Anton a dirty look. "Once she feels she can trust you, then you can offer more. Then let her know how you feel. Don't beat around the bush."

“Just so she knows you have something to offer,” Anton repeated himself. “You know what I mean, right?” And he elbowed me in the ribs and winked. He looked at Seb and they both broke into laughter, although I completely missed what was funny and was too embarrassed by my naivety to ask them to clarify.

In the end, I decided to follow Seb’s advice first, and if that failed, I would consider following Anton’s. After all, Anton had a wife, and Seb was soon to be married, so they must know what they were talking about.

The next time Zipporah came to visit Veronika, the two of them did not invite me to walk with them and quickly disappeared to go where they could speak privately. When they came back, Zipporah insisted that she had to return home and had no more time to visit. I stated quickly, rather than offered, that I would walk her home, and she reluctantly consented to my company.

As we walked, I tried to draw her out to speak with me, but aside from sidelong glances and shy smiles, I could get her to share no more than small talk about the weather. Still, her smiles were so sweet and warmed my heart with hope. I felt it was a simple matter to help her grow comfortable with me. I could always revert to Anton’s methods if she did not. I decided I would walk her home every time she came to visit.

Veronika put a stop to this. The next time Zipporah visited, I was ready to walk her home when they returned. However, Veronika came back alone.

“Where’s Zipporah?” I asked.

“Back home,” Veronika said tersely.

“What? How?”

“I walked her home,” Veronika said casually. “She had to go. She had chores to do.”

“But I wanted to walk her home,” I said.

“Maybe next time,” Veronika said, and that ended any further conversation.

There was no next time, though. Whenever Zipporah visited, Veronika always returned alone after they had gone out together.

"Walking her back home gives us more time to talk," she said. "That's what she comes for, after all."

I decided it was time to be more direct. Under the guise of strengthening my leg, I offered to run small errands for my mother that would take me into town. I walked so as to pass through the Jewish Quarter. Veronika had shown me where Joseph's family lived. It was one of many doors on the narrow lane. When I knocked, Miriam answered and greeted me in a friendly, but reserved tone. I asked to see Joseph, and Miriam led me into their small sitting room. Joseph received me warmly and inquired after my healing. I reported my progress and setbacks as he listened, nodding with a satisfied look. Then, as casually as I could, I asked if Zipporah were at home and whether I could speak with her. She was fetched and stood before me, her gaze averted, her hair, as always, bound by a scarf. I asked if she would walk with me, and she said that she was very busy but had a few minutes. Just to help me exercise my leg.

Once outside, when I suggested a direction to walk, she agreed. I had a destination in mind. "You know, Eleven is not far from here," I said. "Would you like to walk there with me?"

"Eleven?"

"You know, the Forest Gate. We could walk out of the city and stroll in the woods there."

"I'm so sorry," she said after a moment's hesitation, firmly, yet friendly. "I don't have time. Mother depends on me. I must get back. Once we get to the corner, I must turn around."

I returned again three days later, with the same result. By my third visit with the same response, I decided it was time to follow Anton's advice and be more explicit.

The next time I went to her home, I summoned my courage and asked, "Zipporah, you do like me, don't you?"

She pressed her lips together, suppressing a shy smile. "Yes, Ben, you are a very sweet young man. I am fond of both you and your sister. I am grateful for your friendship."

"Do you like me enough to be more than a friend?" I asked, my heart racing. I looked sideways at her and saw her cheeks redden.

"Ben, let us first be friends," she said softly. "We do not yet know one another well."

"We would if we took more time to walk." I was beginning to think that Anton's approach had its merits—if only I could get her into the woods outside Eleven.

"It's time I returned," she said firmly.

Although I was disappointed, I naïvely took her words as encouragement to continue visiting so we could get to know one another better.

Four days later, I was back at her door, full of confidence that now Zipporah knew my intentions. I had every expectation that she would learn to grow fond of me as well. I had put on my best hand-me-downs from Seb. As always, Miriam let me in and Joseph took me into their little sitting room. After asking about my leg, as was our custom, I asked to see Zipporah.

Joseph placed his hand gently on my shoulder. "Ben, Zipporah is not here."

I misunderstood his meaning, and asked, "Has she stepped out for a moment? I could wait."

"No, Ben, I have sent Zipporah away. To my brother Baruch in Zurich. She has gone to live with his family. There are few young people in our community here in Solodurum. Zurich has a larger Jewish community, and I want her to be able to spend more time with young people her own age."

His words made my head spin. "But she can spend time here with me and my sister," I blurted out. "We are her friends and can introduce her to others."

Joseph sighed before saying, "I realize that you have grown fond of my daughter. I am grateful for the friendship you and Veronika have shown her. However, Ben, what you want cannot be."

His words stung and I felt anger welling up. "You don't know what I want!" I declared, a bit too forcefully.

Joseph looked me in the eye. "Ben, Zipporah is of marriageable age. I have sent her to Zurich so she can find a young man of our own faith. This is best for both of you."

A pressure built up in my head as if it would burst. "But we like each other," I insisted.

"She is fond of you," he agreed. "And she is gone. Ben, some things are not meant to be. You are young. You will find there are other young women to catch your eye who are more ... attainable."

I am ashamed to record here that, at that moment, such anger welled up in me I wanted to strike Joseph for having sent Zipporah away. Mindful of what I owed him gave me the strength to restrain myself from a violent outburst. Instead, I stormed out of their home back into the lane without another word. I knew that with every moment I remained, I would come closer to striking him, and I owed Joseph too great a debt to repay him with the anger of my thwarted desires.

That was my last visit to Joseph's home. I had no reason to return. I had gone only as an excuse to see Zipporah. My leg was healed and I was growing strong again. The following week I returned to my duties in the Guard, and it felt good to be thrown back into the brotherly fellowship of my soldier comrades.

From that day forward I bore a growing grudge against Joseph for robbing me of a chance to win Zipporah's affection. This bitterness grew to include all the Jews who lived in our city, and finally extended to embrace the whole of the Hebrew race. The arguments I had grown up hearing others speak now rushed through my own mind: What an odd people with strange unchristian ways. Always keeping to themselves as if they had something to hide. Dressing differently, eating differently, speaking differently. Are our ways not good enough? Why do they live among us if they do not want to mingle with us? Why do we let them grow wealthy at our expense?

In the evenings with other guardsmen at an inn, after a couple rounds of ale, we always descended to voicing our discontent over the latest insult to what we fancied as our dignity. When we ran out of curses and threats against the French or the Emperor, we turned our sights closer to home. First under fire came the gypsies, and when we had roundly abused them with words, with the intention in the coming days to treat them roughly as they so deserved, we turned our attention on the Jews. When my companions ragged angrily at the abnormality of Jews with their self-righteous ways, taking up good living space in God-fearing Christian Solodurum, I found myself heartily agreeing with them. We vowed we would one day get even, although we always left it vague as to what that meant. After all, unlike the gypsies, the Jews had their homes and businesses and were as much a part of the day-to-day activities of our city as any Christian.

# The Guard Tower

In those days, Solodurum was a free imperial city owing fealty to the Holy Roman Emperor. We paid taxes and contributed a certain number of troops to the Emperor, but our Council was clever, and instead of sending them off to fight the Emperor's endless foreign wars, they managed to convince him to use our troops for defending the generally peaceful frontiers and insuring relatively safe road travel between cities.

The Guard in Solodurum at that time was separated into two basic units. There were those who lived in the soldiers' camp outside the city, drilling daily and providing a small standing army for the city, ready to jump to arms at a moment's need. It was financed by the noble families who owned all the lands in the surroundings. Although this part of the Guard owed fealty to those nobles, it was rare in our days to be called to go on a campaign. We are a people of commerce, not of war and conquest. We try not to take sides. In order to thrive, commerce requires political neutrality.

The second unit of the Guard manned the city gates, patrolled the walls, and generally saw to providing security for the daily functioning of life in the city. Aside from making sure that there was never too great a population of beggars at any one time, they interfered very little in the daily life of Solodurum. They stood in the background, ready to step in if needed. New recruits, as I had been, were regularly loaned to the City Guard to toughen them up by patrolling along the periphery of the city walls.

Once I was declared ready for service again, I was transferred permanently to the City Guard. The great advantage of this unit was that we were allowed to choose where we took our meals and given the option to sleep either at the soldiers' camp or at home. I chose to return to my family.

The most coveted duty in the City Guard was to stand post at one of the city gates. There was plenty of distraction with the stream of traffic coming and going, and distraction is highly sought after in the otherwise monotonous life of the Guard. When the weather turned cold, the guards could stand in the passageway and warm themselves at a brazier. When there was little to do, those on duty entertained themselves playing knucklebones. It was strictly forbidden, and, at the same time, generously tolerated.

The next best duty to pull was keeping watch on one of the round city guard towers which stood, if you remember, 111 feet apart, mostly along the northern stretch of the city wall. There, too, you had the company of at least one other, and a brazier was allowed in the winter for keeping warm.

Walking the periphery of the walls was the third duty of the City Guard. Before the battle, I had pulled that duty regularly, so a transfer to the City Guard was fairly straightforward. I already had a foot in, so to speak.

It was to tower duty atop one of the rounded bastions that Rodrigo had me assigned. This was the kindness he did me. He could have just sent me home until I was fit again for regular service, but I would not have received pay while I was out, and it was questionable whether I would even be let back in, since I now walked with a distinct limp. But since I never left the ranks of the Guard, my limp was never questioned, and I was paid my regular pension the whole time. If anything, my limp was regarded as a badge of honor, a wound received in battle. My companions treated me with respect, and those who entered the Guard after me looked upon me with awe as a war-hardened veteran. So, although I was never openly hailed as a hero, I took this favor from Rodrigo as his way of acknowledging that without me, even if I had fallen unintentionally, there would have been no hole at that point in the enemy line to breach.

And if I had not fallen in battle and been grievously wounded, I would never have met my benefactor.

# The Privy Council Chamber

The back of summer had long since been broken. It was a year since I had received my battle wound. I felt healthy and I had easily integrated back into the rhythm of work. The season shifted from hot to warm to cool, and all too soon, miserably damp and cold. My birthday in November came and went, marking a second year of service in the Guard. I had entered the Guard little more than a boy, and I was now, well, if not totally a grown man, at least I was an old hand, and that gave me a sense of confidence and purpose. With my guard duties, I felt like a contributing member of our town's life. I treasured the easy fellowship with my Guard brethren. Although a shift was often mind-numbingly boring, my reward was that every third month my modest stash of groschen grew. It was a matter of patience, and life in the Guard was a good teacher of that, if nothing else.

It was the month of thick fogs and freezing temperatures. On the tower, we were constantly stomping our feet and rubbing our hands to keep them warm. Our ears ached and felt like they would fall off if we touched them. Our noses were numb and ran relentlessly. Although healed, the scarred wound on my leg ached now as if an ice-cold iron were laid against it. Even the brazier of hot coals that we were allowed did little to ward off the penetrating cold. I spent hours with my watch partner devising clever ways to insert the coals into our boots or tunics to keep warm. Of course, these were all fanciful inventions without any practical application. But it helped to pass the time and distracted us from how miserable we were feeling.

By midwinter, the Guard was short-handed. There was a stomach ailment widespread among us. Some said it was from the cold and a miasma in the fog, others from bad water, and still others from the French working witchcraft against us. Whatever the uncertain cause, we were down a third, forcing us to take turns drawing double duty. I had remained healthy, despite those around me falling ill. My father joked it was due to the amount of stone dust I had ingested growing up. Mother was more practical and said it was the garlic she added with a heavy hand to all our soups and stews. Before my last visit with him, Joseph had urged me to avoid drinking from the communal water pot in the guards' Wait Room. It was annoying to bring in my water flask every day and I got teased by my watch companions, but I had come to trust Joseph's advice, even if I was still angry at him for sending Zipporah away. Whatever did the trick, somehow, our whole family stayed healthy through this seasonal epidemic.

One afternoon a stagnant fog lay thick and wet on the city. I was just coming off a long, bone-chilling duty on the tower. Little good it did for us to stand up on the tower in that soup. We could make out only vague shapes down at the foot of the wall. An invading army could march right up to our gates unchallenged—assuming they could find them.

I pulled open the heavy door to the Wait Room. I was smacked in the face by boisterous laughter, a wave of heat, and the heady stench of a room full of gaseous men taking cheer until their next duty. Our diet of raw onions was constant fuel for our intestinal concerts. For once, I didn't mind; I just wanted to warm up. I entered the Wait Room, slapping my arms to quicken my circulation. I had hardly taken three steps when the Watch Master came up to me.

"Benedictus, you're needed," he said.

"For what?" I asked.

"Another duty," he replied.

"But I've just come off watch," I protested.

"You know we're short-handed. We need you," he continued. "Go now. They're waiting for you."

"Watch Master, I'm frozen through from standing on the tower. Give me time to thaw out."

"Then this post will be perfect," he said with a tired smile. "You will be indoors."

That made me curious. "Where?" I asked cautiously.

"The Privy Council Room," the Watch Master said with finality. I had the option to complain, not refuse. He continued, "It's an easy post. You stand along the wall, more as ornamentation, looking like a fine statue of a Guardsman." He looked me up and down, tugging on my gambeson to straighten it. He absently tucked in a loose strap on my shoulder. "The Council likes to have the feeling they are safe from attack. Silliness, if you ask me," he rambled on. I noticed now for the first time that his eyes looked glassy. "But it's a tradition, and we do what we're told. Right? They keep it plenty warm in there. You'll be wishing for an open window and a bracing breeze before your watch is finished. Here, take this token and present it at the door. It's your pass." He thrust in my hand a ceramic disk embossed with the emblem of the city, the imperial eagle, on one side. I was surprised that his hand was clammy.

I looked at him closely. His face was blotchy and beaded with perspiration. "Watch Master?" I asked. "Are you feeling all right?"

As he passed a hand across his forehead, his eyes looked troubled. "Just a little chilled, you know, such a cold day."

"Chilled?" I asked. "But you've broken into a sweat."

He grabbed me suddenly by the lapel of my doublet and looked me in the eye. "Do this shift for me, Ben. Just for today. You'll be back at your regular watch tomorrow. I promise. No more extra duty. We look after our heroes." He patted me on the shoulder and tottered slightly on his feet.

"Certainly, Watch Master," I said, putting out a hand to steady him. "I'll do this shift. You know you can depend on me."

Suddenly the Watch Master's eyes went blank and he turned away without another word and wandered off through the door of the Wait Room.

I stepped over to where my provisions bag hung and unfastened the straps. I had some food inside and broke off a fistful of bread and a wedge of cheese, shoving them both into my mouth. I needed to stop the growling in my stomach before I stood another watch. I chewed wolfishly and washed the food down with a swallow from my flask. The beer inside it was warm, but better that than drinking from the general water can open for all. I took a poleaxe down from its rack along the wall. Then, with the ceramic disk in hand, I made my way up the stairs to the Privy Council Chamber, through three corridors and up another flight of stairs. Outside the door stood a guardsman, holding a halberd. I showed him the disk and tried to give it to him. He refused to take it.

"Tuck it away," he said. "Stand inside the door. I'll fetch you when your shift is over."

"How long?" I asked.

"Until I fetch you," was all he'd say. He opened the door and, once I stepped inside, closed it behind me.

Although I had never been inside it, I knew half of this room well. From my post on the tower, I had a clear view of it through its north window. I recognized before me the immense conference table strewn with documents, and in the corner was the large green-tiled oven. What I hadn't been able to see until now was the wall covered with maps. On an impulse, I was about to step over and study them, but steadied myself. When I had walked in, the four men at the table, who had been poring over a document, looked up and stared at me. After a moment, one of them, a strongly built man with a closely cropped beard, motioned with his hand to a bare spot along the wall and said, "You stand over there."

It was obvious I was to go stand beside a large chair next to the window I had looked through from above. I stood within clear view of the door, just a few steps away. Should someone knock, my duty was to open the door and announce whoever had arrived. Otherwise, I was as much a fixture in the room as the chair I stood beside, waiting for the moment they might wish to make me useful.

The four men went back to their discussion, treating me as if I were a tapestry on the wall. I was surprised how candidly they spoke in my presence.

"As I was saying," spoke a graying man, "it's been over a year and they continue to officially deny having had anything to do with it."

A younger man next to him spoke next. "I had an interview with the Emperor's ambassador a fortnight ago, and he still insists it was a rogue foray by an over-ambitious general, completely disrespecting the Emperor's sanctions."

"Then why has he not been long since removed and replaced?" asked another.

"When I pointed out that this had been promised to us last winter, his response was, 'It's complicated.'"

"I believe that the French showed their hand with that invasion," the graying man was saying. "I don't think anyone argues that—except the French." There was muttered agreement around the table.

"Based on his subsequent actions, it seems that General Frederick has been given free rein to harass the countryside and threaten other towns," said another. "That is as good as the Emperor's royal seal."

"I wouldn't be so hasty," spoke the man who had directed me where to stand. "With the Emperor sitting far away on his throne, it is highly challenging, if not impossible, to control an opportunistic general in the field looking to line his pockets through random looting. I suspect his troops were restless and he offered them some easy marauding. In our case, they ate Solodurum steel instead." There was chuckling around the table at this. "He will not try that again."

The gray-headed man addressed him directly. "I apologize that this is awkward, but I have been tasked with asking. Could this have anything to do with ... um, family relations?" he inquired. "I don't wish to be indelicate, but it has to be spoken out loud. I'm not the only one with this question. We are not served by beating around the bush."

The other replied. "You have every right and responsibility to ask about this. Have no sensitivities on my part. I have always been open about how things stand between us. I will speak plainly. I have made inquiries and have my suspicions, but no one in his service has been willing to be forthcoming. Either they are well-bought or they are terrified of him. I suspect both. Either that, or he was truly not involved."

I had been following their conversation closely since I was certain they were discussing the battle in which I had been wounded. I was intrigued by these last comments. Who was he speaking about?

"Forgive me a moment," he said next, and surprised me by turning to address me directly. "You're new to this duty," he observed. "Yet you wear the livery of the Tower Guard."

"The usual watch is indisposed," I explained. "The Watch Master ordered me to stand in for him."

"Have you been paying attention to our conversation?" he asked pleasantly.

I wasn't sure of the right answer. He asked so agreeably as if he might want my opinion. But then I remembered the stern admonition repeated over and over during my training: We are not paid our wages to think. So I shook my head and replied, "No, sir. Not at all, sir."

"That's fortunate," he said. "Because if any of what we are discussing should make its way out of this room, then we will know it came from you, and you know what will happen then, do you not?"

I must have looked blank, because he continued, "You will be swiftly hanged as a traitor." He waited to see the expression on my face before adding, "That is, after you've been extensively tortured to find out with whom you shared what you heard here. And in addition to whomever you name, we shall hang your brothers and father, and your friends. Your mother, sisters, and your sweetheart, all of them, will be garroted. Have I made myself clear what's at stake here?"

I nodded before I could find my tongue, "Yes, sir." My mouth felt like it was filled with sand.

"Excellent," he smiled, and turned away. "Gentlemen, shall we resume our discussion? Where was I? Oh, yes, my wayward and possibly traitorous cousin. I will continue to report to Edgar here whatever I discover. But we would profit most, I believe, from continuing to track where General Frederick is causing mischief since being so soundly repulsed by our courageous troops."

And with this the four nobles turned to a lively discussion of troop movements. Gazing at the map on the wall I was facing, I was able to follow most of what they said. I was fascinated by this inside look at the decisions guiding Solodurum's Guard. I was only annoyed that I could not leave my post at the wall to stand closer to study the details on the map. Then the nobleman's words of warning came back to me, and I realized that my life, and the safety of my family, depended on how well I was able to pay as little attention as the chair, the oven, or the window could.

Entertained first by the content of their conversation, and secondly by the urgency that I ignore everything they were saying, the time of my post passed quickly. It ended when the four men agreed to break for supper, with an arrangement to return afterward to continue their discussion. They filed out of the room, leaving me behind. They left the table strewn with maps and documents. Closing the door behind them, they left me alone. I wondered whether I was supposed to remain and guard the empty room until their return or whether I was free to leave my post. I was about to go inquire of the guard outside the door when the documents on the table caught my eye. I stepped over to take a look. After all I had heard, what harm done? I had just picked one up when I heard the latch of the door open. I quickly let the document drop and turned around to face the door. The guard from outside stood there and looked me up and down. Then he looked at the now empty spot at the wall beside the chair, and back to where I now stood, as if trying to figure out how I had gotten there.

"I was just coming to inquire if I was required to remain," I said quickly, wanting to distract him from drawing any correct conclusions. I took two steps toward him as I said this.

"You are no longer needed," he said. "You may go. Return tomorrow at the same time."

"This isn't my regular duty," I started to explain, but he cut me off.

"Yes, I see, Tower Guard," sizing up my livery. "If not you, then another," he concluded. With these words, he ushered me out of the room and locked it behind me. Again, I attempted to hand him the disk the Watch Master had given me. "You'll need it," he brushed me off. Without another word, he returned to his post beside the door, halberd in hand, staring resolutely at—nothing. I knew well the guardsman's discretion: *See nothing unless it threatens, hear nothing unless it's suspicious, and always stand your post.* I returned to the Watch Room, quickly gathered my bags, and left for home before the Watch Master could buttonhole me into another duty.

The next day, the Watch Master was missing. Word went around that he was down with chills and a fever. His second-in-command, a surly fellow by the name of Bruno, took over his duties. He announced in the Wait Room that since more guards had fallen ill, we would cover all shifts exactly as the day before, no exceptions. He made it clear that he would be asking some of us to take on more. Before he could stalk off, I caught up with him.

"Acting Watch Master," I said, "yesterday I was asked to step in—" and then he cut me off.

"Guardsman," his voice was hardly more than a growl. "You did hear what I just announced, didn't you? All shifts, *exactly*, as yesterday. Is there something about that you don't understand? Were you offering to stand a third watch?"

"No, Watch Master," I said, quickly stepping aside as he brushed past me.

I had no choice, so following my freezing shift on the tower, I headed back to the Privy Council Chamber. The same guard as the day before stood at the door. When I showed him the embossed disk, he commented dryly, "I know. You had it yesterday. Just tuck it away."

I entered the room to stand guard beside the chair, facing the wall of maps. The four Council members from the day before had been joined by a fifth. They barely looked up as I took my post along the wall beside the chair. I tried my best this day to see nothing and hear nothing and adopt the guardsman's blank stare. I failed miserably. I could not keep myself from following their conversation about reported troop movements. To the wall map they added pins with small paper flags of different colors attached. It was fascinating.

At one point, the nobleman who had warned me the day before had just added a pin to the map when he turned to me. "Do you find this interesting, guardsman?" he asked directly, pinning now me with his sharp gaze.

"No," I stuttered after a momentary pause. "No, not at all. I'm not even paying attention."

He stood there studying me a moment before saying, "That's fortunate. Because your expression is, how should I say, so engaged."

My lips moved, but nothing came out. I didn't know what to say.

"Perhaps you are just thinking about your sweetheart. Yes?"

I quickly nodded my head. With a last penetrating look, he returned to his conversation with the other Council members.

Of course, I had been listening, and carefully. I was able to learn the names of these noblemen. All of them were well-known to me, and I was grateful to place faces with the names. I was particularly interested in the name of the one who had repeatedly spoken to me: Baron Roland de Cornu, known for his committed engagement in the affairs of Solodurum. He was a powerfully built man, with a close-cut beard and a thick head of hair, though graying at the temples. Exquisitely dressed in the latest style, copied from the French, with whom his family was known to have connections, he was a handsome man by any reckoning. It was an open secret that he was outspoken in Council meetings, urging us to join the newly forming Swiss Federation of cities. His praises were sung by the families of fallen soldiers. He was instrumental in legislation that prevented a landlord from evicting the widow and the children of a fallen soldier who could not pay her rent and had created a fund to provide support. It was rumored that he had his hand in our town's lucrative butter production and trade. It was one of our most sought after exports.

I ended up keeping that extra shift in the Privy Council Chamber the rest of the week and into the next. When the Watch Master finally returned from his sick bed, I confronted him about the extra post. He furrowed his brow as if trying to remember. "That's right, Ben, I did send you there, didn't I?"

"So," I asked. "How much longer? When will the regular watch be back?"

The Watch Master shook his head. "He's not coming back, Ben," he said.

Surprised, I asked, "That ill?"

"That ill, and worse," he replied. "I'm asking you to stick with it, Ben, until I can find someone else. Besides, with your bad leg, you should be grateful for such an easy post. All other veterans of the river battle are back drilling in the camp. They could have sent you back there, but with your limp, you would soon be dismissed. You'll manage better here. You have my permission to hold the poleaxe on your weak side and use it for support. No one will know the difference." He patted me on the shoulder and left me standing there.

So I continued this rhythm, stand watch on the tower, shove some food and drink into my mouth, and report to the Privy Council Chamber. I had long stopped trying to show the guard at the door the entry disk. Expressionless, he just waved me in.

# Baron Roland de Corna

Standing guard in a room that needs no guarding is a monotonous task and completely mind-numbing. To keep myself from falling asleep on my feet, my eyes wandered to the documents scattered across the table. Some of them were topped with large-script writing. Although most were upside down to where I stood, I amused myself trying to sound out what was written on them. At one point I realized that I was so focused on working out the words that my lips were moving. I thought nothing of it until I noticed that Baron Roland was staring hard at me.

Not long afterward, he said, "Gentlemen, I notice that we are growing tired. We have labored over this puzzling situation and deserve rest and refreshment. I propose we break for two hours, retreat to our homes to clear our heads, and return for a short session to see if our digestion has provided us with any new insights. Agreed?"

The other men at the table nodded and grumbled agreement. Everyone rose, stretched and, with few words to one another, headed for the door. Only Baron Roland lingered behind. When the last Council member left the room, instead of following behind him, he closed the door and remained inside. He returned to the table as if he had forgotten something. He stood for a moment with his back to me, not more than three steps away. Suddenly, without any warning, he spun on the ball of his foot and lunged at me, his arms extended.

Baron Roland grabbed hold of my tunic with both hands and knocked me backward hard against the wall. He planted himself and nearly lifted me off my feet. He was amazingly strong. Before I could collect myself, he dragged me across the room and slammed me against the far wall, knocking both breath and senses out of me.

The poleaxe I had been holding clattered noisily to the wooden floor. The dilemma streaked through my mind that do what he will, I dare not resist. This was one of the most powerful and influential men in the whole city! My mind raced trying to discover what I had done to anger him.

He threw me against the wall next to the storage room door. He wrenched the door open and shoved me inside, once again hurling me up against the wall, toppling a small table that stood in there and scattering the parchments that were on it. My helmet flew off my head and rolled across the floor. He pulled the door nearly closed, only a splinter of light remained.

Then I felt his knife at my throat and for the first time was truly frightened. Had he dragged me into this closet to murder me? I wanted to speak, question this violent and unwarranted treatment, but I was too astonished for words. Then he spoke and I understood why he had attacked me.

"You can read."

He had, in fact, caught me sounding out words. He hissed in my face, "Confess it now, before I slit open your traitorous throat."

"I can read," I agreed quickly, my voice hardly more than a squeak. I was still in the dark why this would upset him.

"And you're a spy," he continued, hatred lining every word. "Since your first watch you've followed every word we've spoken. I've seen this, you can't lie to me, and I'll see you hang. How much you suffer depends on your leading me to your confederates. I will see them hang beside you. Their deaths will be long and painful. Yours, I promise, will be quick. But you must tell me now all you know."

My mouth fell open with surprise. How could he think me a spy?

"Are you a disguised priest, bent on a Catholic crusade to purify the city? Or are you French, planning your Emperor's invasion? *Allez! Parlez français comme moi. Avouez!* Confess!" He pressed his blade more firmly against my neck. "Confess, and I promise you an easy death."

Stammering, I said, "I, I don't speak French. I'm not a priest." Then the words tumbled out of me, "I am Benedictus, son of Laurentius, the stonemason. I'm a member of the Guard. Solodurum is my home. It's always been my home. I'm not a spy. I meant no harm. I was bored. I was curious."

The pressure at my neck softened. "Learning to read is not part of a guardsman's training," he growled. "Nor of the stonemason's. Why can you read?"

"My grandfather taught me. I wanted to become a scrivener, but I don't have the money for an apprenticeship. I'm saving up what I earn in the Guard."

"Your grandfather? How did he learn to read? Was he a defrocked priest?" The pressure at my neck returned.

"My grandfather grew up with the Benedictines outside the city gates. Thus my name. They taught him to read. He taught me. He was a stonemason."

Now it was Roland's turn to be astonished. I saw his mouth fall open, although I had no clue why. He recovered quickly and asked, "What was your grandfather's name?"

"Valentinus," I replied. I felt his whole body start.

"And his father's name?" he demanded.

"Don't know," I said truthfully. "He was an orphan. Our family name is Waisel. *Orphan*. That is why he grew up with the monks. He never knew his parents."

"Unbelievable," he muttered and, although the knife vanished from my throat, he kept me off balance and pushed up against the wall. "How do I know you're not lying?"

"You can ask my father," I protested, knowing no other manner to prove my identity.

"I've a better idea," he said quickly. "If Valentinus, the Master Stonemason, was indeed your grandfather, what token did he leave behind?"

My mind raced; what token could he be talking about? I could think of nothing. "I—I don't know what you're asking." The knife was again at my neck.

"Then answer me this, what did Valentinus build?"

"The bastions and the wall on the north side of the city," I said quickly. And then I flashed on the embossed disk that served as my permit to enter the Privy Council, and I knew what token he was asking about. "And he placed his visage on the wall below the rim of the center tower, the one beside the Armory Gate."

His eyes lit up. "His visage? *One* image of his resemblance?"

"No, not one," I said quickly. "He placed one to the north and another one looking south. But I've only seen the one on the north side."

"And with good reason," he said, dragging me out of the storage room and over to the window. "The one looking south is visible only from this chamber!" I looked out to where he pointed and saw for the first time in my life Grandfather's visage on the back side of the tower. It looked identical to the one on the north side, with one small difference: There were no subtle horns on this image.

"And why did your grandfather place his face on this side?" he growled, a light in his eye.

I thought a moment, trying to remember something that at the time had made little sense to me. "Because he said there is great danger that can come from without, but the greater threat is from within." And then I added quickly, "But I don't know what he meant by that."

He stared searchingly at my face. "You're telling the truth," he said at last. "Unbelievable. I thought they were just stories." A distracted look on his face, he released his hold on me and turned away.

"But it's on the other side, too," I insisted, misunderstanding his meaning. "Grandfather showed it to me. I can show you." I was worried that he was going to come after me with his knife again.

He turned on me, but he had nothing in his hands.

"Benedictus, son of Laurentius the stonemason, you claim you can read. How well?"

"Very well, my lord. Grandfather taught me. I want to become a scrivener."

"And I want you to prove it to me." He grabbed me by a strap on my gambeson and pulled me from the windows to the conference table. He picked up a document that lay on top and shoved it into my hands. "Read this," he commanded.

I stared at it, deciphering the unfamiliar script. It was very ornate writing with far more swirls than I was accustomed to seeing. He mistook my hesitation and mumbled, "Too good to be true," and was reaching to take it out of my hands.

"Be it known," I stuttered quickly, "that we have given and granted, and by these presents do give and grant for us and our heirs to our well-beloved—"

"Enough," he declared, taking the document and pressing another one into my hands. "Read," he commanded.

This one was written in a less embellished script. I read easily, "In the name of God Almighty, Father, Son, and Holy Ghost, three truly separate and distinct persons and only one divine essence. Be it manifest and known to all who shall see this public instrument, that—"

He snatched this one from my hands as well. "It's true," he murmured. Then he picked up a third one and thrust it into my hands. It was not written in German but, thanks to Grandfather, it was easy to read.

"*In Nomine Domini* Amen. *Honestati consulitur et utilitati publice providetur, dum pacta quietis et pacis statu—*" He gently tugged it from my hands.

"Latin, too?" He said, eyeing me with great interest.

"You see," I said. "Do you believe me now?"

He looked me in the eye, and his own were filled with mischief. "What I believe is that your grandfather sent you as a personal gift to me."

"My lord?"

He looked me up and down. "You wear the livery of the Tower Guard."

"I stand watch on the bastions. I come here after my regular tower shift."

"Effective immediately, I'm assigning you to the Council Guard. By tomorrow I want you wearing that livery. Report this to your

Watch Master and I will follow up with a written order. From now on, you will stand watch only here."

He must have seen the disbelief in my face. He lowered his voice and spoke in a confidential tone. "There is a traitor in our midst, Benedict Waisel, and I have been unable to ferret him out. I hope, with your help, to find him."

"How do you even know there is one?"

"Because secrets are getting out. I thought I had discovered the source in you. You make the perfect spy. A guard who can read."

"Who else could it be?"

"It is possibly one of the other Council members."

"How do you want to find that out?"

"With your help. You will stand duty at different times when I am not present. Even if they are hesitant to speak of treason freely in front of you, they will think nothing of writing a message in your presence, and even give it to you to deliver. You will report everything to me. In this, you can be of great benefit to your city."

I nodded my head. "I understand. I will do as you wish. Just one question, if I may. The other Council members are worried about your cousin. What are the chances he is the one you are looking for?"

"It is very likely. My family has always leaned to the French. Our family name, de Cornu, is unmistakably French. We have a custom of aligning ourselves with French ways, how we prepare our food, how we dress, how we groom ourselves. There are family members who, in private, will speak only French. My cousin Roger would happily throw the Basel Gate open and let the French march in. These conspirators would abolish our Council, end our independence, and make us a vassal city. I will not let that happen. I am committed that Solodurum remains independent. I have been outspoken that we must make ourselves a part of the Confederacy. I have little doubt that Roger is plotting against the city. But if he is the one, someone is feeding him information. I must know who that is."

"And you hope that I can find him out?"

"You will be my eyes and ears when I am not present." He continued, speaking more to himself than to me. "They are unlikely to say anything seditious in your presence. After all, you are sworn to defend Solodurum. But then, so are they. They might try to bribe you." He turned to me his full attention. "Let's make it clear now that I will double any sum they might offer you. You deserve an incentive to withstand that temptation."

"Baron Roland, I would never—" I began to protest.

Roland held up a hand to keep me from saying more. "You would never, nor would everyone else who ever took a bribe. Just let it stand with this: I will offer you more to remain loyal than they can offer to turn you to their betrayal. Agreed?"

I tried not to show it, but inwardly I bristled at the implication that my loyalty could be bought.

"You don't like that, do you?" Roland said, eyeing me carefully. "You feel I question your loyalty. You wear your feelings on your face. I already like that about you. We will do famously together."

I couldn't believe my sudden change in fortune. I was being personally engaged by Baron Roland de Cornu himself. Joining the Council Guard was the most coveted and elite duty of all. The rumor in the soldiers' camp was that it was manned exclusively by bastard sons of the noble families. He was eyeing me carefully. Then he commented, "I've noticed that you limp. Why is that? In fact, how is it possible for you to serve in the Guard at all with that infirmity?"

"I was wounded, my lord. In battle. In the battle of Büren."

"And the Guard kept you on?"

"As a kindness, sir," I explained. "I pull duties only where I can stand in place."

"That is an odd story," he said, his face concentrated. "Many a good man was sorely wounded in that battle, but the Guard did not keep them on."

"Well, I had a small part in helping to make the breach by which we routed their forces."

Roland looked at me with furrowed brow until it dawned on him. "Wait!" he roared. "You're *that* Benedictus?" slapping his hands together. "You've just made this so much easier. No one will question your promotion."

"You've heard of me?" I asked, incredulous. I was certain that Rodrigo had suppressed all rumor of my involvement. "Truly, I played a very insignificant role."

"Oh, my boy, no need to be modest. I'm certain in the taverns they already sing songs about you." He had a glint in his eye. "You have no idea how happy you have made me. Tomorrow, I expect you in Council livery. Understood? Now I must make haste. Tell your Watch Master," he said over his shoulder as he left the room.

I stared after him, astounded at my sudden advancement.

# Deaf and Dumb

I walked through the forest along the faint path that led up the hillside. This was the remote rear entrance to the holy ravine, backed by uncultivated fields and forests. I had intentionally taken the long way around to Martin's gorge to strengthen my leg. I came at last to the hanging bridge, nothing more than ropes and wooden planks to step on, that crossed the deep cut of the gorge. As it swung under my weight, I held onto the rope handrail to steady my uncertain balance as I crossed. I stopped a moment in the middle to stare down at the rushing water foaming white against the rocks. I was thrilled by the deep roar and invigorated by the cool mist rising upward. I had made the uphill climb through the forest and the pain in my leg was faint. I noted with satisfaction my regained strength.

I continued across the bridge and descended into the gorge as it widened out. Coming to the foundations of the small chapel at the bottom, I glanced inside, but it was empty. Only a scattering of votive candles burned. I turned to walk along the narrow, winding path that follows the stream. Even though it was hours before sunset, the light was dimmer here at the bottom of the gorge. I heard voices ahead and slowed my pace. The tone in the voices was harsh and demanding, echoing hollowly off the surrounding stones. Proceeding cautiously, I rounded a stand of trees and came upon Martin, leaning against the trunk of a tree, stock still, facing my direction. His expression was set, his face blank. He gazed at the ground and did not glance up at me. The loud, severe voices were coming from behind him.

"Hey!" a voice bellowed. "I'm talking to you!"

"Turn and look at your betters when you're spoken to," another voice demanded sharply. "Hey! You, scum! Show respect, turn and answer!"

"Must I run you through to get your attention?" I heard the ring of a sword being pulled from its scabbard. I didn't wait longer.

As I slipped past Martin's immobile figure, I was confronted by three men whose faces showed surprise when they saw me. One of them held his drawn sword in his hand. All three of them bore short swords, together with their fine clothing marking them as nobility, although I did not recognize any of them.

"Let him be," I said sharply. "This is Martin. He is the hermit of this gorge and under the protection of Saint Verena. Leave him in peace."

The man with the exposed sword spoke heatedly, "Then why will he not turn and address us?"

"He likely does not know you are here," I explained. "They say he is both deaf and dumb." I turned and placed my hand on Martin's shoulder, gently turning him to face the three strangers. Surprise showed on Martin's face to see them. He lowered his head in obeisance and made a gesture of the cross in the air.

"You see," I continued. "He was standing at this tree in prayerful meditation and was unaware of your presence. It is shameful to threaten a peaceful hermit with violence."

"So, he's not a homeless beggar?" one of them asked.

"He is a holy mendicant, and his home is this ravine."

The men seemed reluctant to accept my explanation. Now that their eyes fell fully upon me, they noticed what I wore.

"You bear the colors of the City Guard," one of them spoke.

"You see rightly," I acknowledged, adding, "I wear the livery of the Privy Council." This got the reaction I intended. They looked suddenly less sure of themselves.

"You have no jurisdiction here," another said warily. There was something in his speech that was not right, but I shrugged it off.

"Nor do I claim any," I replied. "Martin is under far more compelling protection than any the Guard can offer."

This touched a chord with them and they shuffled their feet, looking away. "We meant him no harm," one said. "We merely sought our way and were suspicious of his lack of response."

"Then tell me where you are going and I will direct you," I offered.

"We've never walked here before and wished to know whether this path leads out of the gorge or if it is a dead end."

"You can continue, following the stream to the end of the gorge. I have just come from there, and you will find a rustic chapel and a cave for silent prayer. If you continue to follow the path, you will come to a makeshift bridge where the river turns right and cuts a deeper narrow gorge through the mountain. That bridge will take you to another path through the woods to the next village, hardly more than a few houses and barns. Beyond that are empty lands. There is little there of interest."

"Leave that for us to determine," one of the men replied gruffly. "We will go that way." They filed past Martin and me, taking the path I had come by.

Martin glanced at me briefly and then passed me by, walking the way the strangers had come. I decided to follow the three nobles at a distance, to make sure they did not lose their way, which was absurd, because there was nowhere to go in the ravine but upstream. For some reason I could not put my finger on, I did not thoroughly trust them. I decided they must not be from Solodurum. Otherwise, how could they not know about our hermit who lives under the protection of the saint of the ravine? But then, I reasoned, perhaps they lived such sheltered, narrow lives that they indeed knew nothing of what is common knowledge among the people. I followed them long enough to see them take the path up the hillside and cross the hanging bridge over the gorge and disappear in the forest beyond. Then I turned and retraced my steps.

As I walked, I could not get them out of my mind. I had no reason to be harsh in judging them. After all, seeing Martin's wild hair, ragged beard and shabby tunic, wrapped in his tattered blanket, no wonder they were suspicious when he did not respond to them.

I followed the stream and walked deep into the ravine. Down at its lowest point, the walls of the chasm opened up to my left. I followed the limestone rock wall, spotted with openings, hardly more than hollows, some down low, most high above my head. I came to one that was slightly higher than I was tall. But along the base of the rock wall lay a large boulder. Stepping onto this, I took a firm hold and heaved myself up.

"God's greeting be upon you," spoke a gentle voice from the shadowy recess.

"And God's greeting returned to you," I grunted as I pulled my body over the ledge and squirmed through the narrow opening.

I righted myself so I could sit and look into Martin's face. His features were still set, but for a brief moment I could see a smile in his eyes before he hid it away.

"They were lying to you," he said.

"I was lying to them," I retorted with a snort. "But tell me, what was their lie?"

"They have been here before. Several times. Before now I was able to stay out of their way. This time they caught me unawares. It won't happen again."

"What do you think they were doing here?"

"It was not for prayer and meditation," he said with a wry smile. "I suspect they want a place where they cannot be seen together nor overheard what they are speaking."

"Which is why your presence is uncomfortable for them," I concluded.

"And all the more essential that they think me not only deaf and dumb, but also dim-witted. There is something about them I trust not over much."

"I felt the same mistrust but could not figure out why."

"Did you not hear? At least one of them is not from Solodurum."

Then it struck me what I had found odd in the speech of the shortest of the three men. "I heard it but did not think more about it," I admitted.

"All the more reason for me to be watchful and listen sharply," Martin said.

I unslung the bag I had been carrying and unbuckled the flap. "Is that why it is so important that people think you cannot speak or hear?" I asked as I reached inside to pull out a small package.

"So that I may in watchful silence be the guardian of this holy place," he replied. "Besides, I save my conversation for God and friends alone." He now smiled at me broadly.

I wasn't satisfied. "Martin, you have put yourself in unnecessary peril with this. Every local knows you can speak and hear as well as they can. If these men should inquire about you, they will learn the truth."

"Then let us pray that they continue thinking it is below their exalted station to speak with those who are inferior to them. I suspect that speaking with locals is exactly what they are trying to avoid, unless it be a very particular local."

"What do you mean by that?"

"I'll let you know once I know more."

"Riddles, Martin?"

"Riddles are God's way of revealing to us the glories of creation. It is our task to solve God's riddles."

I smiled as I pulled out the cloth-wrapped package my mother had given me as I left home. "Well, here's the sort of riddle I prefer." I lay the packet on the stone between us and carefully unwrapped it. The aroma of ginger, raisins, and honey filled the small space. "Do we eat it all while it's still warm?" I murmured. "Or save some for later?"

Martin frowned. "Mortification of the flesh," he said flatly.

"Ah, yet a new riddle," I laughed. "Listen, Martin, Mother says you are a hermit and not a priest or a monk. And the truth is, most monks are three of you put together. You are as thin as that rag you wear. You are allowed carnal pleasures, you know. In moderation."

"Your mother is a wise woman," Martin said with the glimmer of a smile.

"She's always had a soft spot for you."

"To my good fortune."

"So no complaining and help me eat this."

Martin now smiled broadly. "So, cut me my crumb already."

I pulled out my knife and cut the treat into several small pieces. I made sure that Martin got the lion's share.

"You wear a new livery, I see."

"I have been promoted to guard the Privy Council."

"Another door closes and a new one opens. Your life seems to be full of the unexpected. I gather this is a position of greater trust and opportunity."

I wanted to tell him about Baron Roland but felt reluctant to speak about our special arrangement with anyone, even with Martin. "It is the opportunity to stand as silent as the furniture in the room," I laughed. "I am grateful to have such an easy post and to be indoors when the weather is extreme. Although, to tell you the truth, the hours drag on sometimes."

"An opportunity for prayerful meditation," Martin smiled with a wink.

"Oh, eat your crumb already," I laughed.

We chatted comfortably until dusk started to settle.

"Go alone," Martin urged me. "We serve no one to be seen together."

I pulled from my backpack some carrots, a small cabbage, three onions, and a little bag. "Here, put these into your own sack."

Martin picked up the small bag. "What's in here?"

"Dried peas."

"This will make an excellent soup," Martin said, already placing the vegetables carefully into the sack he carried slung over his shoulder. "My thanks to your blessed mother."

"Veronika picked them out for you."

"Veronika? How is your sweet sister?"

"Older and opinionated. My mother will sorely miss her when she marries. They are very close."

"Is she engaged?" Martin asked, surprised.

"No, nothing of the sort. But she is such a help at home. And now with Anton married and Seb soon to move out as well, it will just be Veronika and me at home."

"You don't have to return for a duty, do you?"

"No. I'm still dressed in my livery because I stopped home to pick up these treats and did not want to lose more time by changing. And a good thing, too. It caused those nobles to think twice about harassing us. But now I want to get home before the dark pens me in. Martin, take care. I know you want to find out what secrets those nobles have, but I truly fear for you. If they catch you spying on them, they will not hesitate to kill you to keep you from revealing whatever secrets they have. Stay away from them. Please."

Martin lightly waved off my concerns. "Come," he said, "if you are so worried, then turn with me to the Virgin Mother to protect us both. Sing with me the *Ave*."

He knew I could not refuse him—or the Virgin Mary. I had time at least for a few repetitions. We raised our voices together in prayer. Our song echoed off the stone walls in the shallow cavern, helping us to sound like a choir of half a dozen voices. After the third repetition, it occurred to me that Martin might be intent on singing a full rosary. After all, he had all the time in the world, living in God's eternal presence. I, on the other hand, had to make it home in the fading light. As we sang, I caught his eye and my eyebrow asked the question. He lifted his rosary, and when he saw my eyes bulge, the corners of his mouth twitched up in a momentary smile. He quickly flashed his fingers to count out nine. That long I could wait.

"Calmer, now?" he asked when the last tones were finished echoing around us. If he had not asked, I would not have realized how the singing had relaxed me, and I was amazed.

"Now you must hasten. Go in the presence of God." He leaned forward, wrapped his arms around my shoulders and spoke a brief benediction. Then with his chin he indicated that I should go. "Go quickly and come again soon. Bring me more temptations," he said, as I crabbed backward toward the narrow opening. "Next time, I hope to have something interesting to tell you."

As I walked along the stream, my thoughts returned to the three noblemen. Should I mention them to the Baron? Then I wondered if I was just being silly with my suspicions. After all, Martin's behavior was odd. Incautiously, I pushed them to the back of my mind.

# The Crucifixion

My life entered a new rhythm. No longer required to drill, my only duty was standing guard in the Privy Council Chamber. I did this six days of the week, alternating two days on afternoon shifts followed by two days on morning shifts, then two days on afternoon shifts, with Sundays to rest. Baron Roland was not present at every meeting, as there were often subcommittees of the Council that met there. He checked in with me weekly whether I had seen or heard anything suspicious, but I had nothing to report. He told me to stay alert and it would come.

Over the following months, the only break in the rhythm of our family life was when my brother Sebastian married and moved in with his wife's family, since they had more space than we did. On Sundays, following church services and our family noonday meal, I made my Sabbath pilgrimage to the ravine to visit with Martin. As the weather warmed we got to see Martin midweek as well. During the Wednesday market he had the practice of collecting alms in exchange for a wordless blessing and always stopped at our home on his way back to his hermitage. Martin was still following his discipline of silence, but that did not prevent him from showing up so Mother and Veronika could fuss over him a bit and tempt him with some sweets. Wednesday was one of my afternoons off, and he and I could talk once Veronika and Mother were done feeding him something warm and filling his bag with food if he came up short from the market. He always insisted on praying with them first, and this satisfied his need not to be regarded as a beggar knocking at our door. We teased him that he was our personal holy man.

It was a cool spring afternoon. The sun was playing hide-and-go-seek with the clouds. When it was hiding, the air still had the bite of winter in it. But the moment the sun touched me, I felt the warming promise of spring. It was my Wednesday afternoon off, and my parents, Veronika, and I were working the little strip of earth across from the ditch at the foot of the walls. Others like us were busy in their strips of earth allowed to the townspeople of Solodurum to cultivate as our spring gardens. The land was owned by the church, which generously allowed us to use it. In payment, we all tithed to the poor, as directed by our priest.

To our left and right our neighbors were equally engaged with pulling out the winter weeds and turning over the earth. This was our third turning. We had already added horse apples, and the ground was ready for planting. I was given the monotonous chore of planting beans along the fence we had raised to keep out any passing goat or cow. The fence did not keep out the rabbits, though. I spent my childhood lying in wait for them to add to the family's soup pot. Planting the beans was tedious. The only diversion was the pruning knife I had stuck in my belt that kept poking me in the thigh.

I realized that I wasn't paying close attention to my work at hand when I heard my father growl, "Ben, they like to hear the church bells." Of course, I knew what he meant. Beans grow best when planted shallow, not deep. I had been using a stick to punch deep holes into the soil and dropping in the beans. It was enough to poke a hole with my finger in the clay soil.

"Sorry," I mumbled. "I knew better." I was distracted. Something was nagging at me, wanting me to notice it, but I couldn't put my finger on it. I paused to consider what it could be.

"Look, Ben, little Thomas has something," Veronika called out to me.

I glanced up. Little Thomas was walking over to us from the neighboring plot of dirt. He was cradling an animal under his tunic.

"What'cha got?" Veronika asked him.

"Shadow," Thomas replied. He pulled down the neck of his tunic and we saw a furry head the size of a small cat.

Veronika stood up and went over to him. "Can I pet him?" she asked.

"Sure," Thomas said. "He's mostly asleep right now."

"I thought you said you can't keep him," Veronika said, reaching out to stroke the animal's small head.

"Can't," Thomas said sadly. "I've got to let him go."

"Too much trouble?" Veronika asked. By this time Mother had gone over as well.

"I can just imagine," she said. "You can't keep a wild animal."

"I told Papa that because of Shadow we don't have any more mice, but he still says he has to go."

"Up all night?"

"That's why I can take him out now," Thomas explained. "He sleeps all day, but once it gets dark, he goes into action. He tends to get into everything in the night. Papa says he has to go."

"Poor little weasel," Veronika crooned, still petting its head.

"Not a weasel," Thomas corrected. "Shadow's a pine-marten."

The word jolted me. I jumped up like I'd been stung by a hornet. "Martin!" I exclaimed. That was what had been tugging at me. Martin always, *always* stopped by after the midweek market on his way home from collecting alms. "He never came!" I exclaimed. "Mother, did you see him?"

"No. I thought he must have come by while I was out."

I turned to Veronika. "Did you see him?"

She had a puzzled look on her face. She slowly shook her head. "No, he never came. And I never went out. That's odd. Martin always stops by. Ben ..." and her voice died out.

I felt a sudden chill and an unreasonable urgency. "Gotta go!" I declared loudly, abandoning my work.

"The beans," my father protested as I strode out of the garden. "Ben!"

"I'll do them later," I called over my shoulder. "I have to go. Now!" I finally recognized the feeling that had tugged at me all afternoon.

Impending doom. In my limping gait, I sprinted along the deep ditch that ran parallel to the city wall, heading in the direction of the Berne Gate. A part of me argued that I was being silly, but a voice immediately answered, "Better silly than sorry." I walked faster.

When I got to the edge of the city, I headed north, passing through orchards and cultivated land. Fairly soon, though, the path gave way to forests. The way was gently uphill, and by the time I reached the entrance to Verena's gorge, I was out of breath. I didn't slacken my pace. If Martin had failed to show up to refill his meager store of provisions, it could mean only one of two things. He was either sick or injured.

I scolded myself that I was blowing my worry out of proportion. He could have slipped into one of his deep reveries and lost track of time. But Martin and I had been friends for as long as I could remember, and I cared for him and felt I needed to look after him, particularly since his decision to become a hermit and a mendicant. He had always had a strongly pious side and, although this seemed like the natural progression of his character, I worried for his well-being. I followed the stream that runs through the ravine. Martin's hermitage was all the way at the other end.

I turned a corner in the path and was brought up short as if a donkey had kicked me full in the chest and knocked all the wind out of me. "Oh, Martin," I whimpered.

There, on the side of the path, like a crucifix suspended from the branches of two neighboring trees that stood close together, Martin hung by his wrists. A rope on either side was tied around them and then affixed to the trunks of the trees. He hung there stark naked, his head hanging to one side, his feet dangling on the ground. I could not tell if he was dead or unconscious. I ran to his side. It was clear that he had been beaten. His face was swollen and tracks of blood ran down his face and over his shoulder. There were dark bruises along his ribs. I pulled the pruning knife from my belt and cut the rope holding one hand.

He collapsed like a rag doll. I supported him as well as I could so all his weight would not pull on the other wrist. I draped his limp body over my shoulder, reached up and cut the other arm free. As Martin fell full upon me, he groaned. Inwardly I rejoiced. He was alive.

"Martin," I spoke to him as I maneuvered his body so I could carry him. "Martin, it's me, Ben. You're going to be all right, Martin. Stay with me."

I moved him so I could carry him piggyback. He was not in the least bit heavy. Martin had taken mortification of the flesh to heart. He did not whip himself as some zealots do, but he ate so very little, far less than he could have.

I stood a moment considering where to go. I had initially thought to take him to his hut, but then knew that was not a good solution. There was no one to care for him there. It took me but a moment to decide. I retraced my steps back down the stream toward the opening to the ravine.

# Be Not Wroth

For the next day and half, Martin woke only to groan and fall back into a troubled sleep. Mother cared for him, the whole time muttering under her breath about the folly of youth and the wickedness of the world. When she was off attending to other duties, Veronika took her place. She was beside his bed with a single candle the last thing at night, and I found her sitting there in the morning. Whether she spent the whole night standing guard over him, she would not tell me. Her fondness for Martin had always rivaled my own.

I was in the room when, late on the second day, Martin came back to us. His eyes were wide with confusion. "Where am I?" he whispered hoarsely.

"Ben brought you home," Veronika said softly. "You're safe. You're with us."

He seemed to understand and heaved a big sigh, cut short by a quick intake of breath. "That hurt," he murmured with a grimace. Veronika lifted his head so he could drink. His lips were parched and he began to gulp greedily.

"Not too much," Veronika cautioned him, pulling the cup away. "Little sips. Lots of little sips." Martin nodded his head and drank more slowly. When he lay his head back down on the pillows, he belched. Then he farted. Veronika and I could not help laughing.

"Well, it sounds like everything is still working," I said, leaning over my sister's shoulder so he could see me.

"And it hurt only a little," Martin said with a faint smile.

"Martin," I addressed him, growing serious. "Who did this to you? Did you see them?"

He nodded his head. "You did as well," he said.

I pondered this riddle a moment before realizing what he meant. "The three noblemen?" I asked.

"The same," he said. "I was not careful. Got too close. I wanted to hear."

"Why did they beat you?"

"They wanted proof that I am deaf and mute."

"Why didn't they just kill you?"

"I must have been convincing, although one of them suggested inserting a bodkin into my ears to ensure that I am truly deaf. That caused me pause."

"What stopped them?"

"For want of a bodkin," he smiled weakly.

I would have asked more, but Veronika stopped me. "You must let him rest," she insisted. "See? He has already fallen asleep again." I had to agree. Martin's eyes were shut and he was breathing deeply like one sleeping.

I was seething. I wanted to go out and find these cowards and personally eviscerate them. What kind of men would beat a harmless hermit and leave him hanging to die? Clearly, men who had something to hide. The only reason they did not stain their hands with his blood was because he had been able to convince them that he was not a threat. They likely assumed he would be dead by morning without their having to spill his life onto the forest floor. Agitated, I paced the room. If I only knew where to find them! I went outdoors and walked the length of the city wall to cool off.

Later, when I stepped back indoors, Veronika called for me to join her.

"He's been asking for you," she said.

I leaned over and touched Martin on the shoulder and spoke his name. He stirred and opened his eyes.

"Ben," he said in his quiet voice. "I sense that you are angry."

"I am burning like Mother's pot on the fire that is about to boil over," I admitted readily.

"Ben, be not wroth," he said. "In the end, they did my will."

I was puzzled by these words. "Whatever do you mean?"

"So often have I beseeched our Lord. I wished that I might share even the smallest portion of what He suffered, to know that suffering on my own person. These men were His instrument. Our Lord granted me my wish."

"Martin," I exclaimed, incensed. "They left you to die there tied to those trees."

"As our Savior was left to die nailed to His tree."

I stared at him. Inwardly, I rebelled at his magnanimity. It was ill-placed.

"Ben," Martin beseeched me. "Be not wroth with them, though they meant ill. It is all God's will. I forgive them. I ask you to, as well. For the sake of Him who suffered for our sins, sin not again. Find it in your heart to forgive."

Martin's generous heart humbled me, and, pressing my lips together to keep from embarrassing myself, I gave a quick nod, accepting Martin's guidance. Still, it did little to tame the call for revenge screaming in my blood. I decided it was fortunate that I did not know how or where to locate those noblemen, although secretly in my heart I swore they would suffer at my hands if they ever crossed my path again. Then, in the same moment, I heard Martin's call for forgiveness. It was as if one voice, calling hotly for revenge, spoke in one ear, and another voice, Martin's, spoke the soothing tones of forgiveness into the other.

As fate would have it, I was to be tested two days later. I had been on duty in the Privy Chamber all afternoon. As I left, I caught sight of one of the noblemen I had spoken with that day in the gorge, the short one who spoke with an accent. He was walking down the broad hallway in the company of several members of the Elder Council. I did not stop to think about what I was doing. I leaned my poleaxe into a corner and strode after him, drawing my knife. I saw red, and before I ever reached him, I imagined myself cutting his throat and splashing his crimson blood on the tiles underneath our feet. I had no thought for consequences. I had no thought of forgiveness. My blood screamed for revenge.

I was three strides behind him when suddenly Baron Roland was standing in front of me. He seemed to have come out of nowhere.

"Guardsman," he said sternly, grabbing me by the sleeve of my gambeson and giving me a quick shake. This broke the momentum of the blood trance I was under. "Guardsman!" Roland repeated, staring sternly into my eyes. "You will escort me into the vestibule."

He did not wait for me to respond. Roland walked in the opposite direction the nobleman was taking and pulled me along by the arm. He walked me down two floors until we came to one of the doors, and then outside into the cold air. Then he faced me.

By this time I had regained my senses. I took a deep breath. "Thank you," I murmured. "I would have killed him."

"I could see that," Roland said, gently prying the knife out of my still clenched hand. "You had blood in your eyes. What did he do to you? Seduce your sister?"

"Nearly as bad," I said. I told him the whole story about Martin, his vow of silence, the encounter, and how they had left him for dead, hanging between two trees.

"And where is the hermit now?"

"In my home. My sister and mother are caring for him."

"An odd story," Roland reflected. "What were they doing there, I wonder? And why attack a poor hermit, even if he had been listening to them. What did they have to hide? One of them had an accent, you said?"

"French, I believe," I replied. "Martin thought so, too. Just now there were Council members with him."

Roland's eyes lit up with recognition. "Ah, now I know who you mean. He is an emissary of the Emperor, but has lived some years in this region. He has convinced many that we should remain loyal to the Empire and resist further alliances with the Swiss Confederacy. Ben, why did you never mention this to me before?"

"It seemed insignificant at the time. Just some noblemen picking a quarrel with a poor hermit. I thought to tell you, and then it slipped my mind."

"Yet you and your hermit were certain they had something to hide."

When he said that, all the pieces fell together. Of course, this was the sort of suspicious activity Roland wanted to hear about. "I am sorry, Baron. You are right. I didn't realize it at the time. I was too focused on finding the traitor in the Council Chamber. Do you think he is the spy you have been seeking?"

"Perhaps, but more likely that he is the recipient of information than he who has stolen it. Ben, we have to accept the threat can come from anywhere. Even from the direction of the holy hermit's gorge."

"I promise to be more alert after this."

"We must also be clever about this, Ben. You can't attack a visiting nobleman in the presence of the Elder Council." Then he laughed. "You can't go attacking the nobility under any circumstances. What they did to Martin would be child's play compared to what would happen to you. There is no way you can seek revenge without bringing destruction upon your whole family. You have to trust me in this." I must have scowled, because Roland placed his hand on my shoulder and said, "Let's find out first if they were plotting—and what it was. Then I will lend my long arm to avenging our hermit. We just need to be patient and alert. Will you follow my lead on this?"

How could I refuse?

# The Blades of Grass

One morning soon after this, I rose to find that Martin was gone. Mother and Veronika were huddled at the hearth.

"Where's Martin," I asked, expecting to hear that he had only stepped out to relieve himself. That's when I noticed that Veroni was quietly weeping and Mother had been comforting her. "What's happened?"

Mother looked up. "Nothing," she said brusquely. "Martin claimed that he has healed enough. He's gone back to his hermitage."

"He's still too weak," Veroni said in a quiet voice, wiping her tears. "I tried to tell him, but he would not listen to me. He does not believe that he is welcome here."

"I'll get him back," I said resolutely, heading for the door and grabbing my cap.

"In the end, he must decide," were Mother's last words as I closed the door behind me.

I didn't have to go far. I found Martin sitting in a patch of sunlight by the side of the path that leads into the forests skirting the city walls.

"Martin! What are you doing here?"

In answer, he patted the ground next to him. I sat beside him.

"Behold the blades of grass," Martin said with a flourish of his hand toward a small patch of green. "Each one identical to the next. Yet, look closer." With a gesture he urged me to bend over and gaze more closely at them. I stared, not knowing what he wanted.

"What do you see?" he asked after a few moments of silence.

"Grass?" I answered uncertainly. "Really, Martin, what do you want me to see? I am not blessed with your spirit eyes. You have to tell me plainly."

Martin laughed freely. "Then I shall open your eyes to what I see. When we look without trying, all we see is grass. It all looks the same. Fodder for the sheep and cows. Yet when we look closer, we discover diversity. There is variation from one blade to the next in size and even in shape. They *seem* identical, but they are not."

I stared at the grass until I could see what he meant. "All right, I can see that. But does it have meaning? The difference appears insignificant."

"It has immense meaning, my friend. The growth of the grass is inspired by an idea that God holds within His divinity, and every blade of grass strives to emulate that divine idea. So it is with every leaf on the tree under which we sit. It is so between this beech tree and the one next to it. Just open yourself to the wonder of how similar they are, and yet how different." I stood and took a step back so I could study the two trees. He was right. They were both beech trees, yet distinctive in the pattern of how their branches grew. I looked back to my friend and shrugged my shoulders. I still didn't see his point.

Martin continued, "With every tree, every bush, every flower, it is the same. But it does not stop there. Every cat, every snowflake, every horse, every hummingbird, all the way to God's crowning creation, even every human being."

I tried to make sense of what he was saying. "Are you telling me that all living things grow, striving to emulate a divine idea?"

"An idea that is an ideal," Martin celebrated with a tired smile. "And for human beings, it is even more complex. Our lives are a paradox that pulls us first in one direction, and then in another." He paused to look at me and waited.

"Tell me already," I urged him.

"We sense an eternal spirit living within us. That is the human ideal. It guides us to live with compassion, love, generosity and faith. Yet we live in a body that is subject to hunger, cold, jealousy, anger, disease and death. We are constantly pulled between the eternal ideal and our earthly reality. Which do we allow to dominate in us?" With this Martin stopped speaking and his whole body slumped. I could see that he was spent. I placed my hand on his shoulder. "Martin, may I invite you home for a warm bite to eat? So you can emulate the divine ideal of good health?" This brought amusement to his tired face. Then I added, "I have taxed you with instructing me on the mysterious ways of the Lord. You look like you could use some more strengthening."

Martin nodded weakly. "Indeed, I would welcome that. Enlightening you on the intricacies of the divine plan is indeed taxing." He gave me a sidelong grin. "And I must reluctantly admit, I have misjudged my readiness to return to the privations of my hermitage. I am weaker than I expected."

I took Martin by the arm, helped him to his feet, and slowly led him home. Not only did he have a warm bite, he stayed another three nights before insisting it was finally time for him to return to his beloved hermitage. This time, he did not attempt to go alone, but accepted that Veronika and I accompany him. That way, we were able to take a basket full of food and make sure he was well provisioned before we left him to his solitude.

## Connie

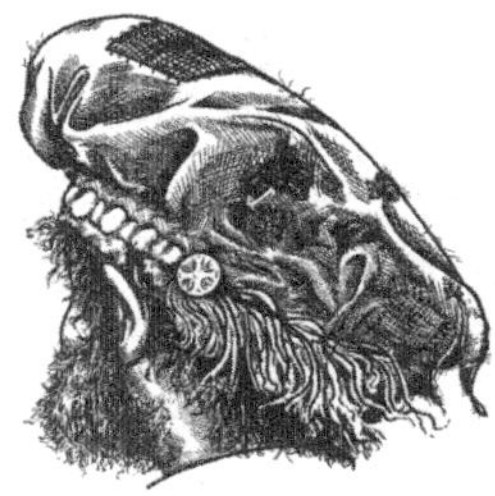

Living at home, I relished the warmth of my family circle. Certainly, tempers flared at times in our small living space, but we were also very forgiving of one another and no one stayed sour for long. My family had accepted my presence in the Guard and even seemed proud that I bore an injury I had sustained in defending the city.

When with the Guard, I was surrounded by the easy camaraderie that we shared with one another. There were always one or two who rubbed you the wrong way, but unless you had to share a post with one of them, it was easy enough to avoid those who seemed to go out of their way to irritate others.

In this way, spring slipped smoothly into summer, and the summer gave way to another autumn as my birthday approached. Best of all, my private pile of groschen continued to grow, and I still held firm to my plan to leave the Guard one day and enter an apprenticeship.

One chilly fall day, the sun was out, yet the breeze spoke of winter, and I was returning from the camp where I had been sent to deliver a message. I had made a point of visiting with Andreas and catching up on the latest gossip before returning. I was walking through the Candlemakers Lane when I heard two unusual noises that drew me to go out of my way. The first was the sound of a saw and hammer, unusual in a city built of stone and not of wood. The second were sharp bark-like exclamations of distress, and I had a strong suspicion who was making them. I came upon the construction first, two men hard at work. One was sawing planks, the second was hammering together the walls of a small structure. Curious, I walked up to them.

"What are you building?" I asked.

The man who had been sawing stopped long enough to look me up and down. His eyes paused on the emblem of my tunic. "What business is it of yours?" he asked in a surly tone.

"Just curious," I said, feeling like I had intruded.

"The Guard has other business to be curious about," he said.

I didn't like the way he had put me on the defensive. I took note of his swarthy skin, the ring in his ear, and a colorful scarf around his neck. A gypsy day laborer. I took a step forward. "See here," I said. "I've asked you politely. The least you can do is give a civil response."

The workman put down his saw and snatched up a hammer as he stepped up to meet me. I wondered if we were about to come to blows. At that moment, the man who had been hammering stepped between us. He took me by the sleeve and led me several steps away. He spoke soothingly, "Don't mind him," he said. "He's often sour. Nothing personal. We're building a latrine, that's all. This neighborhood is in need of one."

I looked at the walls he was raising and saw the truth of what he had said. I glanced at the other workman, but he had gone back to his sawing. "No offense meant," I said. "I was merely curious."

"As you have a right to be," he said, clapping me on the shoulder.

"And you were able to get the permission to build?" I knew from my brothers that all building in the city was controlled. Maybe it was not as strict for structures of wood.

"Everything has been taken care of," he said soothingly. "This quarter is desperate for a central latrine."

Since it was not my place to inquire further, I turned away from them and continued down the street, which at that point took a steep curve. I passed by the fountain of St. Dymphna that provides water for residents in those narrow lanes. The sporadic sounds of distress I had heard before continued to echo off the stone walls of the buildings. Then I saw him, Crazy Connie, standing in a corner where two walls met at an angle. He had his back to the street, facing dead into the stone wall. He was engaged in an animated conversation with his demons, a frequent occurrence. I walked over and, as gently as I could, placed my arm around his shoulders. He whirled around at my touch, his eyes wild.

"Connie, it's me. Benedictus. Don't be frightened."

"Twenty-two," he muttered, his face intense. "*Twenty-two.*"

I knew better than to ask him, twenty-two *what*. Aside from it being twice our town's fetish number, it made no sense. Connie's face was contorted and twitching. He never gave explanations; I had to guess what he needed.

"Connie, have you eaten today?" He looked at me as if I had spoken a foreign language. "Food, Connie. Have you eaten?" I made a motion with my hand of putting something in my mouth. He suddenly grew very quiet. "Show me your purse, Connie," I coaxed. "Let me see if you have money in your purse."

"Lots!" Connie barked with a scowl, grabbing the small purse that hung under his arm and shaking it. I could hear the coins chinging against each other.

"That's great, Connie," I said, gently guiding him away from the corner to walk with me. "Let's get something to eat." Connie let me lead him. I was surprised no one had done this yet.

All the young men my age kept an eye out for Connie. He was not more than a few years older than I was. He was crazy, but harmless. Most of all, he was one of our own, a young man struggling to stay alive. That his struggles were different than ours did not matter. We helped him out of the sense of brotherhood we felt with a fellow sufferer along life's path. And we probably all secretly counted our blessings that we did not have to struggle with the same demons that tormented Connie, in spite of his mysterious well-lined purse.

We had never managed to discover Connie's family. All we knew was they let him wander the streets freely. It made sense, for the only way to prevent him from wandering around town would be to tie him up or lock him in a room. The very thought of being locked up touched a deep chord of fear in each one of us. We all held in high esteem the right to walk around freely. We in the Guard were sworn to that freedom and to defend it for all who lived within the city walls. So why shouldn't Connie have the same right?

As far as we could tell, and we had often discussed this, Connie had someone who made sure he had a purse filled with enough coin so he could buy food during the day. We figured his family must have a certain wealth. Either that, or Connie had a patron who chose to remain anonymous. Connie didn't seem to have a home to return to every night. He often just slept under the Chapel Bridge. He was terrible at looking after himself. During the day he was so distracted by the fears running through his head, he rarely thought of feeding himself. On this day I wondered why he was still hungry. Maybe he had only just emerged from whatever hiding place he had tucked himself into. Since I was headed to the bakery myself, I took him with me.

Using the coins from his purse, I bought him a small loaf of bread. Connie clutched it to his chest, a large grin across his face. But bread alone does not fill a belly. Once outside on the street again, I pulled a fat wedge of cheese from my provisions bag, pressed it into his eager hand, and took a coin from his purse so I could replace it. I walked with him down to the river, and we found a stone bench against a stone wall that caught the midday sun.

"Come on, Connie. I'll sit with you while you eat." I wanted to make sure some ne'er-do-well did not steal the food out of his hands. The poor are not much better behaved than the ducks and swans we fed our hardened bread to. Whenever one got a piece, there were always two or three trying to snatch it away.

We sat with our backs against the stone wall that reflected some warmth and protected us from the chilly fall breeze. While Connie ate, I pulled a piece of dried meat out of my bag, tore it in half and offered it to him. He snatched it from my hand like a wild animal might and stuffed it into his mouth. His eyes glowed with enjoyment. The food in his belly must have calmed the demon that had plagued him earlier. He was now all smiles and the wild look had vanished. How quickly he could shift his moods. Suddenly, there was a mischievous gleam in his eye.

"Bennie," Connie said between bites. "Do you like my hat?"

Connie was always dressed in a hodge-podge manner, usually in what had once been finely-tailored and expensive clothing. He had obviously found other friends who were passing on to him their worn-out hose and doublets. I always wondered if it was out of generosity and compassion or a subtle mockery of an unfortunate young man whose mind would always remain childlike. People could be cruel that way.

Today Connie was wearing a brocaded velvet hat that had no brim. It was tattered and fraying, but must have once adorned the head of a wealthy man.

"It's a beautiful hat, Connie." What I really wanted to say was that it had once been a beautiful hat, but I knew better.

"Does it look good on me?" he asked next.

"It is perfect for you, Connie." In truth, the hat was too small for him. Connie had a remarkably large head. The seam at the back of the hat had split open.

"Does it fit me well?" Connie had an uncanny way of knowing what I was thinking.

"Like it was made for you," I lied.

"It wasn't made for me," Connie revealed. "Do you know who it was made for?"

"No, Connie, who was it made for?" I did not expect him to know, but I usually tried to follow the direction of his questions and answers. It kept him from getting anxious and belligerent.

"For my brother," he said.

I was thunderstruck. "Connie, I didn't know you have a brother."

"Connie not allowed to tell you that," he said looking satisfied, as if he had actually not told me.

"OK, Connie, then you didn't."

"It's a secret," he continued, staring out at the boats in the river. "Not anyone can know. Not even you, Bennie."

"It's all right to keep secrets, Connie. Even from your friends."

"I know," he nodded.

There were a few moments of silence as Connie went back to eating. Then suddenly he turned to me and asked, "Bennie, do you like my hat?"

I took a deep breath. *Here we go again*, I thought.

"It's a beautiful hat, Connie."

"Do you want it?" Here was a new twist.

"No, I don't want your hat, Connie."

"Why not, if you think it's beautiful?" With Connie, sometimes any answer got you in trouble.

"All right, yes, I would like your hat."

"Can't give it to you. Do you know why?"

"Because your brother said you have to keep it?"

"How do you know that?" he asked with genuine surprise.

"You just told me." I was referring to the fact that he had a brother.

"No I didn't. How do you know what my brother said to me?"

"I made a lucky guess."

"I'm not supposed to tell anyone. I'm not supposed to give my hat away."

"Then you keep it, Connie."

"But you'd like it, wouldn't you?"

"Not if I can't have it. Then I don't want it. You keep it."

Connie went back to his food and we sat watching a boat dock at the toll house. When he finished the bread, he turned to me and asked, "Bennie, do you like my hat?"

After a hearty laugh, I heaved myself to my feet. "Time for my shift, Connie. See you around." As I walked away, I pondered a brother who had such expensive clothes to pass on, yet let his brother go hungry and barefoot and live on the streets. I decided that Connie had invented him.

# Redemption

I did not miss any opportunity of visiting Martin to make sure that he had not returned to the austerity of his hermit's life too soon. On this day, I found him sitting in the dappled sunlight on a boulder along the stream. He was gazing into the rushing water and appeared to be deep in thought. I approached him slowly so as not to startle him.

Whereas one moment his face was an unreadable mask, as if his soul was as far away as the stars in the sky, the moment he heard my footsteps he looked up and flashed me a warm, welcoming smile.

"Dear brother Benedict," he said. "Please join me. I am so happy to see you."

"And I am happy and relieved to see you looking well," I replied. "I was concerned that you might have returned to your solitude too soon."

"I hope seeing me puts your heart to rest," he replied. "Come, sit with me and I will share with you the fruits of my meditation."

The boulder he sat on was broad enough to have space for me as well. I perched next to him and he leaned his shoulder against mine. He looked thin and, as he rested against me, he was hardly any weight at all. In contrast, his face shone with a bright light. I was grateful to be sitting beside him and could politely look away, since the look in his eyes was too intense for me. The closest I could come to describing it would be, ferocious. A ferocious light. It was not threatening, but far too fierce to look at for more than a few moments.

Martin gestured to two fir trees of about equal size growing on the other side of the stream. "Do you recall our last conversation?"

"About the blades of grass?" I asked.

"Behold these two trees. They arise from the ideal of God, with the same intent to grow. They look identical, yet when we examine them, we find subtle, telling differences."

I patted his shoulder. "You are a mystic, my friend. They look the same to me. What do you want me to see? That they are the same, or that they are different?"

Martin laughed. "Why, both."

"If you're not careful, people will think you've become delusional from too much squinting of your eyes."

"And I believe that I am a lone realist with my eyes wide open, viewing the world with clarity. Ben, here we see a perfect example of the individual expression of God's ideal."

"And by ascribing to both trees sameness and differences, what is it that you claim to see so clearly?"

Martin's eyes were gleaming even more fiercely. "The grandeur of God."

"In the grass? In the trees?" I asked with a laugh of disbelief.

"If I cannot see God's grandeur in the blades of grass, the leaves, or in the trees themselves, then I will be blind to it everywhere else. We don't experience God when we step into a church where everything is made by man's design. It is when we step out into the world—where everything is made by God's design. That is when we are surrounded by His grandeur and He reveals to us His divine plan."

I laughed, but I was also embarrassed because I lacked the simplicity of his certainty, so I said, "You have a powerful imagination, dear friend."

"You don't need an imagination, Ben. Just open your eyes."

I loved Martin too much to brush him off as crazy, although that was what I was feeling. Had the beating affected his thinking? Or was there something more to what he was saying? Was there a way for me to see the world through his eyes? "Teach me, then, to see as you can. What do I have to do?"

Martin became animated, and jumped up from his seat on the rock. "First, acknowledge the complex variation of nature, yet recognize that it is perfect in itself." He plucked a pine cone off the ground, dug into its core, and pulled out a seed. "Gaze upon this—a seemingly lifeless grain of nearly nothing. Yet it has within it everything it needs to grow into that!" He gestured emphatically to the towering tree he stood beneath. "That means there is a knowledge greater than we can imagine in this little grain of nearly nothing."

He opened his hand and placed the seed in the middle of his palm. "Now here's a further mystery. Leave this seed in the sun, and it will dry up, wither and eventually become dust. Yet bury it in the earth where it is damp and dark, and an unfathomable force awakens that reaches out of the darkness in search of the light."

"The very light that would have destroyed it had it been left exposed," I said, caught up in his enthusiasm.

"Precisely," he exclaimed with joy. "What a delicious paradox to solve! All life hungers for this light and reaches toward it, yet we cannot approach it unprepared or without help. It is the light of God that shines upon us through the might of the sun, so that we might become aware of it. Yet, unlike the sun, God in His goodness and grace shines upon us both day and night."

"How can you be sure?" I teased.

"Oh, of that I have proof," he said confidently.

"Proof that God shines His light upon us both day and night? What is your proof?"

"Because, dear Ben, the plants don't stop growing at night. Nor does the child in its crib."

I pondered this. "You make us seem no different from the plants or the beasts. Yet you have repeatedly called us the Crown of Creation."

Martin grew serious. "Each of God's creations strives to emulate the ideal hidden in God's divinity. In fact, they do so because that is what they are designed to do. That is why one fir tree resembles another one so closely. The animals have no choice to do otherwise. They follow the imprint of the ideal. That is why one cow behaves so predictably like another one. Why one donkey is as stubborn as the next. However, we, the Crown of Creation, have been granted something the rest of creation lacks. It is the dilemma you faced when you wanted to break away from your family's profession. Falling in line with your family's tradition would be acting like the horses or the goats, one following the herd behavior of the next. But you accessed the precious gift that was given to all human beings."

"Free Will," I murmured. "We have spoken of this before, haven't we? It is why you are not a soldier like your father before you. It is why you won't join an order of Brothers."

Martin could see that I was finally understanding some of what he had been trying to teach me. He continued, "By exercising our Free Will, we realize we are not always in agreement with one another. Often, we put our Free Will aside so we can work and live in harmony with others. Our society depends upon us to follow agreed upon norms and conditions. However, when, for instance, we want something different than following in a parent's footsteps, this leads us to act at cross purposes to one another. Unlike the plants and beasts that by their nature live in harmony with one another—yes, they do compete for space and the wolf will eat the lamb—but it is all predictable. Only the human being has the capacity of defying this predictability, thanks to this unique, divine gift."

"Free Will?"

"It has led to great good in the world and, sadly, also to great cruelty and evil."

"What about the light of God?" I asked suddenly. "Does that not pull us upward as it does the plants and the beasts, to strive toward the perfection of what you call the Divine Ideal?"

"Indeed it does," he said solemnly. "Every heart strives for the light of God." Martin turned toward me and placed a hand on my shoulder so he could look me in the eye. "And for this reason I cannot hate the men who tied me between the trees, to hang there and die, but I pray for them with even greater fervor."

My jaw dropped. "So you are earnestly forgiving them for what they did to you?"

"We share the same path," Martin said. What was that expression in his face? Sadness? Resignation? "They, too, walk toward God, though they walk, one might say, backward, gazing at their own shadows and the empty illusion of grandeur that gives. My prayer is that they turn around and face the light."

"Yet, you have not answered me. Do you forgive them?" I needed to know.

"If God can forgive me for my weaknesses, which are many, can I not forgive them theirs?"

When he saw my eyes grow wide, he added, "Does the heart that is turned toward darkness not strive for God as well? We all seek redemption, dear Benedictus."

# The Miasma

Another winter settled on the city, this year with more snow and ice than usual. My life alternated between family and serving with the Guard. I was grateful for my post in the Privy Council Chamber which kept me in the warmth during the cold days. Reports of roving French forces pillaging the countryside were a distant memory.

Spring came early and brought with it a welcome thaw. We reveled in the warmth of spring and the promise of summer. Peace seemed to reign and our lives followed predictable rhythms. All of this was shattered one sunlit afternoon.

It was my mother who first alerted us to the outbreak. I had just risen from a nap when she rushed in the door.

"Pestilence!" she shrieked, waving her arms erratically.

Alarmed, my sister cried out, "Mother, what is it?"

"Pestilence!" she repeated emphatically. "Everyone speaks of it in the market. Where's Father? We must find him."

By this time I was on my feet. "Slow down. What are you talking about?"

"There's a pestilence, I tell you," she insisted, her eyes wide with fear. "No one is safe. We shall starve. We shall all die."

I put my arm around her shoulders. She was trembling. Thinking she was cold, I led her to the hearth and got her to sit down. I stoked the fire to warm her up. "Mother, tell us what you know."

"The dead are lying in the street," she said, looking from me to Veronika. "You must find Father."

"You saw the dead?" I asked, trying hard not to be carried away by her panic.

She shook her head. "Marili saw them. She was on her way to the bridge to the Lower Town. She said there is a miasma and it is killing good Christian folk. They lie in the street." She grabbed me by my tunic. "You must find Father. And Seb. Anton will be safe. He is working outside the city."

"I will go and find them," I reassured her. I rose and stepped to the door. Mother hurried after me.

"Take this!" she said, pressing her headscarf into my hands. "Against the miasma. Cover your face." I took the cloth and glanced at Veroni. She stood there pale and wide-eyed.

In the streets, I did not encounter many people until I neared the market. Everyone I saw there was in a hurry, walking away from the central plaza, most with something, a cloth or a shawl, pressed to their faces. In passing, they glanced at me with sidelong looks and hastened on. I tried to find someone I could ask, but with their faces covered, I recognized no one.

Father was working on a house, so I made for there. I did not get far when, hastily turning a corner, we nearly collided with one another.

"Father!" I exclaimed. "Is it true? Mother came home with a story of pestilence."

"Near the St. Dymphna Fountain," he replied, his voice low and unsteady. "The talk is everywhere."

"She wants me to find Seb. Do you know where he's working?"

"I've already sent him home," he said. "Come, we will go together."

I hesitated. "I should report in," I said. "In case we are needed."

Father was silent a moment and then nodded his head. "Of course. Go, do your duty to the city. Return when you can." He turned and walked away.

I hurried through the narrow streets. I decided to pass through the quarter above the river to see what I could on my way to the garrison. I was taking a shortcut through the Jewish quarter, which is actually just one street, not a whole neighborhood. When I came to Joseph's door, I paused.

I had not visited him since the day he told me that he had sent Zipporah to live with his brother's family in Zurich. I felt a yearning to see Zipporah again, or at least to hear how she was doing, to know that she was safe. Maybe even hear that she had asked after me. Young men can hold on to vain hopes far past any expectation of them being fulfilled. I was no different. I convinced myself that as a physician, Joseph might be able to shed light on the extent of the threat we faced. That was all the excuse I needed. I knocked, and there was no response for so long I was about to continue on my way when the door opened a crack.

"Ben!" I heard a woman's voice speak in surprise. It was Miriam. She opened the door a little more and looked up and down the street before saying, "Come in quickly." She took me by the sleeve and pulled me in. Then she closed the door behind me.

"I came to speak with Joseph," I said.

"I am here," his deep voice sounded behind me. I turned to see him approach. He looked old, his face heavy with cares.

"There is talk of a pestilence," I said. "I am on my way to see if I can help." I stopped. I was puzzled to see numerous bags packed and piled at the door.

"It is not safe for you to be here, Ben," Joseph said, his voice steady.

"Where are you going?" I asked, still staring at the bags.

After a moment's hesitation, Joseph said, "We are fleeing."

"Is it that bad?" I asked in alarm.

Joseph took me by the arm. "Come. We must talk." He led me into their small sitting room with a table and chairs. He invited me to sit.

"First of all, this pestilence, as you call it, is very real, and yes, people are becoming sick and dying." Alarmed, I rose from my seat, but Joseph urged me to sit again. "Secondly, I will instruct you how to avoid getting ill. If you can convince others to follow one simple precaution, they will be out of danger."

I stared at him, my eyes wide. "You know that?" I suddenly wondered if I could trust him. After all, he had destroyed any hope I had for a relationship with his daughter.

"I have seen this before," Joseph continued. "Not here, but when we lived in al-Andalus. The illness is found only around the neighborhood that takes its water from the St. Dymphna Fountain. Its waters are tainted."

"Nonsense!" I exclaimed. Now I knew he could not be trusted. That fountain had flowed with pure waters since before I was born. "That's impossible! Are you saying someone poisoned the waters?"

"Indirectly, yes. Last fall, the neighborhood above the fountain built its own latrine to avoid a longer walk to use the public one two streets further away. The waste from the latrine is seeping into the aquifer."

"Nonsense," I repeated. Now I knew he was making this up. "That new latrine has been in use for months." I recalled the day I had the run-in with one of the surly day-laborers while it was being built.

"Until now, the winter cold kept the waste frozen and contained," Joseph explained. "With the spring thaw, it has seeped deeper into the ground."

I had never heard of such a thing, and I was reluctant to believe him.

"I have seen the bodies of those who have died. Their skin has turned blue. It is an unmistakable sign. In al-Andalus, it was called the Blue Death."

I struggled with the thought that he was making all this up.

"There are two essential actions," Joseph continued. "Close down the latrine, and, more importantly, seal off the fountain until the waters clear. That may take months, years even."

"Would you cut a whole neighborhood off from their only source of water?" I objected. "That's outrageous."

"It is more outrageous to let them continue dying. But I understand your disbelief. The Elder Council will be even more reluctant to take action. I expect that few will understand the connection between the latrine and the water table. Perhaps the Younger Council will be more open to reason."

I thought about this a moment. "Even if this were true, and I am not yet convinced, you said you are fleeing. Why? If you believe in what you are saying, then you will not fall ill if you avoid the water from that fountain."

"It is not the water from the fountain we fear." He paused, clearly uncomfortable to say more. "We are going to my brother in Zurich."

This didn't make sense. "Where you sent Zipporah?" I felt a tension in my chest. Had she asked after me? I could not get the question past my lips.

"Yes, where I sent Zipporah. He will take us in as well."

"I don't understand. Why are you leaving? What are you afraid of?"

Joseph paused before answering. "We fear our fellow citizens."

"That's absurd," I exploded.

Joseph placed a hand on my arm. "You are young and I forgive you your naivety. Before long you will understand the reason for our leaving. For now, I advise that you go on your way, and for the sake of your own safety, take care that no one sees you leaving our home."

So speaking, Joseph stood up and led me to the door. Miriam and their son, Reuben, were there, still placing items into their open packs.

"I am sorry you are leaving," I heard myself speak the words, but in my heart, hardened with resentment, I did not mean them. They were going to see Zipporah. I would not.

"It is for our own good," Miriam said. "You have been a faithful friend to our family, Ben. We will take your greetings to Zipporah. I know she will be happy to hear that you are well."

There was a stab of longing in my heart. "I wish you a safe journey," I mumbled.

"May God bless you and your family with safety as well, Benedict," Miriam replied.

Joseph had the door open a crack and turned to me. "The street is clear. You must go now." As I passed by him, Joseph caught me by my sleeve. "If you know anyone you can tell who might have influence on one of the Councils, the sooner you take action, the sooner this is over."

I slipped into the empty lane and hurried on my way.

I walked the circuitous city pathways to the St. Dymphna Fountain. The streets were deserted and, although I felt a little foolish, I pressed Mother's headscarf to my face to ward off the miasma.

I came to the fountain and found no one there, and no bodies lying on the street. The water splashed merrily as if there were nothing to be concerned about. I stared into the deep basin, wondering if I could see anything of what Joseph had said. I could see nothing suspicious and decided that Joseph was making it up. I impulsively reached out to drink from the waters, just to prove him wrong, but one thought stopped my hand: What if he was right? I suddenly felt a dark sense of joy that his family felt forced to leave the city. And then immediately I was washed by a wave of shame that I would wish Joseph and his family any evil.

With the cloth pressed to my nose, I hurried off and made my way across the river and out the Berne Gate to the compound of the Guard. There I joined the other guardsmen in the mess and heard the swirling rumors. We carefully sifted through the conflicting stories, discarding the outlandish and looking for more details about the plausible. There was no question that citizens in the quarter of the St. Dymphna Fountain were sickening and some had died, two expiring in the street in a pool of their own excrement. There were even rumors that the skin of the dead had turned a hideous hue of blue. But what was the cause? Everyone agreed it was the miasma, a poisoned air. But what had caused the miasma? Did the threat come from without? Was it the French? A scourge from God? Had someone poisoned the waters?

Or did the threat come from within? This was far easier for us to grasp. At first we soundly accused the gypsies, but we could find no motivation for them to bring a pestilence. The gates of the city would be barred to them now, and they would have to trek to another city to find work or beg their daily bread.

Finally, we landed upon the Jews. They lived within the walls of Solodurum. They were not God-fearing, at least, not like good Christians. They set themselves apart from us with their odd rituals, manners and ways of dress. They even favored their own language, which sounded like a thin mockery of our own. They had nothing to lose and everything to gain. Most agreed: It must be the Jews. Before the evening was over, fueled by my smoldering resentment at Joseph, I too was convinced that the Jews must be the source of the deadly miasma. It made perfect sense.

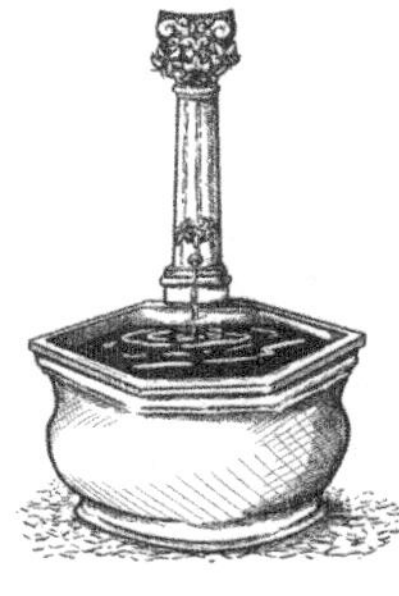

The next day, I arrived for my shift at the Privy Council chamber. A heated discussion was already under way. There were more Council members present than I had ever seen before. Some even stood, there not being enough room at the table. Several shuffled out of my way so I could take my post along the wall. I quickly counted. There were eleven. These were all the members of the Elder Council. I guessed that they were meeting here instead of in the larger chamber to ensure privacy.

Once he had been addressed by name, I realized that among them sat Baron Roland's cousin, Roger. He was a stout, powerful looking man with a closely trimmed black beard. He was dressed in the latest fashion, the Italian cloth of his tunic thickly embroidered with silver thread. Something in his manner made my skin crawl. I tried to figure out what it was. He exuded confidence, but then, so did Roland. He had the air of a man who expected others to follow his lead. Again, so did Roland. I decided to pay close attention to what he had to say.

"It is common knowledge," Roger said slowly and with emphasis. "They mingle carnally with the cursed gypsies who at least have the decency to live outside our city gates. So, too, should the Jews."

Having spent an evening trading rumors with the Guard, I felt a dark satisfaction to hear these forceful words against the Jews. It reflected my own bitterness toward them.

"It is time we reckon with them," said a thickset, middle-aged member, sitting next to Roger, whom I had not seen before. "It is a mistake to show Christian charity to those who reject the Christian faith. They are an unnatural breed."

"These Jews have no fear of God," a red-faced man spoke next. "They never attend church and take sacrament. They never go to confession."

"For there would be no end to the sins they had to confess," the man beside Roger said with a harsh laugh, joined in by others.

Still another said darkly, "It is they who betrayed Our Savior. They mock our faith."

"They are behind the thievery that makes our streets unsafe after dark," asserted the man next to Roger.

"They are the pestilence in our midst and must be dealt with," the red-faced man shouted.

"It does no good to turn a blind eye," Roger spoke commandingly, holding up a hand to quiet the others. "It's clear the Jews are to blame for this pestilence, and we must take decisive action against them. Certainly you've noticed that the illness does not touch them. That is only possible if they are the source of this evil. It has to be said out loud what we have all whispered to be true. They have long plotted the destruction of our city." Several shouted their agreement. I wanted to join my voice with theirs. Fortunately, I remembered my place and restrained myself.

"Nonsense," objected another member, an elderly gray-haired gentleman. "Enough of this incendiary talk. They gain nothing by killing their neighbors."

"They will acquire the empty homes with their hidden wealth," Roger replied vehemently. "We are long overdue to reckon with this foreignness in our midst. They came in the time of our forefathers, few in numbers, asking for a safe haven to live out their lives. Out of Christian compassion and generosity, the city granted it to them, and now look how they have paid us back. They have multiplied and gush out beyond the handsome quarter allotted them. It is clear that they hunger to take over another block, to drive good Christians out of their homes."

"It's true what Roger says," another spoke up. He was young compared with the older gray-haired members. "They become more prominent every year and compete with our youth for good quality work. Next they will insist on representation in our Council."

There were loud mumblings of both agreement and objection.

"Roger, you are taking this too far," argued another, who had kept silent until now. "They do the work the city allows, nothing more."

"They are money-lenders, which the church forbids," still another spoke up. "They enslave us in debt and suck out our life's blood. The only way to be free of our debt is to be free of them."

"What is honorable about that?" Roland objected, speaking out for the first time since my arrival. "The only reason we owe them is because we borrow from them."

"Do not speak about honor, Roland. They are not Christians. The church prohibits Christians from practicing usury. It is an abomination."

"Neither their religion nor the prohibition mattered when you needed a loan," Roland replied sharply.

As I listened to their heated condemnation of the Jews, I was carried away with the wave of justification they were expressing. At the same time, in the back of my mind, there was an irritating nagging that I was betraying a family that had helped me after my injury and brought me back to health—and with no expectation of payment. I shrugged off the feeling, like a biting fly. They deserved this condemnation. Why wasn't I good enough for Zipporah? Why did Joseph have to send her away? Why did she agree to go? I allowed my youthful passion for revenge to override my Christian charity.

"Enough!" Roger demanded loudly. "We must focus on the issue at hand. There is a plague. Good people are dying. The Jews are causing this miasma. They must be dealt with directly, and with a hard hand. We do ourselves no favor being generous with them. Only more Christians will die. A sacrifice must be made. A sacrifice to God!" Roger paused and looked around at the nodding heads before continuing. "We must burn them," he said, his voice low and threatening. "Every last one of them, burnt at the stake. Only this will clear the miasma and end this pestilence. God cries out for a burnt offering."

These words were jarring and my blood ran cold. I had wanted to punish Joseph for sending Zipporah away, not murder him, not murder all the Jews. I frantically searched the faces in the room. Several were nodding their heads in agreement. Others looked startled. One spoke up.

"But we have no proof," objected an elderly gentleman. "We cannot burn a whole measure of our citizenry without any proof. That's barbaric. We're better than that."

"They live among us, but they are not citizens," Roger said severely. "They profit from what we have provided them, and they repay us with death. Once they have been burnt to ashes, and the miasma clears, that will be proof enough that we have acted in accordance with God's will."

"And if the miasma does not clear?" asked another quickly.

"Then we shall try something else."

"And by then we will have blood guilt on our hands," the other replied forcefully.

"My friends," Roger continued in softer tones, but still with urgency. "There is already rumbling among the citizenry to this effect. We must act before they take matters into their own hands and view us as impotent. After cleansing the city of the Jews, we shall turn our attention to the gypsies. We will have done ourselves a favor."

There was a lot of grumbling and side conversation, but I could not tell which way the Council had been swayed.

I felt a sudden panic as I was overcome by a wave of shame. In a flash of clarity I saw that my anger against the Jews was personal and had nothing to do with the epidemic. Killing them, even driving them away, would be morally wrong and an affront to God. I had to do something, but I knew I would be severely punished if I said a word. As a guard, I was part of the furniture, nothing more. But what if Joseph had told me the truth about the water from the fountain? It would be so easy to test. We did not have to turn to such extreme measures.

In the meantime, several voices called out of the general din, "Agreed, it is time to cleanse the city!"

In the midst of this, Roland stood up to speak. He commanded their silence.

"I can see the Council is being led down a slippery slope from which, I warn you, there will be no return."

"The people demand action," Roger confronted him. "The Council is convinced that the Jews are the cause."

"Not all," one of them called out in protest.

"Yet we all agree that we are remiss if we do not act," Roger continued. "It will otherwise lead to unrestrained violence, and it will be on our heads if we do not take decisive action. We must now take a vote—"

"Agreed!" Roland spoke loudly, interrupting his cousin. "The situation demands action. But we surrender our moral high ground when we conspire to murder our neighbors."

"Then what action do you propose?" the red-faced man called out.

"Exile," Roland declared firmly. "We will exile the Jews from Solodurum. Once they are gone, if the pestilence ends, we will know they were the cause. If not, then we will have saved ourselves from innocent blood on our hands."

There was immediate agreement murmured through the room. "Much better! Yes, exile! Send the Jews away." Roland had offered them a way out without bloodshed.

He quickly followed this up. "With the Council's permission, I would like to personally oversee the removal of the Jews."

At this offer, many spoke at once, and I saw Roger glare darkly at his cousin. I wondered why.

"Roland, you do your city a great service to take this on," an elderly Council member said.

"It is better this way," several agreed. Many appeared relieved to have been pulled back from the brink of lethal fanaticism.

"Are you then of one accord?" Roland asked, looking around the room. "Roger called for a vote, then let us have a vote."

Multiple voices cried out "Aye. Aye. Time for action. A vote!"

"I will require the full cooperation of the City Guard," Roland continued.

"The Council places them at your service," several voices confirmed. "Whatever it takes to end this pestilence."

"A vote! A vote!" many called out at once. The vote was quickly taken, and Roland was given full authority for the removal of the Jews from Solodurum with the unlimited support of the City Guard. Roger's call to burn the Jews at the stake was not mentioned again.

Roland was looking around the table at the other Council members when he glanced up and looked at me. His expression clouded over when he saw me, and I guessed that my feelings were showing on my face. He gave me the look I had seen before that meant, *Keep your mouth shut. We'll talk later.* Then he gave his attention back to the Council meeting as he oversaw the drawing up and signing of the documents empowering him to oversee the exile of the Jews. I glanced over at Roger. He was still glaring darkly at his cousin. I wondered if Roland had noticed his expression as well.

Once my shift was over, I went to find Roland. The Council meeting had broken up and he was standing in a knot of men in the Council vestibule engaged in a heated discussion. I stood along the wall and waited until I could catch his eye. Once he saw me, he excused himself and walked away. I followed at a discreet distance, so as not to cause suspicion that we were going to meet. He disappeared around a turn in the hallway, and I found him standing at the doorway to an empty room. We entered and closed the door behind us.

"All right, talk. I have only a few minutes."

I quickly told him everything that Joseph had shared with me.

"I don't know if it's true," I explained, "but it is worth finding out. At first I didn't trust Joseph, but after everything I heard—"

"None of which you may breathe a word of," Roland interrupted, his tone severe.

"I know my duty is to remain silent. And I will. But why would your cousin want to, to ..." I couldn't even say it out loud, it was so horrifying.

"You heard what he said in the meeting. I suspect he is in debt to their deep pockets and saw this as a way out."

"But to make innocent people suffer—"

"If indeed they are innocent," the Baron interrupted.

"But the Jews have nothing to do with this pestilence," I protested. "They hold the key for how to end it. They are not getting sick because they do not take water from that fountain."

"I want to believe you," he said with a frustrated wave of his hand. "I do."

I nearly exploded. "Then why are you letting this insanity happen?"

He pinned me with a ferocious look. "Would you prefer to see them herded together and burned in a fiery hecatomb?" I shivered at the very thought of such an atrocity. "Look, Ben," Roland continued, "you are convinced the Jews are not causing this pestilence, and I am ready to believe it's not the Jews, but what good does any of that do us when the Council and the good, God-fearing citizens of Solodurum are convinced it is the Jews? The populace is suffering, afraid, and desperate to blame someone. They could turn on the Pope. They could accuse the French. They rail against the Emperor, but the fact is, only the Jews are conveniently within reach."

I thought of the talk the evening before with my Guard brethren. I had also been one of those voices crying for their blood. My face burned with shame. Somehow, I had to make it up. "But banishing the Jews will not put an end to the pestilence," I insisted.

"True, if the water of the fountain is tainted, as Joseph claims. It is credible, and I will put it to a test. I suspected it had something to do with those privies all along but had no way of fitting the pieces together. You have done that for me. I will shut down St. Dymphna's Fountain as your Joseph urges. In addition, I will have those public privies removed to lower ground. As it was, they were built without the permission of the City Council. We tolerated them because it was convenient to have them midtown near the markets. People will just have to get used to trekking to the bridge to relieve themselves."

"Information provided to us by a Jew!" I nearly shouted.

"Which is why I asked to be put in charge of their exile. If my cousin had had his way, they'd be piling wood as we speak to burn them all alive. My gratitude for this information is to ensure that their departure is orderly and without violence. I will also have their homes sealed off to prevent looting of their property. Then, once health has been restored, we can welcome our Jews back home."

"But what about the truth?" I was jumping up and down.

In contrast, Roland calmly stood his ground. "Truth is whatever reinforces what we already believe. The Jews must go into exile because the people need someone to blame."

"But this is wrong, so very wrong."

"Which is why I am putting you in charge to direct their evacuation from the city."

"What? Me? But I oppose it!"

"Which is exactly why you will oversee their leaving. You will do it with kindness and compassion rather than with kicks and blows. You will convince them that leaving is for their safety, which in fact it is, and that they will be welcomed back once this madness has passed. I will give the order that all questions concerning this matter be directed to you. Encourage them not to wander away too far. Like you, I do not wish to lose our Jews. They play a more important role in our city than most people will acknowledge."

I flapped my arms in agitation. "I can't believe you are putting me in this position."

"When you see the anger directed at the Jews, you will thank me for assigning you to their protection. Ben, I am depending on you to keep a cool head through all this. Keep your mouth shut and pick your men carefully."

In the end I had to admit that Roland was right. It did not take long before I heard grumblings and loud accusations against the Jews from the citizenry. Even in my own household. My first action was to hand-pick twenty-two guardsmen I could trust and who would not question my command. I was very clear that we were there so the Jews could make a peaceful exodus from Solodurum. I had to replace several when I caught them complaining that they had to protect "the filthy brood that is the cause of our misery."

My next step was to go speak to the Jewish community. Although Joseph had already taken his wife out of the city, one son, Benjamin, had remained behind to tie up his business arrangements. With his help, I was able to gather together the elders and explain the situation to them. They were well ahead of me. They had already seen where this was going, and most families were packing their belongings and preparing to travel. They all seemed to have relatives in other towns where they would be welcome to take refuge. They were sincere in their thanks that their houses would be sealed and secured until their return. I felt I wronged them by receiving their thanks, since I was the one telling them to leave, and for a time had been one of the voices demanding it. Yet they comforted me, yes, they comforted me, saying that they had much to be grateful for in a peaceful departure and with the hope of returning.

They did not all leave at the same time, but in clusters of families, to support and encourage one another on the road. I realized the wisdom of Roland's decision. As the families departed, laden with what possessions they could carry, the good people of Solodurum lined the road and threw insults at them. Some, I am ashamed to say, also threw stones. Fortunately, my chosen guardsmen quickly stepped in and prevented it from escalating. The Jews of Solodurum left without any serious incident.

The day after the last family had departed, under Baron Roland's orders, I assigned a crew to dismantle the public privies in the small town square above the St. Dymphna Fountain. The people living in that neighborhood were not happy, and some of them objected loudly that we had no right to take them down. But there was little they could argue when I presented the edict: By order of the Privy Council. Although they stood around and grumbled angrily, they did not hinder us in our work.

Once finished with that, we sealed the St. Dymphna Fountain. We might have met even more resistance had this not been the center of the area affected by the pestilence. Many of the guardsmen were fearful to take part, so I asked for volunteers. Extra pay was a good incentive. We all wore masks to cover nose and mouth, and I strictly ordered the men not to drink a drop from the infected waters. Without my having said a word, a few of them made the connection between the privies we dismantled and my orders to not drink the water. One of them even stated the obvious one day while we were working.

"So, tell me again why the Jews had to leave?"

Another answered, "Because they were crapping in those privies." There was laughter at this gallows humor, but the point had been made that the Jews were not the source of the pestilence.

As a final deed, and at Roland's order, I set a guard, day and night, to stand outside the homes of the Jews. It made sense. Empty homes were an invitation to looting, not just by those of whom you would expect it, but also by those who during the day looked and acted respectable.

One afternoon, after I had returned to my regular watch in the Privy Council, Roland sought me out. "Double the guard on the homes of the Jews tonight."

"Whatever for?" I asked. It had been so quiet, I had even been considering asking Roland if I could eliminate the guard altogether.

"Double the guard and speak with me tomorrow."

I knew not to question Roland further and did as he ordered. When I checked in with the guardsmen the next morning, I was surprised by what they reported.

"What a stroke of luck you reinforced us last night," they told me. "A gang of drunks descended on us after two bells. They carried clubs, but were no match for our halberds. However, if we had been fewer, they may have overpowered us. Ben, how did you know?"

I reported this incident to Roland, to which he replied, "This may not be the last time, so we must remain vigilant."

"This was planned, wasn't it?"

"And we were ready for it," he said with satisfaction. "And into the bargain, it has raised your reputation among the Guard. Ah, Ben, they will sing new songs about you."

I didn't half mind his teasing. It was true. The guardsmen in my detail now looked at me as something of a prophet.

# The Packet

In this way, spring passed into the warmth of summer. My routine never varied, and I was content with the regularity of my life. As much as we had longed for warmer days, we soon tired of the intense summer heat and now longed for relief. We were not disappointed as summer gave way to cooler autumn weather, the harvest with its festivities, and the change of colors in the leaves. Martin teased me that it is the human dilemma to never feel content for very long. I told him that in my case he was wrong. I was satisfied with the simple rhythms of my life.

How little prepared I was for how my life was about to be turned upside down.

One morning, I was passing through the halls of the Privy Council. My shift was not until the afternoon, but I had gone in early to hear the latest gossip in the Wait Room.

"You, there!" a commanding voice called out. I turned to see Urs, the Baron's personal secretary, walking up to me. He was a thin, wiry man, his hair beginning to gray. He had an intense look in his eye that never seemed friendly. He emanated impatience and haste, which magnified his aura of importance. Urs had a temper, which showed itself when anyone he considered beneath his station was too slow to respond or dared to question his authority. He made it clear that he was the voice of the Baron and, when he gave orders, we were expected to follow them to the letter, and immediately. Urs had a way of never asking us to do anything for him; it was always an order in the name of the Baron. We all avoided him if we could.

"Baron Roland is sending you to fetch a packet for him."

As much as I wanted to, I could not refuse. "Where am I to go?" I asked.

"The Tower Gate," he said. The mention of the dungeons of Solodurum sent a shiver down my spine. I would have asked him to send another, but I knew he would only grow cross with me.

"Present yourself to the head jailor," Urs continued. "Tell him you have come to pick up the packet for the Baron."

I nodded. Then Urs pulled a folded paper out of his waistband and handed it to me. "The Baron wants you to deliver this to the head jailor, understand? To no other. His name is Hans. He'll know for whom it is meant." I immediately noticed that the paper had been cleverly folded in such a way that it tucked into itself to keep from unfolding and revealing the message within. Urs continued, "Baron Roland is anxious to receive this packet, so return with it immediately. Bring it to me at his city dwelling, on the hill. No ale-houses along the way, understood, or you will suffer for it."

I bristled at the implication that I would do that, but kept my peace. It was clear that Urs did not know me or my special arrangement with the Baron. I slipped the folded paper securely behind my belt and said I would bring the packet up the hill to him.

I took several steps away, but Urs called me back.

"What is your name?"

"Waisel, Benedictus," I answered.

"I notice you are limping, Waisel," he said.

"It's an old war wound," I replied. "It's nothing."

"The Baron will not accept it as an excuse for lingering along the way. The Baron holds you as accountable as any other man, otherwise he will see you wearing another livery. Understood? No loitering."

"Understood," I answered and clenched my jaw to keep any further response from slipping out. I turned smartly and strode away, walking as well as I could without favoring my weaker leg. I took several deep breaths to calm myself. I was not going to let his self-importance get under my skin. I knew he was speaking for himself and not for the Baron.

As I walked through the cobbled streets, I pulled out the note Urs had given me. Its foldings intrigued me. I wanted to know how it was able to stay closed without the use of sealing wax. I studied its diamond shape. One side was smooth and without folds. The reverse showed folded edges forming an *X* along the back. I wanted to learn how to fold a note in this way, not sure when it would come in handy, but certain that it could. I hesitated a moment knowing the message was not for my eyes, but I had no intention of reading it anyway. Then I reasoned that if it were private, it would have been sealed with wax. Urs' stinging accusations had already made me more rebellious and reckless than I might have been normally. Slowly I unfolded the paper, making sure I understood each step so that I could put it back together again. It was far less complicated than I had expected. I memorized the steps and promised myself later that day to practice it so I would not forget.

The note was fully unfolded for no longer than the span of two breaths, but in that one glance, I could tell that the writing was not Baron Roland's. His writing was crisp and unadorned with a swift upstroke at the end of words. This writing was well-formed, but more ornate and rounded, with extra curves and circlets. It had not been my intention to pry, but the note was so brief, I could not help but take it all in with one look. It was two short lines of writing. The first line consisted of two words: *November ninth.* Beneath it was written *St. Ursus Fountain.*

I knew the fountain. It was a natural spring along the old and now less traveled route to Zurich. A new road that was more direct had been opened the year before. Since the message had no meaning for me, I paid it no further heed. It was obviously establishing a tryst with day and place. This was Baron Roland's business, not mine. Should it involve me, I knew he would tell me. I refolded the paper carefully along the proper lines, delighted that I had mastered its trick. I tucked it away into my belt.

I approached the Tower Gate with some apprehension, in spite of knowing that I just was being silly. I was filled with childhood tales of what happens inside, the sort of stories parents tell their children to get them to behave. Just the same, whether the stories be true or not, it was a forbidding and impressive fortress. It towered slightly higher than the city walls into which it was built. Round and constructed of massive stone limestone blocks, it had only the smallest slits for windows. Taking a deep breath to steady my nerves, I used the knocker on the large wooden double door. I waited several breaths, but when nothing happened, I knocked a second time. After a second wait, I was about to knock again when I heard the bolts being pulled back, and the heavy door was heaved open with a screeching of its hinges. I was struck by a gust of cold, damp, stale air. A disheveled looking guard stood in the doorway.

"Once was enough, you know," he grumbled. "We're not deaf, you know."

"Oh, sorry," I stammered.

"It's not like I sit next to the door all day waiting for someone to pound on that damn door, you know," he continued.

"Of course, not," I mumbled, and repeated, "Sorry." I pulled myself together. "I'm here to see the head jailor. I am to pick up a packet for Baron Roland."

The unkempt guard stood aside, which I took as an invitation to enter, and I stepped over the threshold. He shoved the heavy door closed behind me, eliminating all sunlight. It shut with a jarring thud of finality that echoed dully in the dark space. I glanced around, seeing little. The entry was lit with lanterns, and I waited for my eyes to adjust to the gloom.

"Wait here. I'll fetch Hans," the jailor said. "Don't touch anything. Don't talk to anyone." In the dim light, I watched him shuffle off. I was startled when, before my eyes, he shrank. What sort of tower of mysteries had I entered? However, it only took a moment to realize that he was walking down stairs that I could not see in the dim light. I laughed at my own jitters.

I waited in that damp, dark space, hemmed in by the rounded stone walls. The stonemason in me admired the skill that had worked the squared limestone blocks, each the size of a sow ready to farrow, into a rounded wall. I wondered if Grandfather had had anything to do with it. I couldn't believe he would.

I struggled to take a breath. The air had a smoky, stale, rancid smell, a disgusting combination. I wanted to open the door to bring in more light and air. I looked around to distract myself. Everything lay in deep, black shadows where the light from the meager lamps did not reach. Before me and to my left lay the stone stairway the jailor had plunged down and out of sight. Hollow sounds echoed around my ears. I was certain I heard low moans. I could hear the scraping of feet on the stones, and from somewhere, the dripping of water. There was the sudden heavy clang of metal. Was that the sound of chains dropped to the stony floor? I shivered at the secret horrors that this tower kept. A shadowy movement to my right caught my attention. Along the stone wall stretched a low wooden bench. Chains attached to rings anchored in the stone wall hung down loosely, waiting to hold a prisoner by the wrists. I peered into the dimness and made out a solitary figure sitting on the bench. He was waving at me.

I did not want to focus on the poor wretch and his miserable fate, so I quickly looked away. What could I possibly do to lighten his suffering? My gut urged me to run away from that place, and I steeled myself to wait as I had been told and leave only once I had received the packet. An instant later, that resolve was shattered when the miserable prisoner on the bench whimpered *my name*. A dark thrill ran through my bowels and I quickly tightened the muscles of my abdomen to keep from messing myself where I stood. I broke into a cold sweat. The voice called my name again. "Ben-*nie*!" I *knew* that voice. It could be only one person in all Solodurum.

"Connie!" I cried out. I could not stop myself. I ran to his side.

Connie beamed brilliantly up at me from where he sat. Instinctively, I bent down and grabbed first his wrists, then his ankles, but he was not bound by any chains.

"Connie, what in all the world are you doing here?"

In answer, he smiled at me even more brilliantly and crooned sweetly, "Ben-*nie*!"

At that moment, the jailor's footsteps shuffled up the stairs. I glanced over my shoulder and saw him appear at the floor level, breathing hard. It was not the jailor who had opened the door for me. This one had something in his hand. I guessed it was the packet I'd been sent to collect.

"Hey, there!" he called out to me in warning. "Stay away from him."

I stood up to my full height, but did not move away. "Look," I said quickly. "I know this man. His name is Connie—Conrad—it's impossible that he has done anyone any harm. He's an innocent, protected by the Hand that stretches over all lost and half-wit souls. There has got to be some mistake."

"So you know this babbling idiot?" the jailor growled. He approached to within one span of me. He stank of something worse than garlic. Although he had come uncomfortably close, I stood my ground.

"I do. I can vouch for him. My friends and I look after him. He lives under the bridge at the river. He could no more steal than read. My friends and I care for him as an act of kindness."

"Then get him out of here and look better after him," the jailor grunted. "He's more clingy than fleas." He looked down at what he held in his hand. It was a cloth sack, bound closed with a thin strip of leather.

"Did you come to collect this?" he asked, holding it up.

"I was told to pick up a packet. For Baron Roland."

"I don't care what fancy-pants baron it's for," he said with a crude gesture. "I'm glad to be done with it," he added, thrusting it into my hands. "Nothing but wormy nuts. Now get out and take your annoying friend with you before I change my mind."

I wanted to make for the door, but I had not yet fulfilled all my duty. "Are you Hans?" I asked.

"What if I am?" he responded rudely.

I fished the note out from behind my belt. "I have a note for him, and for him only."

"I'll take it," he said, reaching out his hand.

I pulled back, not letting him have it.

"I was told to deliver it only to Hans."

"Give it to me already," he said roughly, snatching it out of my fingers. "It has come into the right hands."

"Baron Roland's secretary said you would know for whom it is intended."

"That I do," he mumbled. "Now it's time for you to leave this hell-hole." He walked to the large wooden door, pulled the bolts and yanked it open. The door screeched on its hinges.

I did not wait for a second invitation. I grabbed Connie by the arm and pulled him to his feet.

"Connie, we've got to go," I hissed into his ear, pulling him to the portal, a window of warmth and light. I was already silently praying that this was not one of the days that Connie dug in his feet and refused to be led.

As I pulled him past the scowling guard, Connie craned his neck to look behind him. "Jo-hann," he howled mournfully.

I almost stopped. He wasn't here alone! Although I forced myself to keep moving, under my breath I asked, "Who's Johann, Connie?" Was this a friend from the streets sitting even deeper in the shadows? But I was decided. I wanted out. I needed to get out. I said apologetically, "I can't help anyone else, Connie. I'm sorry. I can't help Johann."

"Johann," Connie whined, continuing to look over his shoulder as I pulled him into the light and freedom. I could hear the jailor's harsh laughter behind us. It felt like jagged glass jammed into my neck. Was he mocking us? Was he mocking Johann's cruel fate, to be left behind while the idiot Connie gained his freedom? I convinced myself that I had done all I could. We burst forth into the bright and harsh light of day. I did not stop pulling on Connie's sleeve until we reached the river. As we walked, my lungs sucked in the fresh air as if I had been held under water.

When I was finally able to quiet my breathing, I asked, "Connie, what were you doing in there?"

He flashed me his disarming smile. "Can't tell you," he loudly whispered. "It's a secret."

If I had time, I knew I could trick him into revealing his secret, but I was under orders to get the packet back as soon as I could. "Connie, stay away from that place, all right?"

In response, Connie pressed his lips together and made a spluttering noise, spraying me with spittle. I wasn't going to get much out of him today. "Do you have food?" I asked.

Connie thrust his hand into the bag that hung at his side and pulled forth half a loaf of bread and offered it to me. "Want some?"

"Not right now, Connie," I said. "I'm still on duty. I've got to go. I'll see you later." I turned to head back toward the center of town.

"Bye, bye, Bennie," Connie called out to my back.

I headed toward Roland's city house to turn the sack over to Urs, his secretary. I was puzzled why I was told a packet and instead received a sack. It hung heavily and when I gave it a shake, whatever was inside rattled. I tried to feel through the soft fabric. The sack was filled with round spheres, a sharp point at one end, with a raised seam. Then I remembered the guard's words, "wormy nuts." Walnuts? Had I been sent to fetch a bag of walnuts? Or had I been given this by mistake?

I was just approaching the Council Chambers when I heard the church bells strike the three-quarter hour. *It will be noon in a quarter hour,* I thought to myself. Council meetings break at noon for their midday meal and a rest. I was certain I could catch the baron there and deliver the sack personally into his hands. It would save me limping all the way up to his city house at the top of the hill and an uncomfortable meeting with the critical Urs.

I let myself into the building and, with my Council livery, was asked no questions when I stationed myself outside the Council Chambers to wait for the meeting to break. I was not disappointed. Hardly had the bells ceased ringing the devout to prayer and the hungry to their noonday meal, than the door opened and the Council members filed out. When Baron Roland emerged, I caught his eye and he came over to where I stood.

"I was sent to fetch a packet for you, as your secretary bade me," I said, handing it to him. "But the guard gave me a sack instead."

"Excellent!" Roland exclaimed. His eyes literally lit up when he saw the bag. "My newest shipment." Eagerly he took the sack and tucked it protectively under his arm.

"Are you that fond of walnuts?" I asked with surprise at his joy in receiving it.

Roland looked left and right to assure that we were alone in the hallway. Then he held up the bag. "Ah, Ben, these are no ordinary walnuts."

"I caution you against being too excited," I said. "The jailor said they are wormy."

Roland expelled a huff of irritation. "The prying old fool. But that's to be expected. Yes, Ben, many of the nuts are wormy. And it is the worms I am after. You know, I expect, what this region's greatest export is?"

"Butter," I said. "Everyone knows that Solodurum butter is shipped far and wide."

"And I predict that these worms will bring new industry and wealth to Solodurum that will rival our butter production."

"Worms?"

"Very special worms, Ben. They are *silk*worms, and I have gone to great lengths to have them smuggled to me."

I was puzzled by his words. "I have heard of silk cloth. It is highly prized and expensive, though I myself have never seen it. What's a silkworm?"

"Silk, to this day, is imported from distant Mandalay via Italy, which is why only the wealthy can afford it. The means of its production has been held secret for centuries." At this, he lowered his voice. "But a group of us have discovered this secret. The silk cloth is spun by a very special worm." He held his bag of walnuts up. "A silkworm."

"Fascinating," I said. "And the worms feed off walnuts? We certainly have an abundance of walnut trees in our orchards."

"Not in the least," Roland laughed. "I have for years prepared for this. I have gone to great effort so that the worms held in this bag should flourish. The walnuts are only a means of secretly transporting them. These worms feed from a very special tree that is not native to our land. I have had a small orchard of these trees planted and cared for. The tree is called a mulberry. It is unique among trees in that it grows fruit very much like berries from a bush."

I flashed on the trees Veronika and I had stumbled upon the day of the French attack on the city. "I have seen these trees!" I exclaimed. "On the edge of town, beyond the Beggars Gate."

A look of irritation showed on Roland's face. "I have gone to great lengths to keep these trees a secret," he said. "I even have a guard set to keep vagrants away from them."

I remembered the peasants we had seen loitering in the woods. "We came upon them by accident," I said. "I had gone berry picking with my sister. Fear not. I have not shared this with anyone. But now I am happy to be able to give a name to a tree I had never seen before."

"Then you have stumbled upon the future wealth of Solodurum," Roland said with satisfaction, tucking the bag back under his arm. "And you'll never guess who provided this treasure for me." When I shrugged my shoulders, Roland said, "Reuben, Joseph's son. Twice now, he has succeeded in sending me a shipment of worms."

When he saw the surprise on my face, he continued. "Reuben trades with caravans traveling far to the east, as far away as Mandalay. I was worried that the expulsion of the Jews would prevent Reuben from getting these to me, but of course, he found a way. One more reason why I look forward to the return of our Hebrew neighbors. I can tell you more at another time. Now I must return to other business. I have chatted far too long." Roland turned to leave.

"Oh, and I delivered your note," I said to his back.

Roland stopped short and turned back to me. He stared at me and blinked his eyes several times, as if trying to recall something. "Note?" he said. "I gave you a note?"

"Urs gave me your note to deliver to the head jailor. A revolting fellow, I have to say," I added.

"A note?" Roland repeated. "From me? For the jailor?"

"Well," I admitted, "it was not written in your hand. I assumed it was—"

Roland did not let me get any further. He said commandingly, "Guard, attend me." He turned on his heel and walked back into the now empty Council Chamber. Puzzled, I followed.

"Shut the door," he ordered. Then he turned on me. "Tell me about that note," he said, his tone serious.

I described the particular way in which it had been folded and how it had intrigued me.

"From your description," Roland said, "I recognize the folding as the work of my secretary. Did you happen to read it?"

I must have turned red because Roland smiled and said, "Of course, you did. You had to figure out how it was folded, didn't you?"

Sheepishly I nodded my head and admitted, "I did not intend to pry."

"It is fortunate for me that you are such a bad liar. Let us hope that no one else ever comes up with the idea of questioning you. Now tell me the contents of this note."

"Just two brief lines," I said.

"Come, Ben, don't hold me in suspense. You and I both know you can read."

"It read *November ninth*. I was particularly puzzled that the number was written out, instead of using a numeral—Baron, are you all right?"

Baron Roland's mouth had fallen open and his eyes had widened. "What was the rest of the message?" he demanded.

"Only a place. *Saint Ursus Fountain*. I believe it is along the old—Baron Roland! What is wrong?"

Roland had gone visibly pale. He reached out to support himself on the table behind him. "Whose script?" he asked faintly.

"Ornate lettering, clearly not your own," I said.

"Indeed, not," he said, his eyes focused beyond anything in the room. Recovering himself, he looked up at me. "Ben, you have done me an invaluable service. You must keep this to yourself." When I nodded, he added, "Breathe not a word of this to anyone. In fact, here," and he handed the sack back to me. "Deliver this to Urs. Do not tell him we have spoken. There is no reason he will ask, so you won't have to lie. Do this for me, Ben."

"Of course, Baron," I replied. "I will be happy to. But can you tell me what is amiss?"

"Better for you that you do not know," he said. "Knowledge can be dangerous and a heavy burden to bear. I do not wish this weight on your shoulders, or the danger that comes with it. Go now. I have a great deal to prepare. Remember, we have not spoken!" With these words he strode from the Council Chamber, leaving me behind, quite bewildered.

I turned my steps to make the climb up the hill to the Baron's town house and Urs' office. It was taxing for my weak leg, but I toughened myself so as not to arrive any later than I already was. When given entry to the house, I presented myself to Urs and turned the sack over to him.

He stared at it crossly. "I told you to pick up a packet."

"That is what the jailor gave me. When I pointed out to him that I had come for a packet, he insisted this was all there was."

"It will fall fully on your head if you have idiotically brought me a sack in error."

"I told you—" but Urs held up his hand and would not let me continue.

"As it is, the Baron is not happy with the amount of time it has taken you to return from this simple errand. A whole man would have come in half the time. I risk my own position by telling you this, but I feel it only fair so you can make arrangements. Baron Roland confided in me that he was ready to release you from the Privy Council service due to your, well, lack of wholeness, shall we say. However, I have beseeched him to overlook your tardiness for the sake of the wound you received in service to your city, and the Baron is willing, albeit reluctantly, to let it pass. This time. You owe me, Benedictus Waisel, and I will expect to collect from you for this favor at a time of my choosing. Understood?"

I was enraged at his boldface lie and his cleverness in turning my infirmity against me and into a way to wield power over me. I wanted to reveal his manipulations right there, but I had promised the Baron to keep secret my arrangements with him.

"Understood," I replied through clenched teeth. "Thank you for speaking on my behalf," and I quickly turned away.

"I have my eye on you, Benedictus Waisel," he said to my receding back.

*What is this all about?* I wondered as I walked away from the Baron's city house.

# Prisoner Delivered

I found out early one evening, about two weeks later. I was walking with Andreas and Christoph, who were on their way to an alehouse. We saw Connie coming toward us down the narrow lane.

"'Leven! 'Leven!" Connie shouted. He sounded angry, but we knew better. Connie often sounded angry when he was anxious or frustrated.

"What's he saying?" Andreas asked. "Did he say 'heaven'?"

"Sounds like 'leaven,'" Christoph said. "Maybe he means leavening. Does he want some bread? Connie, are you hungry?"

"*'Leven*!" Connie shouted with even greater force. "'Leven, 'leven, 'leven, 'leven!" he shouted.

Christoph put his arm around Connie's shoulder. "Come on, little friend. You can come have a bite to eat with us. You'll have your bread and we'll treat you to a tankard of ale, to boot." As they led him away, Connie continued to cry out, "'Leven! 'Leven! 'Leven! 'Leven!"

*He's not talking about bread*, I said to myself. But for the life of me, I could not figure out what he was referring to.

"You coming?" Andreas called out to me over his shoulder.

"Headed home," I called back. "See you tomorrow." I had thought about going with them, but decided to continue home instead. Veronika had promised to bake me one of her special cakes to celebrate my birthday. I decided I preferred having my family around me more than a mug of ale in my hand, as much as I appreciated my fellow guardsmen.

As I walked, I heard behind me the approach of stomping boots. I turned to see a squadron of seven guardsmen marching down the lane, six of them heavily armed with helmet, breastplate, and a halberd on the shoulder. They were on Guard business, and I wondered where they were going that required such a show of force. I stepped to the side of the street to let them pass. They came even with me and pulled up sharply.

The guardsmen in the lead stepped forward and spoke loudly, "Waisel, Benedictus."

"Peter?" I said. I knew him well.

"Waisel, Benedictus," he repeated in a loud voice. Other people in the street were staring and backing away.

"Yes, of course I'm Benedict Waisel. You know me well. What's going on?"

"You will come with us," Peter said, his voice stern and toneless.

"You've been sent for me? What's this all about?"

"The guardsman will fall in!" Peter commanded loudly.

Obedient, yet puzzled, I stepped forward and the six heavily armed guardsmen surrounded me, arranging themselves as we walked, two in front, one on either side, and two behind.

"Where are we going?" I asked. "What's going on? Why the show of force?"

I received no answer. I asked twice more, but when no one would respond, I realized I just had to wait and find out when we arrived wherever we were going.

It became immediately clear that we were not headed back to the garrison. We were walking away from the river, deeper into the city, up the gradual incline of the Upper Town that lay on higher ground. Our route would take us right to the Tower Gate. I was puzzled. There was nothing but open fields past that tower, and beyond the fields were monasteries. Where were we going?

I didn't have long to wonder. We passed through the tunneled entrance of the city gate and under the portcullis. Once we emerged on the other side, the tower came into sight, lit lanterns hanging beside its entrance. We marched right up to the forbidding double doors and stopped. Peter stepped forward and pounded on the heavy wooden portal. After the span of several breaths, with a metallic screech of the hinges, the right-hand door opened and there stood the jailor, holding a lantern. It was Hans. Peter engaged him in a lively dispute.

While Peter was busy with the Tower guard, I stepped back to the guard on my left. His name was Georg. I knew him as an older veteran and a straightforward soldier.

"Georg," I said in an undertone.

He glanced at me. "Not supposed to talk, Ben," he said.

I pressed on regardless. There was half a chance he'd answer me. "Georg, what's going on? Why have you brought me here?"

He struggled with himself for a moment, but when he saw that Peter was still talking, with a quick look at the others, he answered. "Only Guard gossip, you know. Something about murdering a Council member. Passing notes in walnuts. Damn clever ruse, if you ask me."

*Walnuts?* I puzzled. Then I flashed on the bag I had picked up for the Baron a fortnight before. "Wait," I said. "I picked up a bag of walnuts. I picked them up from here."

"Silent, there!" bellowed one of the guardsmen in front of me. He had heard me speak and turned around to put me back in line. "You will remain silent!" he ordered.

"See, I told you," Georg murmured behind me.

At this moment, Peter returned to us and, grabbing me roughly by the shoulder of my tunic, marched me to Hans.

"Prisoner delivered!" Peter announced loudly.

It was November 10th, my nineteenth birthday.

# The Tower Dungeon

"Prisoner?" I exclaimed. "Will someone tell me what's going on?"

No one paid me any attention. Peter put his hand into the center of my back and gave me a shove forward. The jailor grabbed me by my tunic and pulled me over the threshold. The door to the tower closed behind me with a dull thud. The space was dark, damp, and cavernous.

I turned to the jailor. "Look, there's some mistake. I'm a guardsman to the Privy Council. There's been some sort of mix-up."

"Silence!" he bellowed at me. Holding me roughly by the collar of my tunic, he gave me a shake as he walked me to the stone stairs that led down. "Walk!" he commanded. "No funny business."

I put out my hands to feel my way along the wall as I descended the gently curving stairway. I was struck by the overwhelming stench of smoke, moisture, and mold. The smell turned my stomach sour. I fought the urge to throw up. Although the stairs were not lit, I could see a faint light below me. At the bottom, we emerged into a large, circular space. Cells lined the walls, one next to another. I was too startled to look if there was anyone else down there. In the middle of the room was a large wooden structure. I had never seen one before, but based on descriptions I had heard fellow guardsmen give, this was the dreaded rack, on which people were tortured by pulling on ankles and wrists in opposite directions until joints were violently wrenched out from hips and shoulders.

My knees grew weak just seeing it. Next to the rack was a round and raised fire pit, ringed by bricks. Long iron rods stuck out from the ashes at odd angles. I could only imagine what they were used for, and I shuddered. In spite of the dull chill of the place, I was grateful that no fire burned in that pit.

What was this nightmare? What was I doing here?

The jailor yanked me over to a cell and pulled the door open.

"Behave yourself and I won't have to chain you to the wall," he growled and gave me a shove that threw me off balance as I stumbled into the confined space. He had hardly closed the door with a clang of finality when I rushed back to the bars.

"Why am I in here?" I demanded. "Tell me what I've done."

He looked at me from the other side of the bars and a broad grin crossed his grimy face. "As if you don't know. You conspired to murder one of the members of the Privy Council."

"That's absurd!" I shouted. "My post is to defend them. I've harmed no one."

"That's what all guilty men say. The fact is, he's dead, and there's a witness who says you did it. That's all that matters." And he smiled broadly at me again.

I was dumbfounded. "Who?" I demanded. "Who's dead?" My head spun. "Look, get word to Baron Roland. Roland de Cornu. He can clear all this up. Is there a messenger I can send?"

"Very clever, you are," the jailor said, his eyebrows shooting up. "Send a messenger, eh? That's a good joke. Send a messenger to Baron Roland, you'd have to kill the messenger. That's a good joke." He started chuckling coarsely and turned his back on me.

My mind raced trying to understand what he was talking about. Kill the messenger to find Baron Roland? Did he mean ...?

"Jailor! Was Baron Roland the Council member killed?"

The jailor was already beginning to climb the curving stairway. "I said you are a clever boy, and you are. Pretending not to know. But Urs has given witness against you, and he's the Baron's secretary. The Baron died yesterday as he traveled to Zurich. But you know that better than I. Now keep quiet down here, or you won't get any food."

I tried to make sense of what he had just told me. Baron Roland dead? And Urs had accused me of murdering him? I felt my stomach drop to my feet.

I paced the small cell, my heart racing and my mind unable to focus. Like a caged bear I had once seen, I followed the perimeter of my enclosed space. I walked until I was weary, and still I was no wiser. My head grew fuzzier, not clearer. I sank down to rest on the stone bench built into the wall. The stone was cold, but I was too exhausted to care. Utterly bewildered, my head a buzzing wasp's nest of confusion, I slumped where I sat and fell into a numb sleep.

I awoke when something heavy landed in my lap. Groggily, I opened my eyes to see a rat sitting on my knees staring up at me, its whiskers twitching. With a sudden start I swiped the vile creature onto the floor where it scuttled out of my cell. The room was dark, except for a lantern burning on the opposite wall near the stairs. After sleeping on the cold stones in that damp place, my lame leg was aching. In the dim light, I saw two buckets beside the cell door that had not been there before. I limped over to them. One was filled with water. I first smelled, then tasted it. It was spring water, not fresh, but not foul. I drank deeply. The second bucket was empty. From its smell, I realized it was for me to relieve myself. I picked it up and moved it to the furthest corner of the small space.

I wondered what time it was. How long had I slept? Had morning come yet? I had no way of knowing. My head ached with the uncertainty of my situation. Baron Roland dead? Could that be possible? And Urs accused me of killing him? I realized he must be using me to cover up the true conspirators.

The floor was too moist for sleeping. Instead, I curled up on the stone bench. What could I do but wait? My stomach complained and I wondered if I would be brought some food. I wanted to call out to the jailor, but he had been very clear that if I made a fuss, he would withhold my food, and even chain me to the wall. I glanced up at the hanging shackles and shuddered. Best to be patient and wait this out. I only hoped the rats would leave me in peace. I had heard too many horror stories of rats eating away the exposed flesh of prisoners who had grown too weak to defend themselves. With these dark thoughts, I slept again, but fitfully.

When next I woke, I was at first jolted by the stiffness in my shoulder and in my neck. My leg throbbed. That was nothing next to the shock I had when I heard a familiar voice.

"Poor Bennie."

"Connie?" I sat up straight, causing even more pain in my cramped muscles, and looked around where his voice had come from. Had I dreamt it? No, Connie was standing outside the bars to my cell. "Connie, what are you doing here?"

"Poor Bennie," he repeated in a mournful tone.

"Connie, have you also been arrested?"

"Connie comes and goes," he said. "Johann is my friend."

I was reminded of the time I had found him in this tower. As I left with him he had called out a farewell to Johann. I had assumed it had been a prisoner. I now saw my mistake.

"Connie, is Johann the jailor? Hans?"

"Johann is my friend," he repeated.

"Do you come here often, Connie?"

"Johann is a good friend," he replied.

This wasn't going anywhere, so I asked, "Did Johann send me any food?"

Connie bent down and picked up a tin plate off the floor. "For Bennie," he said.

There was an opening in the bars just wide and high enough for the plate to slip through. "Thank you, Connie," I said and eagerly looked at what I had to eat. It wasn't much. A dollop of stiff, cold porridge, a hard barley biscuit, and a small wedge of dried cheese. I grew up hearing my mother repeat a common saying in Solodurum: A hungry stomach is a grateful beggar. I knew the truth of it this day. I wolfed down the food and then drank from the water bucket.

It was not a proper meal, but it took the edge off my hunger and gave my head more clarity. Connie had been watching me the whole time. I wondered how often he came down here to keep prisoners company and watch them in their confinement.

"Is it morning, Connie?"

He didn't say anything, but did nod his head sharply, just once.

Awaking from my sleep, I had had a sudden flash of inspiration, and the chance to check it out had been delivered to my cell door.

"Connie, the last time I saw you, you were really upset. You were upset about something to do with 'leven.'"

I saw Connie's eyes grow large. "Can't talk 'bout 'leven," he said, forcefully. "Not allowed!"

"This isn't about bread, is it, Connie? This is about the number eleven, isn't it?"

"'Leven!" Connie shouted. Then he chanted, "'Leven, 'leven, 'leven, 'leven." Connie took a deep breath and repeated it all over again, hanging onto the bars of my cell and rocking from left to right. "'Leven, 'leven, 'leven, 'leven!" And again, "'Leven, 'leven, 'leven, 'leven! Can't talk 'bout 'leven. Not allowed!" His eyes glazed over.

"Why not, Connie? Why can't you talk about 'leven?"

"Can't!" he shouted so vehemently that his mouth spewed spittle. "Big! Big! Streets will flow! Streets will flow!"

This was a puzzling comment. "The streets will flow? With water? Is the river flooding?"

Connie wrapped his arms around his head. "Can't!" he shouted with inner turmoil. "No more. Said too much! Connie not allowed!"

"Okay, Okay," I said soothingly. "You can't talk. It's all right, Connie, no more 'leven. No more streets running with water."

"Not water," he said, and his eyes gleamed.

"If not water, then what else ... wait a minute, will the streets be flowing with ... blood?"

Connie shrieked. "Too much! Not allowed! No more 'leven," and with that started his chant again, "'Leven, 'leven, 'leven, 'leven. 'Leven, 'leven, 'leven, 'leven. 'Leven, 'leven, 'leven, 'leven!"

I wondered what this meant. Other than Solodurum's fetish number, what could he be obsessing about? And then it dawned on me. Today was November 11th! *Eleven, eleven.* But what were the other two elevens? He was clearly reciting a set of four elevens. Or was he just repeating it as a rhythm? Maybe it had no further meaning beyond his mad ramblings. Yet where did he get the idea that the streets will flow with blood?

Connie had not yet stopped. "'Leven, 'leven, 'leven, 'leven! 'Leven, 'leven, 'leven, 'leven!" I needed to calm him down if I was to get anything more out of him.

I said quickly, "I really like your tunic, Connie. Very handsome, beautiful brocade." And it was. As always, Connie wore the most exquisite castoffs. I always imagined this as the private joke of some wealthy nobility, dressing this mad beggar in his fineries. "And your cloak, Connie. Where'd you get such a fine cloak? Such a beautiful trim. I'd like one myself. Can you get me one like that?"

Connie always liked when I complimented his clothing, and he stopped his chanting to listen to me. "You like it, Bennie?" he asked, breathing hard from his incantations of eleven.

"I sure do. Where can I get a cloak like that?"

"Can't have it, Bennie. It's only for me."

We talked about the decorative stitching and the edging. Then I asked what he had had to eat and where he had slept the night before. I learned that he had gone to a tavern with the two guardsmen, and they had treated him to an ale and a sausage. The sausage was such a prize that he had returned to enjoy it in the solitude of his nest under the bridge. Eventually, I ran out of things to ask him, and we grew silent together.

I sat back down on my stone bench to think it through. I had nothing better to do, and I certainly had nowhere to go. Connie stood at the bars, continuing to rock back and forth, humming tunelessly. Without comment, he abruptly wandered away, back up the stairs. I wondered if I would see him again.

The hours dragged with nothing to do. I tired of puzzling over Connie's obsession with eleven and the terrifying picture of the streets running with blood. What would have to happen for the streets to run with blood? An attack? Who would attack the city? An attack would not get past the gates. For the streets to run with blood, they would have to get inside. How would they do that? They would be seen and stopped before they ever reached the city wall. All these thoughts whirled through my mind in a never-ending circle, always returning to the same question: Who would attack the city? When my head started sagging, I lay down and slept again.

When I next woke, I glanced up and was not surprised to see Connie standing at the bars to my cell again.

"Hey, Connie," I said, groggily.

"Hey, Bennie."

A crazy thought had occurred to me while I slept and it had risen to the surface of my consciousness like a bubble in still water.

"Hey, Connie, do you have a brother?"

He had told me once before about a brother, but I had shrugged it off as invented. Now, I wasn't so sure. At my question, Connie suddenly went stiff.

"Can't!" he said emphatically.

"What's your brother's name, Connie?"

"No!" he said petulantly. "Can't."

"Does your brother give you your fine clothing?"

"Not allowed!" he bellowed at me.

He didn't have to answer me. I finally understood who Connie was and more importantly, who his brother was, not necessarily his name, but his status in the city. Connie had heard secrets he should not have heard, but what did it matter? Who would he tell? Who would believe him?

I was certain now what the first two elevens meant, and dread filled me as I guessed what the two other elevens stood for. If I was right, I had to act quickly.

"Connie, do you know what time it is?" I asked.

He shook his head. Of course, he could not tell time.

"Connie, is the sun still high?"

"Going down," he replied.

I was surprised. I must have slept much of the day away in the stench of this windowless hole. I had no time to lose.

"Connie, do you know where Johann keeps his keys?"

He smiled brightly. "Johann has lots of keys," he announced.

"I'll bet you don't know where the key for this cell is."

He wrinkled his brow before declaring, "Connie knows."

"I don't think you do, Connie."

"Connie knows!" he insisted, his voice nasal.

"I just don't believe you, Connie."

This had the effect I was hoping for. He became agitated. "Connie knows!" he shouted.

"Well the only way I'm going to believe you is if you show me."

"Connie gets the key," and he turned to go.

"Wait!" I hadn't thought this through enough. "Wait, Connie. If you try to take the key, Johann will be angry with you and maybe never let you back in again. You don't want that to happen." Connie's face looked concentrated. I added, "You have to take it without him knowing. Do you think you can do that?"

"Connie knows where to find the key," he said, full of confidence. He left me and slowly ascended the stairs. There was half a chance this would work. My only dread was that Connie would forget and wander out into the city.

Anxious, I started pacing again. My leg was stiff, and walking helped to loosen it. I lost count of how many circuits I made around my small cell. Twice I turned and changed direction. I struggled to keep my breathing regular. I needed to get out, and I needed to get out now. Connie was my only hope. I froze in my steps when I heard his shoes scraping the stones on the stairs. I stood at the bars nearly holding my breath. Connie appeared and had a wide grin on his face. I took hope at this, although in the dim light, I could not tell if he was holding something. He walked straight up to the bars and held up his open hand. In it lay a large iron key.

"Are you sure it's the right one?" I asked in a low voice.

In answer, Connie offered the key to me. So as not to spook him, I reached through the bars and slowly lifted it off his palm. With my free hand I reached around and felt for the keyhole in the door. I guided the key silently into it and very slowly turned it. I could not risk any tell-tale sounds that would alarm Johann. The key met resistance, and I pushed against it. My heart skipped a beat as the lock gave way and I heard the bolt inside slip back. The door swung open.

I had an idea how to get out of there, but I still needed Connie's help. "Come inside," I said to him. "Come sit next to me."

Connie was willing. He came into my cell and I closed the door behind him. We sat side by side on the uneven stone bench.

"Connie," I said. "Can you help me?" I asked adding a whine to my voice.

"What do you need?" he asked, a look of concern on his face.

"I'm cold, Connie. It's so damp in here, and I don't have the right clothing. Connie, could I borrow your beautiful cloak, just to warm up." I could see the worry in his face at this request. "Not to keep, Connie. I just need to warm up. You're not giving it to me. I promise to give it back once I'm warm."

I could read on his face the struggle going on in his heart. I pressed forward. "We're friends, Connie. You know, if you were cold, I would give you my cloak to warm up. I give you food when you are hungry. This is what friends do for each other."

"Bennie's a good friend," Connie said. "Bennie can borrow my cloak." So saying, he took it off his shoulders and handed it to me. I quickly wrapped it around my body. It held his warmth. It was a nice piece of felted wool, in spite of being torn in places. In truth, I had grown deeply chilled and was very grateful for this extra layer. Yet, I needed more.

We sat a few minutes side by side in silence. Then I said, "You know, Connie, I'd love to play a trick on Johann." I saw Connie's eyes light up, so I continued. "I think he'd have fun with the joke. I want to see if I can fool him into thinking I'm you. That'd be fun, don't you think?"

Connie nodded his head and chuckled, "That would be funny to fool Johann."

"But to make it work, I need to borrow your fancy cap as well. Just long enough to make Johann laugh. Do you think I could wear it just that long?"

"Yeah, yeah, that's funny," Connie said, already taking off his cap and handing it to me. "Let's go fool him." And he started to get up.

"We can't go together, Connie," I said quickly. "Otherwise, he would see both of us and know the trick. I have to go alone. But you will hear from down here. And then I'll tell you how it went. We'll both come down and tell you how funny it was. But you have to wait here. You can do that, can't you, Connie? Wait here just a minute while I go fool Johann? After, he'll come down with me and tell you what a good trick it was."

Connie was excited at the prospect of having a good laugh on Johann. He was nodding his head, saying, "That's a good joke. Bennie is Connie. You go now and fool Johann."

I got up, opened the door to the cell, and stepped over the threshold. "Wait here, Connie." I pushed the door to, and for a moment debated if I should lock him in. I decided against it. If he grew anxious from being locked in, he'd start yelling. I had to risk it. "I'll be back as soon as I've fooled him, okay?"

I walked slowly to the stairway, wondering how I was going to pull this off. I was stopped in my tracks by Connie's voice. "Bennie?"

I turned back to him. "Yes, Connie?"

He was standing at the bars and wearing a big grin. "You look like Connie," he said. I only hoped Hans would think the same.

I nodded my head and held a finger up to my lips. I said in a quiet voice, "I'll go fool him now." I walked slowly up the stairs.

Keeping the cap pulled down low on one side to cover as much of my face as possible, I emerged into the upper room. I glanced around and saw Johann sitting against the wall, his head dropped onto his chest in sleep. There was a second jailor sitting with his back to me. He was playing knucklebones by himself. I couldn't believe my good fortune. I walked quietly to the door. I remembered that the hinges screeched, but there was no way to avoid it. I walked boldly up to it, pulled back the bolt, and yanked it open. I knew it would wake Johann up and make the other jailor turn around. Keeping my back to them, I raised an arm in a wave and made my best imitation of Connie's screeching, nasal voice, "Bye, Johann!"

From behind, I heard Johann's groggy voice, "Bye, Connie. See you later."

I shut the door behind me.

# The Challenge

Night had fallen, and there were no guardsmen around. I slipped out of Connie's cloak and took off his hat, laying them beside the door. I had promised Connie I wouldn't keep them, but he would have to fetch them from here. I dashed away, through the Tower Gate, past three guards who barely glanced up, and into the streets of the town. I had no idea where to go, but my feet did, and I soon found myself at the river.

I was seething. Someone had murdered Baron Roland, and Urs was accusing me. I wanted revenge. Even more pressing, I had to stop what I feared was about to happen, but the only person I could turn to was dead. I had one crazy idea, but it was the only one I could come up with. Crazy was better than inaction. I crossed the Chapel Bridge, raced through the streets of the Lower Town, and came to the Berne Gate. I pulled up short when it came into sight. Would they be as inattentive as the three guardsmen in the Tower Gate? Or did the whole Guard know by now I'd been arrested for murdering Baron Roland? News like that traveled fast. What else did we have to do but gossip about the latest, the true, the rumored, and the suspect? I had no choice. Regardless which gate I passed through, there would be guards posted.

My one advantage was that I was still wearing the livery of the Privy Council. I thought for a moment of removing it but decided to walk briskly, as if I were on official business. It was the right decision. The two guards at the gate were at that moment busy with a farmer who had arrived with a cart of goods and wanted to gain entrance to the city for the next morning's market day. He had arrived after dark, and the guards were arguing with him that he would have to wait outside the walls until first light. Without breaking my stride, I walked past them with an arm raised in greeting, keeping my face averted. It worked. There were no voices hailing me to halt.

I made straight for the compound. I whisked passed the guard at the entry gate, who dreamily waved me on. I went looking for Rodrigo. I had a solid hunch where he would be, and I wasn't disappointed. I found him in the mess hall at table, sitting on his cushioned seat underneath the spreading branches of the plane tree. We all knew to never, *ever* disturb Rodrigo when he was eating. He took his meals seriously. For an otherwise uncomplicated and unfussy man, all of this was turned onto its head when it came to food. If there was anything that approached religious ritual for Rodrigo, it was meal time. Rodrigo always ate from the same utensils. He kept his personal bowl and plate on a shelf that no one else could even reach because it was so high. He stored there as well his personal spoon and carving knife. After every meal, he carefully washed them himself and put them away. And as I had learned the hard way on my first day, he always sat at the same table in the same seat. Every day. Every meal. That made him easy to find.

I had come at the perfect moment. Rodrigo was nearing the end of his meal, but had not yet finished. He was never satisfied with only one portion. With his immense bulk and high status, he was tolerated taking as much food as he pleased, a privilege that few others could boast.

As I approached him, I noticed that Rodrigo's left arm was bandaged and that there was a scabbing wound above his left eye. I puzzled what sort of scrape he had been in. Had there been any skirmishes while I was locked up? I brushed the question away. I had to do this before my courage failed me.

I walked right up to Rodrigo's table and waited until I was certain he sensed I was there, even though he did not acknowledge me. Focused on his food, he did not even bother to look up. The others at the table, and it was always the same crew, did look up. One of the lieutenants, surprise on his face, said in a low voice, "Ben, what are you doing here? We heard you're in the tower."

"They let me out," I said tersely.

The lieutenant must have sensed my intention. He said, "Don't bother him now, Ben. You know—" but he got no further, because I had just spit across the table into Rodrigo's plate. I spat right into the middle of it. This got Rodrigo's attention. He sat back in his seat, stared up with an astonished look, and belched loudly. Then his eyes focused on me as if he could not quite make sense of who was standing there.

"Why'd you do that?" he asked stupidly. I figured that he had already eaten so much that the stupor of a full meal with ale was dimming his senses. Deciding there was little chance of his attacking me there and then, I relaxed slightly. Then his face became one big question mark. "What are *you* doing here?"

I laid into him. "Rodrigo, you're a slob and a crass bully. Your cavern of a mouth is only overshadowed by the immense crack in your arse." I glanced around the table at the others. They had turned pale, their mouths hanging open, staring at me, their movements frozen. "Have you gone mad?" I heard one murmur.

The mess hall, usually filled with lively chatter, grew eerily silent. Too late to back down, I forged onward. "You are so immense, you bed down with cows because you would crush any woman idiotic enough to let you mount her. Even the cows groan when they see you coming."

Suddenly, Andreas was at my elbow. I had not expected that. He spoke in a quiet, urgent voice, "Ben, you don't want to do this." He had me by the arm. "Let's go, Ben. Step away." I wanted to shake him off.

"Not only that," I continued, pulling my arm out of Andreas' hold, "you're a coward. You let others, like *me*, open the line in battle because you are too much of a milksop to face the first line yourself. You come only when there is a gap and no one to stand against you. You make me sick. You only dare to pick on men smaller than you."

With that I paused. I had said everything I had prepared and I hit emptiness in my head, probably due to the panic rising inside of me. For his side, Rodrigo blinked several times trying to make sense that

I, of all people, would stand up to him. Finally, he said, "Everybody is smaller than me."

That gave me more fuel. "That makes you an even bigger coward. A giant like you doesn't have to bully anyone. Who can possibly be a threat? I'm so sick of you. It's time to put an end to this. I'm challenging you, Rodrigo." With these words I heard a collective gasp in the room. I was immensely satisfied that I had everyone's attention.

"You're an idiot, Ben," Rodrigo said. "What are you, drunk? Go away before I decide to hurt you. How are you even here?"

Remarkable! The brute was showing restraint. For a moment, I had warm feelings toward him. Then I decided it was the ale that had gone to his head. So I spat again, this time into his cup. This assault on his precious drink startled him. I was darkly satisfied seeing his reaction.

"You're a forest troll!" I shouted at him. "Rodrigo, it's time you returned to your own. Meet me at the Forest Gate at eleven bells. Come armed and ready to fight. If you're late, you not only stink like the latrine you sleep in, but you're a stinking, piss-soaked coward. Eleven bells! Do you hear me? Eleven bells! At Eleven!"

I turned on my heel and rushed away before he could respond. Behind me, the mess hall erupted in a roar of excited chatter. I used the confusion of the moment to slip away.

I was certain that by now Johann had discovered my ruse and raised the alarm. The guard would already be out looking for me. In fact, I was counting on it. I had to find somewhere to hide until it was time for my rendezvous with Rodrigo at the Forest Gate. After a moment's reflection, I knew just the place.

# *Eleven, Eleven, Eleven, Eleven*

Well concealed in the darkness under the bridge, I could hear the bell tower count the hours down. I was not alone. The space hosted half a dozen wretched homeless who had complained when I had entered their night quarters, but they begrudgingly made space for me. I only hoped that Connie would not show up. He would make a stink over how I had tricked him, and that would give me away. I passed the time repenting how I had misused his trust and wondering how to make it up to him. But what else could I have done? There was so much at stake.

I had had a dicey moment reentering the city through the Berne Gate. As before, I had walked briskly, as if I were on Guard business. This time, the two men on duty called out at me to stop. I didn't, but walked even faster. In spite of being hindered by my stiff leg, I was prepared to run. To my relief and good fortune, no one pursued me.

The wait under the bridge was not terribly long, but long enough for me to reflect on what I had done. If I had guessed wrong about what was going to happen, Rodrigo would catch me and gleefully flay me alive. That is, if I ever managed to be released from prison for conspiring to murder one of the most influential members of the Privy Council. Assuming they would release me at all for anything other than being crucified on the walls my own grandfather had built. My bleak thoughts mirrored the darkness in which I sat.

My release from them finally arrived when the bells tolled half-past ten. Yet I did not jump out even then but forced myself to wait a bit longer. It would not do to arrive too early, and catastrophic if I arrived too late. Looking cautiously in all directions in case a guard had been set nearby, I crept out from under the bridge and held to the deepest shadows. At this time of night the streets were deserted. There was some light coming from the upstairs windows across from me, and in it, I could see my breath steam in the cold night air. But I didn't need that to know it was mid-November. Sitting in the damp under the bridge, my fingers, feet, and ears had grown numb with cold.

I mapped out in my mind a route to the Forest Gate with possible detours in case the way was blocked. There was no need. I spooked three cats but did not encounter another soul along the way. I had a tickling in my gut when I heard the bell toll the three-quarter hour and still saw no one. Was I on a fool's errand?

As I came in sight of the gate, I saw a small crowd of men, a Solodurum dozen, the early birds, gathered to see me mashed into pulp. I was dismayed to see no swords among them. It flashed through my mind that this was clearly the gaping hole in my plan. Then my spirits lifted. Behind the knot of men and to the side against the city wall stood a patrol of five guardsmen, all wearing full armor and carrying halberds, two with lanterns. I was certain they were there in my honor, ready to arrest me again. I would have preferred six—or eleven for that matter—but they would do. If I was delusional and had misinterpreted Connie's chanting, then I would welcome their protection when Rodrigo showed up to break me in half. In spite of that, I was annoyed that there was no sign of him. Was he going to stand me up?

All I needed now was a sword.

I walked through the cluster of men right up to the guardsmen. It was Peter again who stepped forward as patrol leader.

"Ben," he began. His tone was apologetic this time. He was off his guard, and that was the window I was looking for.

"I'm sorry for the trouble I've given you," I said, and took a step to come within an arm's length.

"We've got to take you back," he said. "Orders."

"I know," I replied. I closed the gap between us and performed the prettiest swivel on my foot, swinging my right elbow against the side of his jaw. We had practiced this maneuver often enough in camp that it came naturally to me. Peter was taken offguard by the unexpected blow to his chin and stumbled backward into the other guardsmen. As I pivoted, my left hand grabbed the pommel of his short sword and I pulled it free from its scabbard.

I raised his sword above my head and cried out loudly, "Brothers, draw your weapons!" I only hoped they would grab sticks and stones off the ground. "We are under attack! Save the city!" I pushed past the astonished crowd and rushed onward to the gate, still another thirty yards ahead.

I could detect movement in the dark shadows. I had come too late! Traitors were opening it. "For the city!" I cried out shrilly. "Fight for Solodurum! For your wives! For your sweethearts!" Would those behind me think me mad? Perhaps I was.

But there was clearly a milling around the gate. I saw the faint glimmer of dark lanterns. I could not tell how many were there. Three? Five? Traitors all. They were surprised at being discovered, but quickly regained their wits.

I was desperate to get that gate shut and barred again. I fell on one, giving him a stunning blow to the side of his head with the pommel of my sword. He crumpled to the ground with a grunt. Amid shouts, a second one shoved me hard against the wall. I literally bounced off the stones and slipped behind him to confront those who were starting to enter. The gate stood wide open.

I hacked at the neck of the first man to come through, and he fell at my feet, his armor clanging. However, the sight of the man behind him caused me to hesitate. He had just ducked through the open gateway, high enough for any average sized man, but for him far too low. He stood a moment and stretched to his full height. He was huge and every bit as large a man as Rodrigo, if not larger. Covered in rustic armor, his hair long and matted, his thick beard bristling wildly, his eyes gleaming malevolently, he could have been a rock troll stepped out of the forest. All the rest of the invading force was behind him. He did not have a sword in his hand. Instead, to my horror, he held a hammer, a war hammer of immense size.

I took several steps back, giving ground. My eyes took in the hammer's arc, already in full swing, and although I jumped, I was too slow to avoid its reach. The hammer smashed into my thigh, sweeping my legs out from under me. I fell hard. The force of the blow twirled me around and knocked me onto my face, but I was determined not to have a sword thrust into my back, and with an immense effort, I rolled over. I found myself staring up the legs of this Goliath. He paused, straddling my body, and bellowed defiance at those who had followed behind me, more out of curiosity than in opposition. The group of onlookers had reached us by this time and saw for themselves that an armed enemy force had breached the gate. But how long could they hold out, without weapons, against a monster swinging a hammer the size of a wild boar? I held onto the vain hope that more guardsmen were on their way to arrest me.

Still standing over me, the troll bellowed his war cry again, raising his hammer for the next blow. In a moment he would move on. I could sense him shifting his weight to his forward leg. He was clothed in armor from his head down to his feet. Armor is wonderful protection from blows coming from before, from any side, even from above. But armor offers no protection whatsoever from below. It has to have gaps, otherwise one would not be able to move. I still had Peter's short sword in my hand. I found myself staring up at the monster's groin. Suddenly I heard Joseph's words that first day he came to me after my battle injury. "There is a vessel ... along the inside of the leg ... that if cut ... in a matter of minutes."

Without thinking, lifting myself onto one elbow, I thrust upward. In battle, this vulnerable vessel was nearly impossible to reach but, from where I lay on the ground, it was in full sight and my only hope. I yanked the sword back and thrust again. Then a third time. The giant roared in protest and pain as the blood poured down onto my shoulders and into my face, first in spurts, then like a torrent, soaking me, blinding me, and knocking me back. My head swam and I thought bitterly, how ironic, I am about to drown while lying on dry ground.

I came to my senses gasping for air. Without my own effort, I was moving, as if I was being raised up. I was drowning and my breathing was a choking splutter. I wanted to lift my hands to clear my eyes, my nose, my mouth, but my arms were leaden. I felt a hand not my own wiping my nose and mouth free and with a great cough and gasp of air, I could breathe again. I forced my eyes open and my blurred vision found a beard, and above the beard was Rodrigo's face. He noticed me looking at him.

"Like a babe in my arms," he chuckled harshly. Around us was the hue and cry of battle. Rodrigo carried me away to safety and lay me down on the cobblestones. "Stay here, clever little stonemason," he commanded. "We still have some cleanup to do." And with that he was gone. I heard his terrifying war cry rise above the din of battle. My head was full of confusion and the whole left side of my body felt numb. I welcomed unconsciousness, and it did not disappoint me.

# "We Soldier On"

I hovered in a void between pain and delirium. Every time I approached wakefulness, the pain sent me back to a world of terrifying dreams. When I tasted the bitter liquid between my lips, I recognized it as my drink of forgetfulness. I swallowed it greedily, though I knew not the hand that put it to my mouth. I welcomed the numbing sleep that erased the pain and silenced the disturbing dreams.

I could avoid wakefulness only so long before it demanded my attention. When I finally submitted to the inevitability of waking up. I found myself in a small, bare room. At the curtained door stood a guard. Sitting beside me was an old friend.

"Joseph!" I cried out hoarsely. "You've returned!"

"I was summoned out of exile to attend to you," he explained. "I replied that, in spite of my fondness for you, I could come only if my family and all of the other exiled families could return to their homes."

"And?"

"Well, I'm here," he said with a warm smile. "And my family did not return alone."

"With all the other families?"

"Yes, we have been welcomed back to the city. As you must be well aware, once the latrine was closed and the fountain blocked, the pestilence dissipated. We were absolved of all blame."

"Do you know who convinced the Council to grant your return?"

"Baron Roland, of course. He persuaded the Council that human waste from the privy—"

"Baron Roland is dead," I interrupted. "He was murdered in an assault as he rode for Zurich."

Joseph lay a hand on my arm. "Baron Roland did not die, although he was attacked. I attended him yesterday myself. The wounds he received were not life-threatening. He will recover fully."

I could not make sense of his words. "But they told me ... I was arrested ... They put me in prison!"

"I wish I knew what to tell you. Baron Roland is as alive as you, and far less grievously injured. I am deeply grateful for the action he took after we were forced to leave the city. It is thanks to the guards he placed before our homes that few were looted. Most of our neighbors treat us as if nothing had happened and we had never been sent away." Joseph continued talking, but I stopped listening. I was trying to make sense of what he had just told me. If Baron Roland was still alive, why was I put in prison for his murder? He had to know that I had nothing to do with the attack on him. I was his man, his personal spy!

I was brought back by Joseph's comforting hand on my arm. I looked up as he handed me a shallow bowl filled with a dark liquid. Its aroma was familiar. "Drink this," he said gently. "I can see I have overtaxed you with my jabbering."

The painful throbbing in my leg held my attention. "Will it put me to sleep again?"

"Yes, but more importantly, it will dull the pain. This wound will challenge you, I'm afraid. Far more than before. You will have to endure the poppy this time, but I will be strict when it is time to wean you of it. I will not sit by and see you addicted to the poppy. "

I reached down with my hand, afraid of what I might find—or not find. But my leg was still there, thickly wrapped.

"I still have my leg."

"If it were up to the garrison surgeon, you would not. He declared it a waste of our time to try and save it. We think it was worth our while."

"We?"

"I had the honor of taking counsel with Baron Roland's personal physician. He gave me the lead in treating you."

"How is that possible? I thought, being a Jew, I mean, aren't you excluded from those circles."

"There are thinner boundaries in medicine than in politics or religion. He recognized that he could learn something from me, and I assured him we could learn from each other. Perhaps the world is slowly changing. However, this leg of yours did present us with quite a riddle. There were moments we wondered if the garrison surgeon had not spoken the inevitable."

I was already feeling the pull of the drug, but this comment brought me back awake with a start. "You might still have to take it?"

"I don't think so," he said, patting my shoulder. "Let's give it a chance to heal. You are young, and our bodies have a miraculous ability to mend themselves. Time to go back to sleep now. We will talk more later."

I remember closing my eyes and nothing more.

The next time I awoke, Veronika was sitting beside me.

"Is this a dream?" I asked groggily.

"I hope not," she said with a laugh.

"How long have I been out?"

"Since last night. You missed the morning. The birds sang a beautiful concert."

"Joseph?"

"He was here earlier and changed the bandages on your leg."

"How does it look?"

Veronika paused before saying, "Not pretty." She started to tear up. I put out my hand and took her arm.

"Are they going to take it off?"

Veronika shook her head. "Joseph said it is not festering, and that is a good sign. I don't know what any of that means." And with this she began to weep in earnest.

"Stop, Veronika. Please." Her crying was weakening my own resolve to be strong. "Your tears don't help. I'm still alive. Even if they have to take it, I'm still alive."

She sobbed even louder and I had to give her a little shake to make her stop. "I know," she said, taking a ragged breath.

"Veronika, I need you to be strong for me."

She nodded her head. "That's what Joseph said."

"Then be that for me. Please."

She wiped her eyes on her sleeve. "Mother and Father were both here this morning. We are preparing for when you come home. I will nurse you."

"I look forward to that," I said sincerely. I meant going home.

"I will nurse you, and clean you, and cook for you, and be there for you," she said.

"Dear little sister," I sighed. "Thank you. I can't wait to get home. Will Mother and Father come again?"

"Yes, in the morning."

"Joseph?"

"He will return before the day ends, I am sure. He promised to deliver to you another sleeping draught. He doesn't trust what they would give you here."

"I'm lucky to have you both," I murmured. I glanced up at the curtained entrance. As before, a guard stood there. I was puzzled what he was guarding.

After a moment's silence, Veronika said, "You had another visitor while you slept."

I waited, but she was reluctant to keep speaking, so I had to nudge her. "Who? Tell me already."

"Baron Roland."

This startled me. "He came here? Are you sure? You know what he looks like?"

"He was here. He introduced himself. He was very kind to me and spoke nothing but praise about you. He thinks very highly of you. However, when he saw that you were not about to waken, he left."

My mind raced. "Did he leave any message?" Veronika was clearly uncomfortable. "You have to tell me. I must know."

"Baron Roland said that your service in the Guard is over," she said stiffly.

I laughed roughly. "I could have figured that out on my own. Did he say anything else?"

"That you are to go home and heal. These quarters are only for members of the Guard. He did not say it unkindly. More as a matter of fact." Veronika was silent for a count of four before she burst out, "And I think it absolutely horrid that they treat you like this. Why, if it hadn't been for you, the French would have breached the gate! Everyone speaks of it. Don't they realize what they owe you?"

I held up my hand. "Stop!" I warned her. "There is a reason for guidelines and rules. We may not agree with them, but we are obliged to follow them."

"You can stop being the good soldier, Ben. They've turned their backs on you."

"Rules and laws are there for the safety of the whole, not the individual." Even as I spoke these words, they sounded hollow and tasted bitter.

"But, what you've done!"

"What I've done was my duty," I forced myself to say. "Nothing more. Now cause me no more grief by speaking further." Veronika opened her mouth to continue, so I added, "Please, Veroni. Until I'm stronger. We can argue about it when I'm stronger." Her tears welled up again, and she nodded her head in acceptance. I closed my eyes to keep her from saying more. I must have been utterly spent, for I fell asleep without Joseph's brew.

When I woke up, I was startled to see an immense shadow looming over my bed. As my eyes cleared, I saw it was Rodrigo.

"How's my clever little stonemason?" he asked. There was no bite to his words. He had meant it kindly. That was simply his name for me.

"I am told I will limp," I said.

"You already did limp," he said tonelessly.

I smiled thinly. "Worse, then."

"Limping is good," he said with a shrug. When he saw the surprise on my face, he added, "It is a step up from not being able to walk. We have to be grateful for what we have and make the most of it. We soldier on. That's what we do."

"I can't stay here," I said. I realized how much that frightened me.

"I know," he said. "I tried to arrange a special dispensation, not completely unusual, but was blocked by someone from the Privy Council. They wouldn't tell me who. Seems like someone wants you out of the Guard, and the sooner the better."

"I'm not too surprised. I'm a liability. I did, after all, escape from prison."

Rodrigo's rough features broke into a broad smile. "I think that was a first. You're the talk of the garrison."

"I did it for a good reason," I pointed out.

"A very good reason," he nodded in agreement.

"Just not good enough to keep me in the Guard with a serious limp."

Rodrigo's face darkened. "It's more than the limp, you know. I've only heard mess hall gossip, but considering him," he said, inclining his head toward the guard standing beside the doorway, "you're still not cleared." I had not made any connection until now.

"You mean, that's not a regular post?"

"In your honor, I'm afraid," Rodrigo said.

"Are they worried I'd escape?"

"The order is to keep you under guard, day and night. That's all I know."

"How am I going to run away?" I said, gesturing to my bandaged leg.

"Still, that's the order. You know the Guard. Follow the order, don't question it."

Bitterness rose up in me, a bitterness I could not spit out. "You don't think I'd plot against Baron Roland, do you?"

"I'm sorry, little stonemason," Rodrigo said calmly. "That's not my call. I just follow orders."

I sank into dark thoughts, but after a moment Rodrigo pulled me out of them. "Anyway, I came to tell you, first of all, that I forgive you for spitting in my food and then in my drink. I wanted you to know that I've decided not to break your scrawny neck or any other part of your feeble body. I realize you were just trying to get my attention."

I couldn't keep myself from grinning. "And I apologize for having resorted to such extreme tactics. I couldn't think of anything better."

"It worked," he said, nodding his head thoughtfully. "Although you hardly needed me. You dispatched that elephant of a man all by yourself. Very handy work."

"I thought I would drown," I said, remembering the moment.

"Which is why I plucked you out of there."

"I'm glad you didn't toss me this time."

Rodrigo chuckled. "I could see you were in a lot of pain."

"I owe you." I sincerely meant it.

"Consider us even," he said. I never knew he had a magnanimous side. "Anyway, now that we have all that cleared up, I also came to tell you that I will miss you from the ranks. Not that you were a very good soldier. As a soldier you were average." He must have seen the look on my face and said, "Don't pout. You have the courage of a lion, but you took risks that should have cost you your life. I will miss you because you attract more than the average amount of good luck, and I like to keep men like that around."

My defenses were low and his words touched my aching heart. I had held this question for so long. I overcame my embarrassment and asked, "Is that why you saved me, pulled me out of the fray at Büren?"

Rodrigo laughed in a carefree way. "The first time I pulled you out of the mud and the blood of battle, at that little skirmish by the river, I saved you for the sake of the debt the city owes to your grandfather for the beautiful city walls he built. I love those walls. I believe I told you that at the time."

"Fair enough," I said. "And this time?"

"This time, I plucked you out for the debt the city owes to you that we still have walls to defend. This time you earned it."

I felt great pleasure at these words. It must have shown on my face, because Rodrigo added, "Although I feel compelled to point out that you did fall on your face again."

# *House Arrest*

Three days later, two guardsmen appeared at my bedside. "Time to go," one of them said. It was the older veteran Georg, who had been part of the patrol that had arrested me. He was a burly man with a grizzled beard.

I had dreaded this moment. After speaking with Rodrigo, I was uncertain of my fate. "Are you returning me to the tower?" I asked, doing my best to sound as if I didn't care.

Georg glanced at the other guard, Johannes, a man with whom I had often shared watches. "Bless me, no, Benedict. We're taking you home. To your family. Your sister has everything set up for you."

Flooded by a wave of relief, I had to fight back the tears. "Rodrigo told me I'm still to be ... confined ..."

Georg had a concentrated look. "We are to deliver you to your home and, and ..." he seemed at a loss for words.

"And continue keeping me under guard," I finished for him.

He gave a quick nod of his head. I appreciated his reluctance. It meant they still saw me as one of them.

"For your own good," he added quickly. At the time, my head was too fogged up from the poppy to make sense of this, but it would have saved me a lot of anguish if I had asked then what he meant.

They picked me up with far more care than I expected and carried me to a donkey cart waiting outside. They laid me into the cart on top of thick cushions. "Thank you for the pillows," I said sincerely. Still in a lot of pain, I was not looking forward to the bumpy ride.

"Only the best," Georg said with a broad smile. "I hope you like your royal carriage." He and Johannes shared a chuckle. They sat up front and I rode facing backward. I watched the garrison's House of

Healing slowly recede until it was out of sight. They held the donkey to a walk to minimize the bumps. I closed my eyes and dozed for the rest of the ride.

Apparently word had been sent ahead. My parents and my sister were waiting at the door when we arrived. The two guardsmen, gently once again, carried me inside to my bed.

"If you need anything, Ben," Georg said. "Just give a holler. One of us will be standing at the gate."

I was confused by his words. He made it sound like the guard was there for something other than to keep me confined to quarters. The truth was that I was utterly in the dark about what was really going on. I came to numerous false conclusions, and I was deluded by youthful conceit that I already knew the answer to any questions I might ask. As it was, I was so exhausted and in pain that I just shrugged off trying to come to any clarity over the presence of the guard.

My mother fussed over me, and my father, looking helpless, hovered awkwardly in the background. I reveled in it all, just happy to be home. Once I was settled, my parents went about their daily business. Only Veronika stayed with me.

"Ben, you tell me what you need when you need it. I am here for you."

"Thank you for taking care of me, Veroni. Until I get my strength back."

"I've made a decision, Ben," she rushed on. "I will never marry. I intend to take a vow. I will take care of you for the rest of your life."

Startled, I protested , "Nonsense. Of course you'll marry. This is just practice for when you have children. Lots of children. You raise children, and one of them will care for me." I hoped she would like my joke, but it fell flat.

"Then I shall only marry a man who lets me bring you with me," she said, her face set seriously.

I couldn't let this continue. "You do that and I shall kill myself. I really will."

"Ben!"

"Veronika, Joseph assures me that I will walk again. I will limp, but I will walk and take care of my own needs. I just need your help until I'm strong enough and back on my feet again. I'm not staying an invalid for life. That much, I promise you."

Getting back on my feet was more challenging than after my first injury. My leg healed slowly, and for long stretches I doubted it was healing at all. As winter descended on Solodurum, I burrowed in as if I were a hibernating bear. Every morning I would awaken from troubled dreams to find Veronika at my bedside with a bowl of hot broth. Once I had eaten, I would sink back into sleep again. When I next awoke, my mother would be waiting with a bowl of stew. This repeated itself throughout the day. I wondered vaguely if they took turns between the stew pot and my bedside. After dark, I would find my father sitting beside me. Most of the time we did not speak, but his solid, grounded presence alone was a comfort. On Sundays, even my brothers stopped by, which was a boost to my spirits. My injury did not stop them from pointing out that, although I had saved the city, I was an idiot for getting in the way of that troll's hammer. What had I been thinking? A question only a brother would ask. I had no answer.

I often had terrifying dreams, usually of being slammed in the leg by the war hammer. Sometimes it hit me in the chest or in the head. I'd wake up breathing hard, sweating freely, and in a panic would check that my leg was still there. I never had a peaceful night. If it was not a bad dream, it was the pain that roused me from the oblivion of slumber. This cycle lasted all through the dark, cold winter months.

Over time, with Joseph's discretion regarding how much poppy I was allowed to drink, my periods of wakefulness slowly increased. He lectured me, in no uncertain terms, that it was time I returned to the land of the living. The poppy was solely for my comfort at night, and he left me to suffer the throbbing pain during daylight hours. I didn't like to hear it, but he insisted that getting up and moving around would help with the soreness and the intense itching that I could find no way to relieve.

I was certain that moving around made it worse, but Joseph ordered Veronika to make sure I did not lie around all day. The only time I ever cursed her was when she came to get me out of bed. She was a clever sister. When I refused to get up, she told me it was just fine to lie in bed because she was never going to marry anyway and would care for me the rest of my life. This never failed to get me on my feet, accompanied by language fit only for the barracks. I was determined not to live my life as a burden in my dear sister's care. Later, I apologized very sweetly for how I spoke to her, and she generously forgave me.

After I had been home for nearly a fortnight, I wondered out loud why Martin never stopped by. I ached for a chance to speak with him and feel the comfort of his calm presence.

"He's not been in town since the night you stopped the breach of the Forest Gate," Mother explained.

"Do you know why? He might not be well and may need help." The memory of the attempt on his life was still all too vivid.

"He is fine, as far as we can tell," Mother went on. "Veronika and I went out to check on him and take him food. We found him deep in prayer in one of the shallow caves. He broke off his devotion long enough to speak with us."

Veronika continued. "He said that something had happened, though he would not say what, something that affected him deeply, and he felt compelled to intensify his devotion. It is by choice he has given up coming to town. He explained that it is no longer necessary, as more and more people bring offerings to him in exchange for prayer and a blessing, even in the winter months."

"So he spends all his time praying?" I asked.

"He has become in word and deed a holy hermit, alone in his solitude," Veronika replied sadly.

"I wonder what happened," I mused. A vision, perhaps? "What is his mood?"

"As somber as the cold wind," Mother answered. "But he has earned the respect of those who doubted him. The neighbors know we look out for him, and they bring us food and clothing. We make sure he gets it, but we can't force him to do more to care for himself."

Hearing this gave me a new motivation for being able to walk again.

With my mother's good food and Veronika's devoted care, I did slowly mend. Thanks to Veronika's persistent pestering, by March I was hobbling around the house and using the neighborhood latrine in place of the night pot. That was when I discovered that the guard outside never wavered. Often it was a veteran I knew. Veronika assured me that they stood their station at our gate through the long, dark days of winter. They stood there in snow, rain, sunshine, wind, night and day. Whenever I came out the front door, they snapped to attention. I tried to make sense of that and decided that they wanted to make a point that they were vigilant and I wasn't going to go anywhere, which annoyed me to no end. Where did they think I could go?

That led me to wonder if my trial had been set. Were they waiting for me to grow strong enough to return me back to the tower? But I didn't wonder so much that I asked. In truth, I did not want to know and just wanted to be left in peace. As it was, managing my pain and learning to use my leg again demanded my full attention. With time, I managed to sit in a chair more than lie in bed, and I pulled out my crutch so I could be more independent.

At first Joseph came daily, then every other day, and in the end, once a week. True to his word, he weaned me off the poppy, except for a small dose for the times when I woke in the middle of the night and the pain would not let me fall back to sleep. At least this time around, I had already learned how to be patient with the pain.

"Get out of the house," he ordered me. "The weather has turned to spring, and I want you out in the sunshine and walking around. Exercise will help with the pain. Your leg will tell you when it's had enough. Sit inside all day and all you will think about is how much it hurts. Get out. You're young. You're tough. Get out."

He was right, of course. The more I moved, the more I hungered for more exercise. I was sick of staring into the hearth. One day, as springtime was in full swing and the mud in the ways was dried, I limped to the gate and confronted Johannes, who was the guard on duty that day. "I want to walk up and down the lane," I said. "To get my strength back." Then I added, "It is what my physician wants me to do."

I expected Johannes to turn me right back around. Instead, he nodded and said, "Good idea. I'll walk with you. Good to see you on your feet again."

We had been compatible watch companions and I enjoyed his company now. I remembered stories about his family. Johannes freely shared with me the latest news of his brother, who also wanted to be a guardsman, and his sister, who worked with their father, a tailor. When I got tired, he took my arm and told me to lean on him, so I had the crutch on one side and Johannes' strong shoulder on the other. From that day on, I walked with the guardsman on duty, and I was able to catch up on the latest natter in the life of the garrison. Stupidly, I avoided all gossip about my situation. I did not want to sour the easy relationship we had. Besides, I was convinced I already knew everything there was to know about my status: I was under guard and confined to my home.

Every day, I made a point of walking farther. I had a reason for this, although I kept it to myself. I wanted to build up my endurance. I waited until the rotation fell on Georg and the weather was friendly. The day was warm and trees were wearing their new gowns of tender green. I hobbled out to the gate where he stood watch.

"I want to go to the ravine," I said, ready to argue with him.

"To where the hermit lives?" he asked.

"Martin is a friend of mine," I explained. "I wish to go see him—to seek his advice—and to visit the holy places there. It will be good exercise for my leg."

Instead of disagreeing, or simply giving me an order to stand down, Georg said, "Grab your crutch and let's go. Take an extra layer for warmth. You know how quickly the weather changes this time of year."

It took me a moment to register that he had just agreed to let me go. "Right," I said. "Let me tell my sister. I'll be right back."

The walk was longer and more strenuous than with two sound legs. But I was determined to see Martin. If I were to turn back before getting there, I had no way of knowing if another guard would be as willing as Georg. When we finally came to the entrance of the ravine, I was in a full sweat, but Georg made no comment. He just settled himself on a large boulder.

"I'll wait for you here," he said. "I reckon you'll be wanting some private counsel with the holy hermit."

I was puzzled. "Not worried I'd run away?" I asked.

He waved off my comment. "Stop that nonsense. Anyway, the bridge at the other end is down," he said curtly. "No danger coming from that way. Go on, now. I'll stand guard here. Be mindful I want to get back before the next shift starts. Don't want them to come and find us missing. No reason to make them worry, you know."

I could not make sense of Georg's carefree attitude to guarding me and once again brushed it off. I had totally missed his comment about the bridge at the other end of the ravine. Leaning heavily on my crutch, I followed the path along the stream. It was slow going along the broken path. However, I did not have to go far. After two turns in the way, I saw Martin walking toward me. I hailed him with a wave, and he hurried to come meet me. He enfolded me in a warm embrace.

"Martin," I began. "I am so sorry for not coming sooner."

"You need say no more," he said, beaming at me. "I know all."

"How fortunate that you happened to be coming this way. I don't know if I would have made it all the way to your chapel."

"I have been expecting you," Martin explained. "I made it a practice to come every afternoon in anticipation of your visit. I had heard that you were back on your feet and growing stronger."

"Oh, Martin," I exclaimed, my eyes filling with tears. "I am so happy to see you again."

Martin settled me on a stone in the dappled sunlight. I shared with him everything that had happened since I had last seen him—my imprisonment, the end of all my dreams of advancement, my conversations with Connie, my escape, and my challenge to Rodrigo to meet me at the eleventh gate. I even shared Veronika's offer to take care of me for the rest of my life. Martin listened intently to my desperate story, all the while emanating understanding and care.

"Assuming they acquit me from plotting against Baron Roland, and I swear, I never did plot against him, and they don't seem terribly worried that I will run away, even if I am guarded day and night—the fact is, I refuse to live as an invalid with my parents forever. Or worse, expect Veronika to adopt me into her home when she marries. I told her in no uncertain terms that she may not do that. Once I'm released from suspicion, I need to find a way to earn a living. With my injury, as well as the accusation that I plotted to kill the Baron, the Guard is closed to me. Nor can I return to setting stone. I can barely lift my own body, let alone a dressed stone." All of this, and more, tumbled out of me. Just speaking it lifted a weight from my shoulders and raised my spirits. Martin pondered my words before speaking.

"There is a third path I see, which does not involve the Guard or stone masonry."

Expectant, I looked up, anxious to hear what he would say. "You can read and you can write, my friend. Don't overlook the gifts and talents you have."

I threw up my hands in surrender. "I don't have the money, Martin. The money I would need for an apprenticeship. That is what sent me to the Guard in the first place."

"Then take orders," Martin said firmly. "The monks will welcome you with open arms. In the eyes of our Lord, we all limp."

I paused before replying. I did not want Martin to take offense at a too hasty refusal. "After all I have seen and experienced, I don't think I'm suited for a monk's solitary life of work and prayer. I lack the faith you are blessed with. I've been jaded by the world."

"You won't know until you've tasted those waters," Martin replied quietly. "You may find they replenish you and bring you peace. It is not a sudden decision, you know. One never takes orders immediately. You live among the monks, first as a novitiate. Only when both the novitiate and the Order feel the decision is right do they embrace you into the fold."

"Martin, you always told me that when God closes a door it is because He is opening a window elsewhere, and that He closes the door because that is His way of nudging us toward something we would not otherwise have considered."

"And this open window leads you into His waiting arms."

"I just don't share your faith, dear friend."

"You don't need to, Ben. Simply walk the path, and faith will come of its own accord."

"I will walk it with a serious limp."

"Better limping than crawling."

"Oh, Martin."

We spoke of many other things, but as the day was waning, it was time for me to leave. I did not want to annoy Georg. After all, I was there by his generous good graces. Before parting from Martin, I asked, "I heard that you no longer come into town. Are you determined to hold to this discipline?"

Martin grew somber and his smile vanished. "By my own choice, I am confined to my solitude here. I must do penance."

This surprised me. "Penance? Whatever for? You spend more time praying than the Bishop."

Martin looked at me with alarm, glancing at the trees around us as if they had understanding. "Guard your words against blasphemy, dear friend!"

I laughed at his caution. "I only meant to ask, are you not pious enough?"

Martin looked grave. "I will share with you another time. I have taxed you enough with our chatter. Come again, so I can look forward to our next visit."

I departed with a promise to return in a week's time. I found Georg where I had left him. He sat with his back against a boulder with his eyes closed. He was following the soldier's creed: Why stay awake when one can nap? At the sound of my shuffling footsteps, he opened his eyes.

"Do you need to rest before we head back?" he asked.

"No," I lied. "I sat while we visited. The day is waning. Best if we make use of the light." In truth, I was spent.

We had not walked a quarter hour when my head began to spin. In my desire to meet with Martin, I had overestimated my strength, and I collapsed heavily onto a boulder at the side of the path.

"Georg, please," I begged. "I just need to sit and rest a bit." I was in a sweat again, and panting.

Looking up at the sun descending behind the trees, Georg said, "Won't do if we come late. Everyone will be happier if I am there when the next shift arrives." Wearily, I nodded my head. He'd been so kind to let me come, I had to do my part. I steeled myself to stand up again when Georg offered me his hand. A stocky soldier, he grabbed my arm at the elbow and pulled me up forcefully. Before I could react, he had spun around and hoisted me up onto his back, a common move for carrying the wounded off the battlefield.

"Georg," I protested. "What are you doing?"

"Keep a firm hold on your crutch," he said, already walking along the path. "And your other arm around my neck. I'm getting fat just standing guard in front of your door. I need the exercise. I'll set you down when we're in sight of the first houses. Don't want to embarrass you, you know."

Georg's kindness brought a lump to my throat. Brothers in the Guard look out for one another. I was still one of them.

I needed two weeks of healing before I was ready to make the long walk to visit Martin again. Standing guard this day was Peter, the very same who had arrested me. He and I had marched together in the Guard from the beginning. We had fought in the same line at my first battle. I decided to see if he would be willing to let me go visit Martin. When I limped out through our small vegetable garden to the front gate, I saw he was just finishing up a plateful of food. The moment Peter saw me, he placed the plate down and stood at attention. It never failed, for reasons I was too thick-headed to understand, every guard stood at attention whenever I emerged from our door.

I nodded a greeting to him. Then I asked casually, "Where did you get the food?"

"Your sister," Peter replied. Then he looked worried. "That's all right, isn't it?"

So, my family was now feeding the soldiers guarding me. Uncertain how I felt about that, I brushed it aside. "I would like to go to the ravine," I said. I was about to explain that I had been allowed to once before, but Peter spoke before I could.

"Georg told us. I am ready to go whenever you are."

I had not expected that, but at the same time it did not surprise me. In the Guard, we gossiped about everything. I had a sudden thought. "I can go alone, you know. It's not like I am going to run away with this game leg."

Peter shook his head. "My orders are to watch over you, Ben. I'm coming with you. Besides, Georg told us to be ready to give you a hand on the way back if your forces fail you."

I stared at him. Seemed like there were no secrets. "Let's get going, then."

This time, I could tell I had more endurance, even though my leg was still stiff and hurt with every step. Relying heavily on the crutch, I was again in a sweat by the time we arrived. As with Georg, Peter sat himself on a boulder at the entrance to the ravine and said he'd wait for me there. I did not go far before I found Martin sitting in a patch of sunlight. He rose and greeted me warmly. We chatted for a bit about my recovery, and I realized only then that, since my last visit, I was no longer as severely plagued by the uncertainty of my situation.

"Seems like you've become my father confessor," I teased.

"I'd prefer you'd think of me as your brother confessor," he said with a wink. "Are you strong enough to go further? I have some refreshment at my hermitage that I'd be happy to share with you. People have been very generous and I have more than I can eat. I dislike the idea that it will spoil. Besides, I want you to admire the foundations I have laid for a small chapel. I've decided to dedicate it to my namesake."

"You will call it Martin's Chapel?" I asked.

He nodded and laughed. "First I have to finish building it!"

As we walked, Martin quizzed me what I knew about the breach at the city gate.

I had not spoken of it, not even to my own family. It felt good to talk about it. "It's the strangest thing," I recounted. "I have had a lot of time to hear the latest from the soldiers who stand guard at my door. Although the rumor was that the French were invading, in truth, it was hardly more than a raiding party. There were not enough of them to be any significant threat. Even if we had not stopped them as we did, sooner or later they would have been overwhelmed and cut down. There was no larger force behind them, nor even any trace that there had been one that retreated. Since none survived, we were unable to determine their eventual plan. We thought perhaps their stratagem was to enter the city and open another gate from within, but the Guard never found any sign of a larger force."

"Perhaps it is best not to know," Martin suggested.

His comment made no sense. "Whatever do you mean?" I asked.

"Sometimes it is better not to know," he repeated, but would say no more.

Martin accommodated my slow pace as we walked to the edge of the ravine where the canyon walls cut a sharp right angle above us. The stream below cooled the air as it splashed and thundered in its last large drop before leveling out and growing calm further down the gorge. But, something was missing.

"Where's the bridge?" I asked, staring into the gap at the foaming water below and the forest beyond. There had stood at this point a narrow rope suspension bridge across the ravine that led to a path into the forest beyond. I had crossed it many times. The two posts were still standing, but the bridge was gone. Suddenly, I remembered Georg's comment upon my first visit. He had told me outright that the bridge was down.

"There was some high water," Martin explained. "It took out the bridge. Not a big loss. Few travel this way."

I limped over to the nearer of the posts. Something about it was odd. The wood was hacked, as if someone had taken an axe to it. I looked at the other post. It had also been hacked by an axe. I looked across the gap at the two posts on the opposite side, and saw the remains of the bridge hanging down into the chasm. I looked back at the two posts on my side.

"Say, Martin, have you ... did you see these marks? It's as if ..." and then it hit me, and in a momentary flash everything became crystal clear. I stared at my friend. "The larger force!" I stared at the hewn posts and back at Martin. "The missing reinforcements! They tried to cross here. To come undetected. You?"

Martin's head was bowed, and he avoided eye contact. "Those who were standing on the bridge when I cut it were washed down the stream where I could pull them out. I gave them Christian burial and I pray daily for the salvation of their souls ... and for mine." He had spoken this in a quiet voice. "I arrived here a moment too late. They were already starting to cross in single file. I told them to return to safety, but they would not heed me, nor did they view me as a threat."

"So there *was* a larger force," I whistled. Then I made the connection. "The noblemen who tortured you—they were scouting out a back door to the city so they could enter through the Forest Gate. When you cut the bridge, they were unable to cross and pass through the ravine. Martin! You saved the city."

Martin grasped my arm with both hands. A frantic light burned in his eyes. "Benedictus, I have lived with one single wish for which I daily and fervently pray to our gracious and beneficent Lord for fulfillment. It is to live a life dedicated to prayer and non-violence and protecting this holy place. I have failed miserably." He let go of his grip on my arm and his shoulders slumped. He turned his face away. "The weight of my guilt lies heavily on my heart. I took human life."

"Yet you did it to protect the gorge," I pointed out. "That is why you are here."

"Agreed," he nodded, his gaze directed inward. "In spite of that, I will pay penance for this deed for as long as I take breath. It is not enough that I sinned against our Lord by taking lives I had no right to take. Do you realize on what day I committed this heinous crime?"

I thought a moment before speaking, It had been the day after my birthday. "November 11th?"

"And November 11th is ...?"

After a moment, it came to me. "Oh!"

"That's right. November 11th, Saint Martin's Day, my namesake."

I could feel my dear friend's anguish. "Martin was a soldier before he became a saint, you know." I hoped with this to soften his pain.

"An officer, in fact," Martin replied. "And out of compassion for the suffering of another, in the icy cold of winter, he cut his single cloak in twain to give to a beggar. And on that day, he gave up his commission as an officer. Legend says that he lived for a time in this very gorge. His spirit has been witness to my ungenerous deed."

I bit my lip. I could see how hard this was for my friend to reconcile. "You did save Solodurum," I said quietly. "And I choose to believe that it was St. Martin who guided your hand. Once it becomes known, you will be hailed a hero."

He looked up sharply. "As dear as you are to me, Ben, like a brother, if you breathe a word to anyone of what I have done, I swear, I will lame your other leg. I swear it." The ferocity of his gaze made me catch my breath.

I nodded. "Understood."

# The Summons

Looking back from where I am now, I am amazed at my naivety. I had been so clever in figuring out the clues hidden in Connie's chanting the number eleven, but I was blind to deciphering what was happening to me. However, that is the advantage of being older and looking back, since my hindsight now is remarkably clearer than what was right before my nose at the time.

I was in intense physical pain, and my heart hurt as well with the loss of my position in the Guard. I was bitter at having been imprisoned for a murder I had neither planned nor committed. In retrospect, I see that believing in the worst was my way of not having to process any of what had really happened. In truth, I already had too many worries to keep me awake in the night with the loss of my income and the prospect of spending the rest of my life an invalid in the care of my parents, and later my sister. I had too much time on my hands, and I spent a lot of it repeating over and over in my head what I had convinced myself to be true. Besides all that, I was still just a green lad of nineteen.

When I received the first of what I thought was a summons to Baron Roland's hall, I barely bothered to read it before I threw it in the fire. I was angry to be reminded that I stood accused of plotting his murder. When I received Roland's note, it awoke my outrage that I had been thrown in prison in the belief that I had actually murdered him, and he must have believed I was part of the plot, since he did nothing to exonerate me. If he planned to interrogate me in search for the truth, he'd have to send more than a summons. It was reckless of me, but the fact was, I didn't know what to say beyond claiming my innocence. I had no proof that I had had nothing to do with it.

The following week, a second summons arrived—once again, my assumption. I stared at this one for a long time, never really reading it, just admiring the clear, crisp lettering with strong upstrokes. I was surprised that it had been written in Baron Roland's own hand. I had seen it often enough to remember the distinctness of his letters. This seemed unusual. Why was Roland not writing to me through his secretary? Aside from the brief notes he had left me as his personal spy, it was his custom to dictate official business to his secretary. When I tired of puzzling this out, I threw this summons into the fire as well and watched it burn with a certain dark sense of satisfaction.

Two days later, there was a knocking at our door. Mother fetched me from my bed where I was resting. I hobbled over to find Georg and Johannes, fully armed. I glanced over their shoulders. There was no one standing post at our gate.

"Benedictus Waisel?" Johannes asked.

"You already know that, Johannes," I said with a bolt of fear running through my gut. "What is this about?" Was I finally being returned to the tower prison?

"Official Guard business," Johannes announced, standing up straight.

"As you know, I am no longer in the Guard," I said, petulantly.

"And the worse off we are for that," Georg said.

I barely suppressed a smile and nodded my appreciation for his sentiment. "What is the Guard business?" I asked, softening my tone.

"We are entrusted to escort you to Baron Roland's hall."

For a trial? "Am I under arrest?" I asked, defiance in my voice.

"Ben, don't make it worse," I heard my mother hiss behind me. "Just go with them."

I half turned to shush her. "Mother, please. Don't interfere."

"She gives good advice," Johannes said when I turned back to him. "And to your question, no, you are not under arrest."

"Who'd be so stupid to go and arrest the hero of Eleven ..." began Georg, but at a sharp look from Johannes, his words died on his lips.

It seemed my deeds had not been totally forgotten in the rank and file of the Guard. My heart was lightened by the old veteran's words.

"Give me a few moments to change," I mumbled and returned to my cot to find something appropriate to wear.

I struggled into my best tunic, the one with the least amount of stains, and Veronika fussed over my unruly hair so much I had to laugh in spite of feeling no humor whatsoever in the situation. "Let it be, sister. Just give me a hat to wear. They won't care what my hair looks like when they're forcing my hand into the hot coals." I heard Veronika's sharp intake of breath and realized my mistake. I turned to her and said quickly, "I didn't mean that. He's not going to hurt me. He just wants ..." but the truth was, I didn't have a clue what he wanted. Maybe he really believed I had plotted against him. "Why *does* he summon me?" I asked out loud.

"To thank you," my mother said, who stood in the doorway. "And you will be polite about it."

I took a deep breath so as not to speak the rash words that were already on my lips. I knew it was good practice for what was before me. I let my breath out slowly. "I will," I agreed. Then I took my crutch and presented myself to the guardsmen waiting outside our door.

"I'm ready," I declared. "I hope you have the morning free. It will be slow going for me. It's a steep climb."

"We've brought transportation, Ben," Johannes said, gesturing to the small cart that stood in the narrow way before our gate. Different from the one they had brought me home in, it was nothing more than two wheels with a seat for two behind a donkey, and a seat looking backward for two more.

"That's for us?"

"For you, mostly," Georg said. "Sit up front with me; it's less bumpy. And that way Johannes will have the pleasure of two seats all to himself in the back."

Georg took his seat and, together with Johannes, one pushing, the other pulling, heaved me with my crutch up onto the bench beside him. Johannes jumped on behind and, with a flick of the reins from Georg, we were off. I felt like royalty transported through the cobbled ways and byways of Solodurum. I actually enjoyed the stares of people in the street who stopped to gawk and let us pass. Street urchins left their games and waved their hats, some running beside us, whooping boyishly. When we reached the steep ascent to Baron Roland's hall, Johannes jumped off and pushed to keep the donkey from getting stubborn pulling the heavy load.

"Pull, Minos!" Georg encouraged the donkey. Then, "Push, Johannes!" giving equal encouragement to his two companions. He called this out with such gusto the three of us laughed with abandon. At one point, Minos rebelled and would go no further, stood his ground and brayed. Johannes went around to the front to pull on his harness. "Pull, Johannes!" Georg bellowed. When Minos continued to be stubborn, Georg handed me the lines, jumped out and joined Johannes tugging at the harness to get Minos to budge.

"Smack 'im with your crutch," Georg grunted, leaning backward, but to no effect. I gave Minos a whack on his haunches and, with a spring, the little donkey lurched forward, knocking Georg and Johannes to the side. Now relieved of the weight of the two guardsmen, Minos took the rest of the ascent at a brisk trot, leaving the two men running to catch up. All three of us celebrated with whoops of triumph. I was laughing so hard, I could barely hold onto the reins. Oh, how I missed the comradeship of the Guard!

Once at the top of the hill and before the door of the patrician mansion, I brought Minos to a halt. I climbed down carefully from my seat and stood there, leaning on my crutch. By this time the two guardsmen had caught up. Now in front of the hall, they resumed their official tones.

"Thank you for the ride," I said, still grinning from ear to ear. "I appreciate not having to make that walk using this third leg of mine."

"Don't thank us yet," Johannes said in a dead-pan. "We still have to get you home in one piece."

"You're going to wait for me?" I hadn't expected that.

"Are you daft, or what?" Georg said. "Of course we're going to take you home again. And besides, it saves us a shift on the walls. This is like time off. Give a holler when you're finished. We will give Minos some refreshment around the corner and if we're lucky we'll get some, too."

Now I was truly puzzled. Maybe I was not going to be interrogated after all. I hobbled up the few stairs and rang the bell. A guard in household livery opened the door and when I announced myself, he let me in. I had been here before. In spite of my previous visits, I could not help but gawk at the window and door frames painted in gold, at the tapestries decorated with complex designs that hung on the walls, and the stern portraits of Baron Roland's ancestors. The tile work on the floor had a complicated geometric pattern. It was exquisite. The French influence was everywhere.

The guard ushered me into a small greeting room to the right of the entry and then left. Through the window I could see Georg and Johannes sitting on a bench under a tree. The cart was nearby, with Minos still in his traces, already munching on the high grass that grew there. A serving maid had brought the two guardsmen something to drink, and I had to admit that Baron Roland might be a nobleman, but he was a considerate and caring one. The two guardsmen wasted no time and were already flirting with the serving maid, who appeared to enjoy their banter and attention.

Now that I stood waiting, about to face my former patron, I felt my heart harden. Perhaps Mother was right, and I was only here to receive his gratitude. But that did not explain why I had been accused of murdering him, or why I had been thrown into the tower prison, or the armed guard at my gate day and night. I now know that if I had only allowed myself to ask, I would have learned the truth long before this moment.

I was stuck on Rodrigo's words: I had to soldier on. I could not afford to waste my strength on self-pity. It only robbed me of the resourcefulness I needed to move on with my life. Likewise, I did not feel any desire for the Baron's gratitude, as well-intentioned as it might be. If he was so inclined, then he could exonerate my name and let me get on with my life. I resolved to be polite and gracious and to get out as soon as possible.

The door opened abruptly and Baron Roland swept into the room. He appeared to be fully recovered from any wounds he had received in the attempt on his life. He exuded strength and confidence, qualities the city needed from him in his role as one of the leading voices of Solodurum.

"Ben!" The Baron exclaimed. He crossed the room quickly and grasped me firmly by the shoulders. "I am so glad to see you again!"

"I had nothing to do with it!" I blurted out. "I would never plot against you. I swear it!" I had not intended to say any of that, of course. But at his friendly gesture, I had to assure him of my innocence.

When the Baron looked surprised, I could not stop myself from continuing. "Baron, I have been faithful to you from the beginning. I did not return your kindness and trust with lies and intrigue. That is not who I am."

Roland took a half step back at the unexpected force of my words. "No, I agree," he said quietly. "You have always been faithful and honest with me. You are—and have always been—someone I can rely on."

I was not prepared for this response. I had expected him to confront me with my crimes. "If this is what you believe, then why was I arrested for your murder and locked in the tower?"

Surprise showed on his face, but I did not have time to ponder it. He asked, "Do you not know why you are here, Ben?"

I nodded. I hardened my heart, prepared for the trials ahead of me. I had to be hard. My life was hard.

"Baron Roland, I am here at your summons," I said tonelessly.

"Summons?" he exclaimed. "I have sent you no summons. Twice, I sent you an invitation to visit me. I was under the impression you can read, or was I mistaken?"

Was it possible that I had misinterpreted his notes? Suddenly embarrassed, I remembered that I had thrown them in the fire without reading them through. I had been convinced that he had turned against me. My mind buzzed. Roland continued, "Twice you ignored my invitation. At first, I assumed that you did not feel you had healed enough for the long way. But when I heard that you had repeatedly made the trek to St. Verena—"

"You know about that?"

Baron Roland paused a moment before saying, "Are you so naïve to think you were my only eyes in the city?"

I realized that I had been just plain stupid. I knew he engaged many. "I am aware, Baron," I admitted in a subdued voice.

"When I heard you were well enough to walk to the holy ravine, I thought it must be your hesitancy to make the long climb up the hill. So I sent you conveyance."

"The guard said it was official business," I pointed out.

"Well, if I'm going to take two guardsmen off their posts and have you escorted up here in a cart that is usually reserved for aging Council members, I had to make some excuse, didn't I?"

I tried to settle all the buzzing thoughts whirling around my heart like a swarm of biting flies. "Baron, do you believe me that I had nothing to do with the attempt on your life?"

"To the contrary, Ben. You had everything to do with it." Hearing these words, my heart sank. I was doomed. Then he added, "If it had not been for your involvement, I would not have been alerted to the plot and they may well have succeeded in killing me. I owe you a deep debt of gratitude that I am still alive."

Stunned by his words, I nearly shouted, "Then why was I arrested for your murder?"

"Oh, that," he said with a smile. "It was a ruse, Ben. Forgive me. I had to make them think they had succeeded and, at the same time, believe they had gotten away with it. Once news of my death arrived, they would likely have eliminated any allies I had, and as careful as we were, I'm sure there are those who suspected I was using you for my own purposes. If for no other reason than insurance against any more meddling, it would have been a simple thing to knife you in a dark alley. So instead, I had you accused of my murder. It also served to distract them from going after any of my other informants."

Seeing my blank expression, he added, "It was to keep you safe, Ben. The tower was the one place they could not get to you, or at least, wouldn't bother. Of course, leave it to Ben not to stay safely locked up." He gestured at my crutch.

As astonishing as this revelation was, I was still puzzled. "Then why am I still under arrest?"

"Under arrest?" Roland asked, his brow darkening. "By whose authority?"

"The guard!" I exclaimed. "Day and night a guard stands at my gate. I can go nowhere without them, in spite of being an invalid. The guard that brought me up here to you."

Roland considered me and his face now betrayed amusement. "Has anyone ever told you that you are under arrest?" he asked.

"What?" I asked more sharply than I intended.

"What have they said to you? Has any guardsman ever used that word?"

I took a breath. This was much too confusing. The swarm of biting flies in my chest grew thicker. I rubbed my face and took another breath. "Well, Rodrigo said ... he said they were under orders."

"True, they are under orders. And what do the guardsmen themselves say?"

"They say ... they tell me that they are there to guard me. Their own words."

"And it's time you learned that they vie with one another for the honor of a shift to stand guard at your gate. Tell me, how do they treat you?"

I thought for a moment. Always friendly. Always my brothers-in-arms. Ready to let me lean on them when my leg buckled. Only one action never made sense. "They snap to attention whenever I appear."

"You were a guardsman. What does it mean to snap to attention?"

I blinked several times before replying what I suddenly knew was the truth. "It is a sign of respect."

"If there was the slightest suspicion that you were a traitor, that you had plotted against me, against Solodurum, how do you think they would treat you?"

I thought of the laughs we'd shared, the gossip, the camaraderie, even carrying me when I was too exhausted to walk further. What an utterly blind fool I had been!

"Oh," was all I managed to mutter.

"Yes, indeed, 'oh.' Ben, they've been keeping you and your family safe. You prevented the breach of the gate, and likely a bloody invasion of the city. However, not all those involved have been caught yet, or even identified. Those at the center of this plot must be livid with rage that you foiled their treacherous and careful plans, so perfectly thought-out that they could not imagine failing." Baron Roland explained all this in an even tone. I had no idea. The very thought sent a cold shiver down my spine.

"With or without your leave, I set a guard to protect you and your family from any attempt at revenge. You were, after all, acting as a faithful member of the Guard. I had to ensure you were not in danger and would not suffer for your loyalty."

When I realized what Baron Roland had done, my body was flooded by a deep gratitude that he was keeping my family safe from reprisal. Armed assassins could have knocked at our door, and I would have had nothing more than a crutch with which to defend my family. I lowered my head humbly, "Thank you, Baron. I had no idea. Please, forgive my stupidity."

"Forgiven. I sometimes forget how young you are. I will take the blame for your misinterpretation of the guard at your door. It was my mistake not to contact you earlier, but I wanted to leave you in peace to heal. Besides, in my mind, the purpose of the guard was obvious. Once you had returned home, my status prevented me from coming to visit you. It would not have looked right. It would also have attracted unnecessary attention."

I felt my face redden. "I've been a fool."

"Perhaps, but not when it counted," the Baron said lightly, brushing away my embarrassment. "I do have one riddle you could solve for me." I looked up. "However did you do it? How did you figure out their plan? How did you know they would breach that gate, on that day, at that specific hour? I had you safely locked in the tower, far from contact with anyone else."

I smiled. "I had help," I admitted.

His eyebrows arched. "Do tell, so I may thank him."

"There is a beggar," I explained. "A madman, if you will, who lives on the streets." I told Roland about my puzzlement over Connie's fancy clothing. "I came to the conclusion that, in spite of living on the streets, his clothing and daily replenished purse pointed to a noble house. Of course, I had no idea which house, but that mattered little. What was clear was that he had access to the conspirators."

"You're speaking of Conrad, unless I'm mistaken," he said.

I stared at him in surprise. "How can you know his name? Unless … Are you telling me—?"

"Yes, Conrad is my cousin."

"And so that makes him Roger's brother." I was nearly panting at the revelation. "Connie was the key to everything."

"Which helps explain why Roger left Solodurum so suddenly the morning after the botched breach of the gate. Do tell me more."

I laid out for him everything that Connie had told me and the guesses I had made. "I probably would not have figured any of it out if the day before had not been my birthday, November 10th, eleven-ten. The second two elevens were wild guesses. If I was wrong, I figured the worst that would happen was that the guard would haul me off to prison again."

Roland listened to my whole story with rapt attention, nodding his head as he put the pieces together.

"Raise your head high, Ben," he said. "Solodurum owes you a debt it can never repay. Sincere thanks are the most it can offer."

At the word *debt*, my reflex was to harden my heart. I agreed. There was no way the city could repay the debt it owed to me. My injured leg was a hindrance, and I had no way to support myself, let alone a family. I had become a burden to all those who knew me. Baron Roland must have seen the anger mixed with despair on my face.

"Tell me, Ben. What are your plans now?" Roland asked, as if he had been reading my mind.

"I'm forced to leave the Guard," I said. "Rodrigo told me he tried to get me a special dispensation so I could remain and serve in my limited capacity, but one of the members of the Privy Council vetoed it. Do you know who that was? Maybe, if you spoke with him, you could get him to reconsider."

"It was I who vetoed that request," he said.

I was stunned. "But why?"

"Your time in the Guard is over," Roland said firmly. "To remain enlisted with an injury of your severity sends a poor message. Imagine all the others who sacrificed life and limb for the city. We can't show favoritism. Leave the Guard behind you, Ben. What other prospects do you have?"

I exhaled heavily. "I have a friend, Martin—" I shrugged.

"Saint Verena's holy hermit? How does he counsel you?" Roland asked.

"To take orders," I said without enthusiasm. "With my ruined leg, what other choice do I have? I cannot return to my father's profession where I would need four sound limbs."

Before I could say more, Roland asked, "How bad is your pain?"

"Ebbing, though constant."

"Are you weaning yourself from the poppy?" he asked.

"I take only one draught now. A small portion in the night to ease my sleep. None during the day."

"However much it is, cut it in half," he said sharply, exactly the same stern instructions Joseph had given me just the week before. I bristled at being told what to do. It was my pain, not theirs.

"Why should you care?" I challenged him.

"Don't fight me," he said, his tone gentle. "Just do it. When you are free of the poppy, we can argue if I counseled you well or not."

I stiffened at this unwanted advice and was about to respond rashly. But then I remembered where I was and before whom I stood. I realized I had to control my temper, just as I had to control my pain. If I crossed Baron Roland, he could crush me, and there would be no one to raise an objection. I lowered my eyes and quelled my desire to fight. "Yes, my lord."

Baron Roland smiled broadly. "You didn't like my advice, did you? You never have learned to disguise your disagreement. I like this most about you: You wear your feelings on the outside where I can plainly read them and address them. I don't have to play guessing games. And even better," he laughed, "when you lie to me, I can see it."

At his words I could feel my face redden again, though I was still too young and inexperienced to understand why. I didn't know what to say to this. What did he care, anyway? When was he going to let me go home?

"So, Martin counsels you to take on the cloth."

"He says, rightly I suppose, that with my ability to read and write, the monastic Brothers will accept me with open arms."

"In all likelihood, they would. And is this your wish?"

"Less my wish," I said bitterly, "and more the only window left open to me after the door to the Guard has slammed shut."

"Window? Door?"

I described to him Martin's simplified view of human destiny.

"I understand something of this as well," he began. "You know, Benedict, I have learned that more than one open window can blow a door closed. It might not be just one."

I was puzzled. "What do you mean? More than one window?"

Baron Roland stepped over to a small writing desk. On it were several parchments, an ink stand, and several writing quills. He picked one of the plumes up, contemplating it before saying, "Tell me, what if you had another choice? Different from the monastic life. Would you consider it?"

What other choice did I have? Was he just being hypothetical? "I don't have another choice," I declared stubbornly.

"But if one were there, would you consider it, or is your heart set on joining a community of Holy Brothers. Believe me, I understand its attraction. Your lame leg has no stigma before the eyes of the Lord, only in the eyes of men."

"That's what Martin says," I admitted. Was he mocking me and offering false hopes? I had to know. "What other choice do I have?" I demanded.

"I'm glad you ask," Roland said, looking satisfied. Still holding the goose quill, he stepped closer to where I stood. "I was afraid you might have lost interest in this complicated and dark world of intrigue, lies, manipulation, and trying vainly to read the future. It so happens that I am in need of a personal secretary. Someone I can trust implicitly. I was hoping you could help me find the right man. I have until now always known you to be remarkably resourceful. Headstrong, but with sound instincts."

I would have been embarrassed anew by his compliments had his words not puzzled me. "What happened to Urs?" I asked.

"Ah, the clever Urs. I depended on his ability to keep my secrets. That is, until he couldn't. I thought he was immune to bribery, but I was mistaken. Urs was paid well to betray me. And he would have succeeded, except for you. He never imagined you could read. That was always our little secret. And when you casually shared with me the message he had you deliver in my name, I realized he was being paid to shift his allegiance."

"What message?" I asked. So much had happened since that day, it had slipped from my memory.

"The message you gave to Johann, the head jailor in the Tower Gate."

Then it came back to me. But I still could make no connection, and I asked the Baron to clarify it.

"Do you remember what was written on that note?"

I thought back. "A date, November ninth."

"There was more, was there not?"

"Yes. Saint Ursus Fountain. More not."

"And now think back to when the attempt was made on my life."

"Do you mean the highwaymen who attacked you?"

"It was made to look as if they were highwaymen."

I was shocked. "How can you be sure?"

"I extracted a full confession from the one who was still alive."

"From one of the highwaymen?"

"Let's call them what they were: Assassins. And, had it not been for your curiosity how the paper was folded, and Urs' confidence that you were as illiterate as every other guardsman, they would have succeeded."

I was flabbergasted. “Will you fill in the missing pieces for me? I still do not see what I had to do with this.”

“Gladly. The message you delivered gave a date.”

“November ninth.”

“Exactly. With *ninth* as a word instead of a number, I remember you remarking. So should you or anyone else have seen it, nothing of it would make sense. I was beset by the assassins in the evening of the very day I set out on my journey to meet with representatives from Zurich and Lucerne to discuss a treaty of common interest in war and commerce.”

“November ninth?”

“The very day. And do you know where they attacked me?”

“I will hazard a guess. At Saint Ursus Fountain along the old road to Zurich?”

“Yes. And at the time you delivered that note, only one person aside from myself knew my plans. In an attempt to avoid exposing myself to the perils of the common route and attracting too much attention, I had decided to take the longer and less trafficked road that would take me by the Saint Ursus Fountain. It was the perfect place for a concealed attack.”

“How did you avoid falling into their hands?”

“I went prepared and placed everything into the competent hands of one of the battalion captains. I suspect you know who I mean. He was brilliant. The plot was foiled. He may well have earned my patronage and his knighthood with this.”

It was then I remembered the injuries on Rodrigo’s face and arm when I had baited him in the soldier’s mess. Puzzled at the time, here was the answer.

“So Urs was behind this?”

“Indeed, my trusted secretary. And to erase doubt of his loyalty, he handed you the note himself. He never imagined that he had entrusted it to the one person who could undo his plans. Albeit, unintentionally. Which is not to say I am ungrateful. I owe my life to you.”

"But Urs' influence was immense."

"In truth, I had placed a great deal of trust in him. Perhaps, incautiously so."

"Where is he now?"

"Urs is no longer in my employ."

"He left?"

"Believe me, you will sleep better not knowing." With these words, Baron Roland's eyes flashed for a moment with such ferocity that it took my breath away. I was reminded of how he had manhandled me when he suspected that I was a French spy.

Roland continued, "Suffice it to say that I am in search of a new secretary. Someone who will keep my secrets. Someone I can trust." He was tapping the palm of his hand with the writing quill for emphasis.

"And you want my help?" I asked, to be clear.

"Indeed, I do," Roland confirmed.

This was a task I was prepared to take on. It was not charity. He was offering me the job of identifying his next secretary. Hope flashed in my heart that maybe he would consider me. At the same time, I knew that was silliness. I'd had no training to qualify me. "Fine," I said with a quick nod. "I will help you."

"Excellent," Roland clapped his hands. "I was hoping you would."

"Then we can begin now," I said, inwardly relishing having a purpose after such a long period of inactivity. "Do you have anyone in mind?"

The Baron gave me a knowing smile, but what he knew was still a mystery to me. "It needs to be someone who can read and write," he began, "who can keep his counsel as well as mine, speak to me honestly and directly, who can keep his head in the face of danger and support wholeheartedly Solodurum's move toward independence."

I laughed. "That is asking a lot from one person." I silently wondered if I could rise up and fit that description.

"I agree," Roland said gravely. "For that reason, I think the position would be best handled by a family member."

My heart dropped to my knees. Any hope I had of offering myself was turned to ashes in the wind. How foolish I was to think that I might have a chance. I had been trained to be a guardsman, nothing more. But I took satisfaction that at least he trusted me to help him find Urs' replacement. Maybe, somehow, if I did a good job, he would consider me for other small tasks that did not require two sound legs.

"I do not have much knowledge of your relations," I admitted. "Only your two cousins." Then I looked at him with alarm. "Certainly, you are not considering him?"

"Roger? Working for me? He'd rather challenge me to a duel. Besides, if he ever shows his face in Solodurum again, he will likely be charged with sedition. His execution would be uniquely spectacular and spoken of for years to come."

I was surprised by this. "But how can you be certain of Roger's role in this? Connie gave me riddles to solve, not proof."

"I was recently able to confirm what I suspected—that Roger was deeply in debt. Do you remember how strongly he advocated in our Council meeting that exiling the Jews was not sufficient, but they should be burned at the stake?"

I recalled it clearly. "He was convinced they were the cause of the plague."

"He was more convinced that by murdering the Jews, he would free himself from repaying the money he had borrowed from them."

Roland saw my eyes widen. "You are innocent in the ways of the world, Ben. Not only did Roger think that by immolating the Jews he would never have to repay his debt, he had planned to confiscate their homes and rent them for his own profit. He hired thugs to loot the homes so they could be declared ransacked. Then he would have stepped forward to generously offer to renovate them. He would have made a tidy profit."

At this revelation, my mouth fell open.

"That is why I acted so swiftly to take on an orderly departure of the Jews. As you well know, I also had the Council empower me to use the Guard to protect their homes until they should return."

I remembered the night that Roland had told me to double the guard. "So those drunks ... they were sent by Roger?"

"Likely they were drunk, and yes, I have evidence that Roger provided the drink."

"However did you know?"

"Ah, Ben, remember, you are not my only eyes and ears in Solodurum. He spun his webs very well, my cousin did."

"But what does all of this have to do with the attack on Eleven?"

"Ah, yes, the attack on the city. When his plot against the Jews failed, Roger's need for money became more desperate. With the Jews gone, he could not turn to them for more. So he looked beyond the limits of our city and landed upon the French. They have long wanted a foothold in Solodurum and a Council friendlier to their own aspirations. They deplore all this talk of an independent Swiss Confederacy of cities."

"So Roger betrayed us to the French?"

"I have just returned from several months traveling through the Empire and was able to confirm much of what I only suspected. He hoped the French would set him up as their puppet dictator. With that, his ambitions for power and money would have been satisfied."

I could only shake my head in disbelief. "Where is he now?"

"I suspect that my cousin Roger has gone to live with our French relations."

I felt a wave of relief that Roger was no longer a complication in Roland's life, but then I flashed on someone I cared about.

"Wait. What will happen to his brother?"

"The same who have always looked after him will continue to do so. Roger treated his brother like a dog. Aside from giving him his castoff clothing and loose change for his purse, he provided little. He also took him for granted. Hearing your story, I believe that he had allowed his conspirators to speak freely in Connie's presence. That was his undoing, since it was Connie who clued you in to their great joke of attacking the city of elevens at eleven o'clock on the eleventh day of the eleventh month."

"At the eleventh gate," I added. "It was a clever plot."

"Diabolical," Roland said, but he was not smiling. Then he continued. "To ensure his care, I have adopted Connie into my own household. I don't doubt he will prefer living on the streets, but at least he will have money, food and, in winter, a place to warm himself other than inside the Tower Gate. He has earned more than that for his part in helping to thwart the attack on the city, but there are limits to what he is willing to accept."

I was relieved to hear this. "Then, regarding your search for a new secretary, aside from Connie and Roger, I don't know any other of your relations," I admitted.

"Nor is there any reason you should," Baron Roland agreed. He gestured with the quill still in his hand that I take a chair. "I have made you stand far too long. Please." Then he added, "Let me use this opportunity to give you a picture of my family."

I gladly took a seat, stretched out my aching leg, and made myself comfortable. I knew that the nobility make much of their genealogies and I expected I was in for a lengthy lesson in family history. I wondered how far back he would go.

"My grandfather had four children," he began. He saw my surprise and added, "For our purposes, I need go no further back than Grandfather. You shall soon understand why. He had three boys and a girl. One of the boys, the eldest, Ernst, was my father. A second boy, my Uncle Peter, was Roger's father. My aunt Matilda never grew to adulthood, but died of a fever when she was young, so I never knew her." With this, he stopped.

When he did not continue, I asked, "You said there were three boys. Did the third son also die young? You haven't mentioned him yet."

"I'm glad you were paying attention. Yes, there was a third son." And he stopped again.

"You seem reluctant to speak about him. Was there something wrong with him? Was he born with a deformity? Was he like Connie?"

"No deformity, but there was something terribly wrong with him. He was not born to my grandmother. He was the child of one of the serving women, a bastard son. Not uncommon among the nobility, even today, I'm sure you know, but we hate to admit these indiscretions. My father and Uncle Peter never met him. There were only whispered rumors regarding him. Every family deals with these accidental children in their own way. As an act of mercy, our grandmother had the woman sent away to the convent where the child was born and raised."

When he saw my surprise, he added, "I call it an act of mercy because she could have sent her back to the peasant family she came from or, more cold-heartedly, had her quietly garroted." He waited a moment to see if I had something to say, but I knew better and swallowed the words that wanted to come out. He continued "The woman was warmly welcomed by the Holy Sisters and eventually became one of their number. When the boy was old enough to be separated from his mother, he was sent to live among the Benedictine brothers, who contentedly raised him as one of their own. This was a common enough practice." When he stopped and looked at me, I assumed he was waiting for me to ask a question, but I had none. So he continued.

"The independent spirit in our family apparently ran strongly in his blood. When he came to the age of majority, instead of humbly taking orders and living out his days in monastic obedience, he left the safe confines of the brethren and sought out a life to work with stone. Grandfather, it seems, had not forgotten him, and opened some doors of opportunity. Through his own industry and innate skills, the young man raised himself from stone cutter to stonemason, and eventually to Master Mason." With this, Baron Roland paused again and watched me for a flicker of comprehension. I had none. I had listened to the story with interest, since my own family followed this profession, but otherwise it meant little to me. Bastard sons from noble families were constantly gossiped about in the Guard. Talking about them was one of our favorite diversions.

When I did not react, Roland added, "Although we never met this uncle, we did know his name. It was Valentinus." He looked at me as if this should mean something to me.

"Valentinus," I repeated, trying to understand how this was important.

"Yes," Roland said. "Valentinus." He waited a moment, but when I said nothing he continued. "And this Valentinus is a memorable and highly regarded figure in the history of Solodurum. He is credited with designing and overseeing the building of the fortifications along the north side of the city."

Something in my mind still resisted making sense of this. Confused thoughts began to swirl in my head, and the ache in my leg distracted me. "And this Valentinus placed an image of his visage high in one of the towers along the north wall," Roland continued, raising his hand and pointing with the goose quill, as if the tower were before us. "A head that bears a barely visible pair of horns. Most likely his subtle way of declaring his paternity." My thoughts were like summer gnats, hovering, but refusing to land. "Twice, in fact. One image facing north, away from the city, and the other turned into the city, facing south."

My face still a blank, Roland finally said sharply, "Pick up the pace here, cousin. I'm growing gray waiting for you."

It was like a door bursting open. "Valentinus!" I exclaimed, springing to my feet. "You mean *my* Valentinus? *My* grandfather? Are you telling me—" but I could not find the words.

"My illegitimate uncle," Baron Roland said, "was nothing but an unconfirmed rumor and source of family gossip until you came into my life."

"Your family name! De Cornu! *Horns* in French! We're related?" My head was spinning.

"It would seem so," Roland said with a sly smile. "The world is full of surprises, is it not?"

"How long have you known this?" I was still reeling.

"Since our first conversation in the Privy Chamber. When you told me about your grandfather."

"But why have you never said anything to me before?"

"We do not give family secrets away easily. Especially when they have been so well kept. Had my bloodthirsty cousin Roger heard of your existence, you and all your family would have mysteriously disappeared one night. Your bodies would have been fished out of the Arola far downriver where no one would even care who you had been. My cousin does not suffer competition of any kind."

I paled at the thought that my whole family could have been wiped out over a family relationship about which we were completely unaware.

Roland continued. "As it is, don't ever expect me to acknowledge our familial connection in public. Should you breathe a word of it, I would loudly and vehemently deny it and bring suit against you for the shameless and baseless slander of my good name."

"Then why tell me at all?" I protested, stunned by this revelation.

"Because I've learned that you are proud as well as stubborn and would likely refuse any offer from me as an act of pity born out of guilt ..."

"What offer?" I was still so clueless.

Roland continued, "... but as a member of the family, you might be more willing to accept my offer of employment. As I said, I am in immediate need of a private secretary. I want someone I can trust to keep my secrets and carry out my business. As I told you, I would much prefer it be a member of my family." Baron Roland walked up to me and offered me the writing quill he had been holding. I stared at it dumbly. "I am looking to you, Benedictus Waisel. You have proven to have in abundance all of the abilities I have named as prerequisites for this position: You read, you write, you are honest and loyal to a fault, you are a terrible liar, and at the same time you are amazingly resourceful. You also inherited our family's stubbornness and independent thinking. So tell me, are you willing?" He again offered me the feather.

I was dumbstruck.

"Just nod your head, cousin," Roland suggested with a smile. "And take the damn quill, already."

And so, my dear children, my narrative draws to a close. Soon after my interview with Baron Roland, I entered his service as his personal secretary. With my new employment, and limited by my battle injuries, my days of adventure were ended. Not that my life became uninteresting. Crises and intrigues rise up and settle down as regularly as the seasons come and go—and far more frequently! I have assisted Baron Roland in weathering many of them. I feel I have also played a part in moving Solodurum toward membership in the Swiss Confederacy. The repercussions and benefits of this momentous step will be instrumental in the future destiny of our city. I heartily agree with Baron Roland that it is the only forward-looking move we could rationally make.

It was while serving the Baron that I grew close to one of the housekeepers, a certain Jolanda. I was drawn to her ready smile, her cheerful disposition, and her steadiness in all things. Whereas others behind my back either mock me or pity me for my limp, your mother accepted it as much a part of me as my black hair and blue eyes. She has never wavered. She has blessed our union with the five of you, and not only manages our own household, but has risen in her position to oversee the Baron's housekeeping and the comfort of his guests. But this you know well. Your mother has my enduring love.

I hope that now as well, you have more understanding for the times I hobble home without my cane, only to relate that it has been stolen by Connie. You have often wondered why I am never upset. The truth is that, when the mood strikes him, Connie asks to hold my cane, and even though I know what is coming, how can I refuse? He claims that he wants to pretend to be his good friend Bennie, and once he has my cane in hand, he runs away, knowing full well I cannot chase him. He must have quite a collection of them by now. How can I be angry with him? I did, after all, break his trust that day in the dungeon. In his simple way, he has decided he will never let me forget it.

With this, my children, you now have the written account about my youth that you have so long requested from me. I know you have heard some of these stories over the years from your dear aunt, my sister Veronika, but there are details even she did not know, which I have now included herein. This account will also give you a clear understanding of our family's lineage and history. Now perhaps, it is no longer such a mystery that when there are no guests of State, we are welcomed at Baron Roland's table and dine together *en famille*.

To my sons, as you approach majority, I am pleased that your interests are varied and yet true to family tradition. You, Valentinus, wish to follow in my footsteps and take up the work of a scribe. The Baron has assured me we will have the money for an apprenticeship. And, Conrad, you love the physical rigors of a life outdoors and wish to follow the family tradition of masonry. For you, we have our family connections and will arrange a good apprenticeship with one of your uncles. And the youngest, Andreas, you wish to seek your fortune in the City Guard. My dear friend Rodrigo, whom you know is the Commander of the Guard, will be delighted.

You have my blessings, my sons. I can tell you from personal experience, all three are noble professions.

And to you, dear Sophia, I assure you a generous dowry that will attract a crowd of suitors from whom you are free to choose one that will provide you a secure and stable home life. I know you have been a constant support to your mother and look forward to managing your own household one day. And to Clara, our youngest, I accept from our many conversations—and disagreements—that you will require no dowry at all. Like my dearest friend, Martin, the hermit of the holy gorge, you wish to devote your life to prayer and good works in service to God and your fellow human beings. How can I object that you follow the urgings of your own Free Will when, by following mine, I was allowed to lead the most fulfilling life a man could ever wish? You go with my blessings.

# *Historical Reflections*

Readers familiar with the charming smaller cities of Switzerland will immediately recognize that Solodurum is a thinly veiled version of the beautiful Baroque town of Solothurn, perched on the banks of the Aare River. It lies strategically along the road between Zürich and Bern.

Solothurn is my wife's home town, and one summer while visiting family, her sister arranged for the three of us an early-evening snack on the top of one of the guard towers along the old city wall. She had access to it through the offices where she worked which had been built into those medieval walls. Standing on the tower, I could gaze toward the north, to the line of the Jura Mountains not far distant. Turning to the south, I looked down at the roofs of the Old City. It happened that, as I stood there innocently taking in the sights, I received the initial inspiration for this story.

It was a nearly overwhelming experience as I was suddenly flooded with images, none of them quite connected, but all clamoring to have their story told. The next day, still affected by those chaotic visions, I returned to the guard tower and gazed up to take in its height. It was then I saw the face in the wall for the first time. Benedict's grandfather solidified in my imagination, and the backstory was born.

I never intended to write a work of historical fiction, and discerning readers may argue that I did not. Originally, I merely wanted to use an anonymous medieval city as a backdrop for the story I was inventing. Then the unexpected happened, which lent magic and mystery to the process of creating this story.

I would write whole episodes as they flooded in on me, and only afterward dutifully do my research to ensure that I was not taking too great liberties with time and place. I did want the story to have the realistic and accurate feel of a small, fourteenth century Swiss town struggling with the lure of independence from the Holy Roman Empire to parallel Benedict's own story of breaking with family tradition. Imagine my surprise when I discovered, repeatedly, that there was historical precedence for many of the events that I thought I was inventing.

In order to ground the story as believable, I did make use of factual truths. The city of Solothurn actually does have a fetish around the number eleven. They boast three times eleven steps leading up to the portal of the Saint Ursus Cathedral, and inside, there are eleven altars. Eleven beautiful, monolithic fountains are sprinkled throughout the Old City. In medieval times there were eleven bailiwicks, or regions, surrounding the city, each with its own bailiff. Solothurn lies along the banks of the Aare River, which, in the time of our story, was called the Arola. In addition to the eleven fountains, according to city tour guides, there are indeed eleven churches and chapels, and eleven towers along the city defensive walls. Added to all of this, Solothurn was the eleventh Swiss canton to join the Swiss Confederacy in 1481. Was this the origin of the attraction to the number eleven, or merely one more instance of its powerful grip over this gem of a city on the Aare?

It seems that eleven had a hold on Solothurn long before it joined the Confederacy. In 1350, the city was guided by an eleven-member Council of Elders, and a twenty-two-member Younger Council. Eleven guilds controlled the working of artisans and professions. When a twelfth guild was eventually added, it was folded into one of the already existing guilds to keep the total number at eleven. All of this emphasizes the spell the number eleven had cast upon the city.

These were all features of old Solothurn, originally known by its Roman name, Salodurum. Modern Solothurn has continued its fondness for the number eleven. There is a local brewery called Öufi (impossible for a foreigner to pronounce on the first try), which is Solothurn dialect for "eleven." It produces a beer by the same name. There is even an Öufi Uhr, an "Eleven Clock," mounted on the outer wall of the Coop supermarket located beyond the Biel Gate, just south of the Amthausplatz. The clock sports only eleven numbers and tells time quite accurately—at least as accurately as a clock with only eleven numbers can.

This is a city well worth your visit. It lies along the placid Aare River with the Jura Mountains to the north. The beautiful medieval limestone walls still encircle three sides of the Old City. The visage of a clean-shaven man on the first tower east of the Franciscan Gate on the north side of the city is very visible if you look up. You can go and puzzle over it for yourself.

The buildings of the old town of Solothurn are indeed built from the beautiful limestone quarried from the Jura Mountains to the north, the Weissenstein. A modest museum, appropriately called the Stone Museum (*Steinmuseum*) is dedicated to the usage of limestone throughout the history of the city. The immense monolithic basins for the eleven fountains are truly impressive and must have been the envy of the surrounding towns. The historical buildings in the old town, as well as the long defensive walls, are built from Solothurner marble and shine white when warmed by the sun. It gives the city a noble look.

Walking distance from the Basel Gate is a sacred gorge, the Verenenschlucht. According to legend, Saint Martin lived in this gorge in the 4th century. In honor of this, the small chapel there today is known as the *Martinskapelle*. The first mention of a hermit living in the gorge comes from 1442, later than the time of my story, but lack of documentation does not preclude the presence of an earlier hermit who sought the holiness of solitude. To this day there is a hermit living in and caring for the holy sites in the gorge.

Solothurn had a small Jewish community until 1348, when, due to an outbreak of the plague, there was a pogrom that eliminated it. Were they driven into exile, as in my story, or was there bloodshed as well? Did they return? History does not elaborate.

With these known facts as an underpinning, the fictional part of my story unfolded.

I wrote *Eleven* relying on an imperfect memory of the city. In many cases I brazenly created my own reality, using a Solothurn of my own making. I invented Benedict and his family. I made up Baron Roland de Cornu, Roger, Connie, Martin and Rodrigo. No individual in this story is founded in historical documentation. I resisted the temptation to use names of families that hail back to the time of my story. I did not want anyone feeling I had slighted or misrepresented their ancestors.

I fabricated the Baron's manor house and, although the city is built on an incline down to the river, I invented the non-existent hill on which his house stood. The path leading from one end to the other through the Verena Gorge was not completed until 1791, long after the time of my story. Today the water running through the gorge is but a quiet brook, though the steep sides of the canyon and the many cataracts along the way are witness to a time when larger amounts of water washed through with greater force. I added the bridge over the deep cut in the gorge that Martin hacks down where there is neither a deep cut nor a bridge, and alas, if an eleventh Forest Gate existed in the city walls, I have not been able to verify it.

So where is the history? Imagine my surprise and delight, after I had written about the failed plot to breach the Forest Gate, when I discovered that a similar event had actually happened. On the night of November 10, extending into the morning of November 11—unbelievably, this is the recorded date—in the year 1382, a certain Baron Rudolf II of the house of Kyburg, deep in debt, attempted an armed takeover of the city. He had co-conspirators inside the city ready to open the gate in the dead of night for him and his forces. How the plot was foiled is a story all its own.

A peasant, Hans Roth von Rumisberg—Rumisberg being a village west of Solothurn—happened to be in an ale-house on the evening of November 10th. It was a cold evening, and he had cozied up behind the oven. He overheard the conspirators, who thought they were alone in the ale-room, lay out their plot to take over the town. It was at this point they discovered that Hans Roth had heard their plans. At first some considered knifing him, but others did not want his blood on their hands. Instead, they made him swear not to speak a word of what he had heard to a living being, which, to save his life, he readily did. When they were satisfied that he would not break his vow, they left him and went on their way.

Hans Roth knew he had to do something to prevent the bloodshed of an attack on the city. He set out that night for Solothurn. It was a snowy evening, so to disguise his steps, the story tells, he placed his wooden clogs on backward so in case anyone might find his tracks, it would look like the footsteps in the snow were leading away from Solothurn. Once he arrived at the Berne Gate, there was no one around at this late time of night except for the Watch, who probably eyed him with mild curiosity. What was he going to do?

This was at a time in history when a pious man took his vows seriously. If he had vowed he would tell no living person, then he would stick to it, come what may. However, one also knew that a vow sometimes had a back door. No one told him he could not speak of the plot, as long as he was not addressing another person. So, standing before the gate and pondering how he could save the city without breaking his vow, Hans Roth caught sight of a statue of Saint Ursus, patron saint of Solothurn, embedded in an alcove in the tower above the gate. This was the very thing he needed. Speaking as loudly as he could, he opened his heart to the saint and related everything he had heard about the imminent attack, including the vow that prevented him from telling the guard on duty.

This had the intended effect on the Watch. Not wanting to take the chance that Hans Roth might not be crazy, they raised the alarm and were able to prevent the co-conspirators within the city from opening the gates to the attacking force. The eldest male descendant of Hans Roth has been honored in Solothurn yearly from that day to this.

I have been unable to determine the actual identity of the man whose face is depicted on the bastion wall, which I attribute to Benedict's grandfather. Who knows, perhaps the face on the tower is that of Hans Roth. The walls were renovated in the 1970s, and I read one account that there was no record of a face there before the walls were renovated. Perhaps the chief mason placed his own visage there, just as I have Valentinus doing. Still, that does not solve the riddle of the subtle appearance of horns on his head.

As a writer of fanciful stories, I have a version of my own: The chief architect of the renovation of the 1970s replaced an older image that time and the elements had eroded to an indistinct profile, and that weather-worn image had been the Master Stonemason who had overseen the original construction of the walls. But that is just the storyteller's yearning to round things out.

I experienced numerous other coincidences in my tale when a storyteller's inspiration actually stumbled upon truth. For instance, I had no idea that the chapel in the holy gorge is named after St. Martin. I had chosen the name for Benedict's devout friend randomly, as a placeholder until I might find a more suitable one. Imagine my surprise when I discovered that my choice was serendipitous.

There were indeed marauding French incursions in the 14th Century, and Solothurn was one city of many who marched out against them. There was a particularly noteworthy victory at the town of Büren, about ten miles west of Solothurn. In my story, it was at that battle that Benedict opens up a hole in the line by falling on the spears of his opponents. At the time I invented that scene, I was unaware that there is a Swiss national hero who acted precisely in this valiant manner. Every Swiss school child knows his name: Arnold Winkelried. He performed this deed in 1386 at the decisive battle of Sempach, thus solidifying the survival of the still young Swiss Confederacy against Habsburg pressure. An armed force from Solothurn also took part in this decisive battle. Unlike Benedict, Winkelried actually intended to neutralize several of the enemy pikes by falling on them. He did succeed in creating a breach in the line that allowed the Swiss forces to overwhelm those of the Habsburgs. However, he was less fortunate than Benedict and did not survive his courageous and sacrificial fall onto the spears of his enemies.

In this manner, time and again, when I thought I had invented some aspect of the story, I discovered in my research that indeed there was an historical precedent. The events just did not all conveniently happen in one person's lifetime. So my fiction was to condense many events to fall within one story and connected to the life of one young man, whereas in reality they are spread out over time and involve multiple individuals. In this way, though, I discovered that Fiction and History could indeed be happily married at the altar of Imagination.

# Other books by the author

## The Star Trilogy

### The Dragon Boy

Gold Medal:
Moonbeam Children's Book Awards: Best First Book

Mom's Choice Award for Fantasy, Myth and Legend

Finalist: Young Adult Fiction Eric Hoffer Book Award

### The Dragon of Two Hearts

Silver Medal:
Moonbeam Children's Book Awards for Young Adult Fantasy

Mom's Choice Award for Fantasy, Myth and Legend

### The Dragon, the Blade and the Thread

Bronze Medal:
Moonbeam Children's Book Awards for Young Adult Fantasy

Finalist: Ben Franklin Award for Young Readers

Finalist: Colorado Book Award for Young Adult Literature

Mom's Choice Award for Fantasy, Myth and Legend

### At the Hot Gates

Teen & Young Adult Ancient Historical Fiction

New insights on the famous tale

Excellent reader for 5th grade

### The Yonder

Grand Prize Finalist

Honorable Mention in Young Adult Fiction

Eric Hoffer Book Award

**Available to order at www.donaldsamsonbooks.com or from your favorite bookseller**

Made in the USA
Monee, IL
02 May 2024